Literary editor of the *Irish Times* for sixteen years,
Terence de Vere White is also a highly acclaimed
novelist and contributor to various journals.

THE RADISH
MEMOIRS

Terence de Vere White

Futura

A Futura Book

Copyright © Terence de Vere White 1974

First published in Great Britain in 1974 by
Victor Gollancz Ltd, London

This edition published in 1986 by Futura Publications,
a Division of Macdonald & Co (Publishers) Ltd
London & Sydney

ISBN 0 7088 2934 1

Printed in Great Britain by
The Guernsey Press Co. Ltd,
Guernsey, Channel Islands

Futura Publications
A Division of
Macdonald & Company (Publishers) Ltd
Greater London House
Hampstead Road
London NW1 7QX

A BPCC plc Company

For
Anne and Philip Weld

"What dire Offence from am'rous Causes springs,
What mighty Contests rise from trivial Things"
Alexander Pope
The Rape of the Lock

Chapter I

"I SEE RUNTY is going to publish his memoirs."

"Where did you see that?"

"Here. Look for yourself."

Eleanor Hartley took the newspaper which her husband held up to her, and looked longer than even her short sight demanded at the columnist's paragraph.

The publishing event of the year will be the Radish memoirs "My Thousand and One Days". I hear they are going to be launched at a party for which special accommodation has been booked at the Savoy by John Jackson, whose firm won the auction for this publishing prize. The amount paid has not been disclosed. Sir Romney tells us that he intends to donate a substantial proportion of his royalties to Misericordia (the society for the relief of homosexuals who fall foul of the law, in Africa especially) of which he is life-President.

The two volumes will be published at a monthly interval; a party will be given in connection with each, so as to enable the author's innumerable acquaintances and friends to celebrate. This is a break-through in publishing practice; and we asked John Jackson what it was like to handle a book by a man of such diversified interests as Romney Radish. Jackson was in expansive mood. "It's a pushover. Once in a century an opportunity like this crops up. Just think what it must have been like when the Authorised Version of the Bible was first put on the market. I don't say the Radish Memoirs are quite so significant as that; but I would like you to tell me of any other book, published in Britain, of more universal interest than Runty's."

(Mr Jackson uses the name by which Sir Romney is known only to intimates.)
We had to confess we were stumped for an answer.

"I see plenty of trouble ahead," Lionel Hartley remarked. He had swallowed down the mild irritation he always experienced watching his wife reading without her spectacles. It was less than if she had gone looking for them.

"Well?" he said, sensing that she had come to the end.

"I hadn't heard a word about this."

"Everyone knew he was going to, some day or other. Publishers must have been dogging his footsteps for years. We will read it all beforehand in one of the Sunday newspapers, I dare say. I suppose you will get a presentation copy."

"I should be very much surprised. Runty was never one to cast his bread upon the waters. He knows damn well we will rush out to buy one. And anyway we haven't been seeing one another. How long is it since he was here?"

Lionel Hartley consulted the guest book. "Four years. He came that week-end when we had the General. Don't you remember? Runty brought along three rather sinister-looking Arabs. You didn't know whether they expected to share a room or not."

"I remember. He brought them to upset me. The General was anxious to consult him about the scientific background of the Atom bomb for his history of the Japanese campaign. Runty pulled his leg, and wouldn't help at all."

"Why did you remind me? It was hell. It rained all the time. Runty insisted on playing the gramophone non-stop. Pop records. He borrowed one of my Conrads when he was going away and never returned it. The set has no value now. I daresay we shall have to buy it back at the auction."

Eleanor smiled. "Not a hope. Runty will live for ever."

"I saw him in the Athenaeum the other day. He was lunching with a Greek millionaire. I thought he went out of his way to avoid me."

8

"Why should he avoid you, Lionel?"

"He was probably feeling guilty."

"Not Runty. His conscience congealed long ago."

"He may not have a conscience, in the ordinary meaning of the word, but he is as cute as a fox, and if he is spilling the beans about you he may well be wondering whether there is likely to be any retaliation. Runty doesn't mind a certain amount of not too painful martyrdom if it has publicity value, but there's nobody I know who dislikes personal inconvenience more."

"I don't see what it has to do with you, Lionel."

"Well, I don't know; but many people would think that to have a man trumpeting to the world that he has had an affair with one's wife is of more than marginal interest."

"You must have crossed that bridge long ago."

"That doesn't mean I welcome its being broadcast now, more especially when your name will be bracketed with so many others that it will read like a list of successful mounts in the life history of a champion jockey."

"Everybody knows about me and Runty."

"Not everyone. Not my doctor nor my tailor nor my groom nor the man who repairs my watch."

"Everyone we *know*."

"I have an old-fashioned prejudice against the washing of dirty linen in public."

"You don't think I want it, do you?"

"I should have hoped not."

"I don't mind telling you I'm worried. If one could only trust Runty. I wouldn't mind if he did it in such a way that the brighter type of customer could read between the lines. But he is quite heartless and—isn't it peculiar, have you ever noticed?—there's a vulgar streak in his make-up."

"I have. It is curious. I wonder if there was any funny business in the background. His mother was not averse to a certain amount of dalliance. He had elder brothers. None of them had any talent at all."

"I must say I have often thought it was a most unlikely

stable for the best brain in the land to come out of. The old father was very keen on genealogy and astrology; but I've always heard that he was as woolly-minded as a sheep. The brains come from the mother. She was half Italian."

"Has Runty ever speculated about this?"

"No. It's an area in which he is rather conventional. He's proud of the long descent of the Radishes. The first came over with the Conqueror. He was in charge of the commissariat. They have always been stinking rich."

"I see. We won't have any mud thrown at the Radishes: but I am to expect a handful. Well, I suppose I must put up with it. I've put up with more than most men in my life. Would you mind giving me back my newspaper, if you have quite finished it."

Eleanor did as she was told; but she did not return to the flower-arranging on which she was engaged when her husband had thrown out his news. Her face, which ordinarily showed nothing on its beautiful and marvellously preserved surface, was creased. Her eyes—large beautiful innocent ones, which ordinarily reflected only the face that looked into them—were now like pools into which someone had thrown, not a pebble, but a tin or old boot. Common anxiety was a stranger to Eleanor. She had never had troubles over money or health or the state of her soul. People had been the only occupation of her life, preferably people connected with the arts; she was not so proud that she didn't enjoy the friendship of celebrities; but she took a special pleasure in—as Lionel described it—"picking winners". Her ear was ever close to the ground, and she could almost hear the first faint burgeoning sounds of a reputation. It was made easy for her really. Anyone who knew her—and who that mattered did not?—made a point of bringing along writers and artists of talent.

People spoke of "staying with Eleanor" or "staying at Bloomdale". Eleanor Hartley cropped up in all the arty reminiscences of the Thirties. No one mentioned Lionel. He was always there—friendly, hospitably in the background, as if he were some relation who had come to stay and (from sheer absentmindedness) had never taken himself off, become part of the household. He belonged to a banking family, had his seat on the board, attended quietly to his nominal duties, and was consulted by his wife's friends on practical matters.

If a promising poet won an award, for example, Eleanor was apt to advise him to ask Lionel what to do with it. The poet, nourishing a wild hope that this would produce a plan for immediately doubling the sum, would listen impatiently while Lionel carefully outlined the relevant advantages of various securities. "Are you concerned principally with income? or with capital growth?" he would say, taking out little books and making calculations. The poet, knowing that the money was already owing several times, and in the meanwhile having decided to buy a second-hand car or travel to Japan—spend it on anything in fact but what Lionel was looking up with such kindly care—would pretend to listen.

Sometimes when Eleanor's absorption in some new talent had run its course, Lionel exhibited a continuing interest. "What happened to that young fellow's play?" he might ask, long after everyone had forgotten the evening when it had been read aloud to a captive audience. He had gone bail more than once for Eleanor's former protégés. He bought the pictures of artists who gave their first canvases to Eleanor, and often paid handsomely for portraits. Was ever a face so familiar as hers?

The troubles of the world disappeared at the front gates of Bloomdale, where there was never any conflict except over opinions. Eleanor very seldom—except in matters of the heart—met any set of circumstances which she couldn't manipulate and even where emotions were concerned she had a disinclination for intensity, preferring variety. She was a plant, she liked to say, that did not flourish in too hot an atmosphere and required fresh water regularly if it was not to wilt.

"Talk to me, Lionel. I must talk to somebody. I'm worried to death."

Appealed to like this, her husband responded at once. Such was his way. He lowered the newspaper without abandoning it, and looked at her over his spectacles.

"Still worrying about Runty?"

"Of course. For your sake."

Lionel put down the paper.

"Now, why?"

"He is quite capable of putting me in such an odious light that it will reflect on you. You'll seem too—how shall I put it?"

"Complaisant."

"I suppose so."

"Well, damn it, I was. Wasn't I? We worked that one out."

"It is impossible to explain to everyone that it all meant so little to me really, and nothing at all to you. The difference between you and other people is that you realised in the beginning what so many people only come to understand after they've worn themselves out: love-making is terribly overrated, really—compared with an evening at the ballet, for instance."

"I can only speak for myself. If you didn't like it, why did you give up so much of your time to it? You were never at home during that year when Runty was on the list. Surely you were getting some sort of satisfaction out of it."

"The way you say 'it'."

"I didn't think it was necessary to spell the word out."

"I have never been able to explain my attitude to you. Even that poem I wrote to you—but I daresay you've forgotten that long ago—even that didn't bring home what I meant."

"I remember the poem very well. I can still put my hand on it. At the time I was impressed by the fact that you had such literary skill. You had never let me know. I felt all the more unworthy of the wonderful woman I had married."

"Lionel, too generous, as always!"

"Not at all. Not every man—very few I suppose—would have put up with what you asked me to put up with. This poem—and various announcements of yours at the time—explained that for you religion, art, music, nature, etc. etc. were all symbolised in what, by itself, you regarded as an insignificant ritual akin to brushing the teeth; either, done thoroughly, involved the same amount of time and was accompanied by much the same residual phenomena."

"You did understand. We were in one mind about it all really; but in my case it served a higher purpose. You expressed yourself in your orchids and your Ayrshires."

"Quite. My performances were on public exhibition at agricultural shows."

"My life has always been intensely private."

"I don't know how you can say that when your name appears in every other book of reminiscences."

"As a hostess, as an encourager of talent, as a patron in a small way—and there all the credit should go to you, dear one. You pay."

Lionel shrugged good-humouredly.

"No. I insist. You are too diffident, Lionel. I think we are the happiest couple in the world, and it is all due to you, to your understanding, your patience, your kindness, your sympathy—I could go on for ever. I only wish you had let me persuade you to go into parliament. When Robert used to come here, we often used to discuss it. He said that you would be the greatest Home Secretary of all time."

"Very good of him. I would certainly not be up to Foreign Affairs. I can't travel without feeling unwell. I might have been a success as Minister of Agriculture. I like farmers and country people. You won't be offended if I say that on the whole I prefer them to geniuses."

"Genii."

"I don't think so. I'd prefer my way."

"Never mind. I'm glad we've had this talk. It makes it so much easier to deal with the Runty business. Dearest, oh, I am seriously worried. Of course, he may make me look a fool by not mentioning me at all. He has had so many that he will have to restrict himself or the book will become like one of those in which the lady traveller gets raped on every page. Not that there was much of the Sheik about Runty. I often wondered why he went in for women so much. It was as if he were trying to prove something to himself. He looked very funny. I used to find it difficult not to laugh."

"Please."

"I won't go on. You are so beautifully sensitive, dear. I've had a lot to do with people who traded on their sensibility, but really none of them came within miles of you in that respect."

"I'm glad you use the past tense."

Eleanor blushed. She hadn't thought about syntax. That was one of the traps in life. The things people observed when you weren't trying to deceive them. And she blushed because this was the third morning that she had rushed to the post to see if there was a letter from Freddy Parker. And there wasn't. And he came back from New York last week. He lunched at Rules on Fridays. Today she planned to send him one of her quizzical notes, tender and playful and a little sad. She had developed the gift. There might be some explanation.

"I forgot to tell you that that new friend of yours wants me to back some sort of show he's putting on."

Eleanor went white; less damning than a blush, but her mouth fell open, and that was a familiar sign. She didn't pretend not to know to whom Lionel referred. It was uncanny how he seemed to read her thoughts. Freddy's writing to Lionel on business and ignoring her was the most hurtful thing that had happened to her for years.

"I hope you are not going to be such a fool. Freddy is wildly impractical. He won't study what people will pay to go and see. I've told him again and again."

"I thought you might want me to cough up. I'll tell him I'm broke, shall I?"

"Tell him anything you like. He shouldn't have tried to touch you like that behind my back. He came down on my invitation, and I think he has a cheek to go bothering you, without even consulting me first."

"I didn't take to the chap. I suppose he's all right in his own way. I'm always put off by a middle-aged man in a wig."

"Freddy hasn't a wig."

"He looks as if he had."

"I wish you wouldn't keep wandering away from the subject of Runty. Do you think it would be a good thing if I were to write to him and refer to the paragraph in *The Times* and ask him if he were by any chance planning to make references to me? I could say that I would like to see what he intends to publish. If he dodges me—as he certainly will if he is up to mischief—I can ask your solicitor to write to him. I don't particularly fancy mentioning the matter to that awful Mayberry. Perhaps you would, should the occasion arise."

"Runty is as mad as a hatter, if you ask me. I know he has tons of brains and talents and all the rest of it; but he was always the oddest fish. His public record is like something out of *Alice in Wonderland*. How everyone else takes him seriously beats me; asking him what he thinks China's intentions are, and what is the future of marriage. You'd think the man was Socrates, when the fact is that he has never been able to hold on to an opinion or a wife for more than a year, so long as I've known him."

"That's an exaggeration."

"Not much of a one. A tiny piece of embroidery if you compare it with any pronouncement of Runty's."

"Shall I write?"

"Let me put it this way : if the book is about to be published it's too late if you are in it, and you'll feel terribly small if you write to him and then find you aren't."

Eleanor brooded over this. She valued Lionel's judgement enormously. But in the present instance he was handicapped by lack of information. He knew she had been one of Runty's women — and for longer than most — but he didn't know the details, and she would be embarrassed to tell him, stoic though he was, angel though he was. He had his pride and she her dignity. Both had been put at risk. What a fool she had been!

"If you will forgive me for saying so, particularly at this stage in the game, I could never understand why you let Runty have a fling. He had pinched so many bottoms by that time, and he was always like a marmoset to look at."

"When such a marvellous brain offers himself—with all the world to choose from—it is very flattering, very hard to resist. One is so impressed by all that knowledge and—I suppose I must say—fame plays a part. One's vanity is touched. Try to see the matter dispassionately. Think of me as someone in some sort of social role in the past and Goethe, say, begging me to go to bed with him and we—you and I—having worked all that out with a perfect understanding; can you say I should refuse him? In the eyes of history wouldn't I look a priggish fool?"

"It all depends. To begin with I refuse to see any comparison between Runty and Goethe. Nobody except himself and the baser hirelings of the popular press would ever draw such a comparison. In the second place, Goethe was a fine-looking chap. That would have made it easier, I should have thought. But even having made those allowances, I can't subscribe to your theory that if a man is illustrious or notorious he should only have to nod to a woman and she must lie down."

"I didn't say any such thing. I had in mind some sort of appropriateness in the couple. I do hold a certain position, I suppose."

"Of course, in your own right, and as my wife."

The silence that followed was broken by Lionel. There was no edge to his voice. "There's a fallacy in your argument anyway. It is a piece of pure romanticism. You say Goethe: he was famous and handsome and a poet. Suppose you substitute Mr Gladstone or Darwin or Karl Marx—would you think a woman—even one so distinguished as yourself—should have made herself available if any of those great men dropped a hint? Napoleon, perhaps, the Duke of Wellington at a pinch, Byron, of course; and I'll grant you

Mozart and Chopin, but not Ibsen, not Kipling, not—even as an experiment—Freud. The truth of the matter, my dear, is that after you acknowledge a difference in talent or brain or whatever, we are all very much the same in pyjamas. I'm telling you this; but you should really be in a far better position to tell me. Runty, for example. I bet there was nothing Jove-like about him. In fact you said just now he made you laugh."

"You ticked me off for saying it."

"I know. How inconsistent one is."

"You make the matter seem so simple, but it isn't. Darwin and Freud—to take two of the people you mention—were domesticated and disciplined and didn't make passes at women. But either of them might have fallen in love after he married—many very respectable people did—John Galsworthy for instance—and if it only happened once to them and one innocently were the person to arouse the affection, I should think it would be ungenerous—and history would condemn the woman—if she let the man suffer, even if she was not in love with him and was married to someone else. Take Fanny Brawne; doesn't everyone wish she had given herself to Keats?"

"I never considered the question, I must confess."

"Don't pretend not to understand."

"I think you are doing a job of special pleading. You have assured me that the men in your life since you married me, don't really count. They don't affect our marriage and our affection for each other, our friendship and comradeship—"

Eleanor took the hand that was not holding *The Times* and kissed it.

"I've accepted that; but I haven't liked it. I was aware from the start that I couldn't give you everything you wanted, and I'm not such a curmudgeon as to grudge you looking for it elsewhere; but I never enjoyed the arrangement. It has not been a source of gratification to me. You had very fairly offered me my freedom; and I will now admit that I went once to Fanny Aspern's bedroom at her invitation; but her appearance, undressed, reminded me so forcibly of a plucked turkey I had to beg to be excused. I never made the same mistake again. My help has since taken in every case a more practical—or should I say?—negotiable form."

"That explains why Fanny used to look at me so very venomously. She was awfully snakelike. I used to wonder what riled her. Did she think you might have told me about the fiasco? I don't think you've given yourself a fair chance if Fanny Aspern is the extent of your enterprises."

"I would prefer not to re-survey that aspect of the matter. I told you about it only to deprive you of any illusions on my account. I have not been noble; but am fortunately neither jealous nor envious by temperament; and of all people those I most abhor are the husband or wife who resent their spouses getting elsewhere what is not supplied at home. If I had known more about myself I wouldn't have married you. It wouldn't have been fair."

"I'm glad you didn't, then. Ours has been a wonderful marriage and I've had a son. I don't like Gerald very much, but I'd have hated to be a barren wife."

"Gerald is a very good fellow. We never had a moment's trouble with him. When I think of what other parents have had to put up with, I can't be sufficiently grateful."

"You are always very nice about him. He is the one thing I did give you all for yourself. I never let a man touch me from the day we were married until six months and three days after Gerald was born."

"I never doubted he was mine, if that's what you mean."

"I should hope not. He's a Hartley all right. I can't see a drop of my side's blood in him, except his height. Grandfather was enormously tall, remember. Gerald must have got his grotesque height from him. The Hartleys are small. But he has the eyes and chin."

"Pale eyes, no chin, you mean."

"I didn't say that."

"You never say anything that is unkind. That is why I shall resent it very much on your account if Runty does you down. In the old days I'd have called him out or horse-whipped him."

"I've got it. Why don't you write to him and warn him that if he publishes anything you object to you'll. . . . You needn't be specific. But you could frighten him. He's a craven at heart."

"Suppose he writes back and says that he isn't going to mention your name. Think of the fun he'll have handing my letter round. I won't be able to show my face in London. No, my dear. I'm afraid that we must stick it out—wait and see —then, if he does behave infamously, it will redound more to his shame than to ours. He can't go too far. He will be restrained by fear of libel actions. The publishers will see to that. I hope you didn't write him any silly letters. But I forgot; he can't publish them without permission. I think we haven't much to be afraid of."

Eleanor, as always, was soothed by her husband's practical wisdom, but she still sat unnaturally upright and sometimes her eyes wandered round the room as if in search of a way to escape. Lionel, who noticed everything, noticed this. Why was she so concerned? Sex was a subject in which he took very little interest, less than anyone he knew, except the housekeeper who complained to him frequently about the amount of attention given to it in the Sunday papers, "even the posh ones". "I'd like to take a strap to those hussies," she was wont to say. Lionel parted company with her there. He could not see himself using a strap without hopelessly com-promising himself. Even Frank Longford would see the point of that.

Gentleness was the essence of Lionel. His—Eleanor told him—was a Chekhovian character, laced with sound business instincts, a perfect combination for a husband.

"Don't worry, darling. We shall see it through. Listen to this. I was reading the lines to myself only this morning. I wake so impossibly early. This is exactly how I feel about the matter."

He took a book off the sofa table and started to read in his pleasant modulated voice:

> "Where it concerns himself,
>   Who's angry at a slander makes it true."

"I know the rest of it, dear." Eleanor had heard the telephone.

Lionel opened his post unhurriedly and put down each letter before he had read it through so as to divide his attention equally between correspondence and breakfast. Eleanor, by contrast, gave to her mail the excited attention that she lavished on any art form; she thrust her chair back at an angle, and a quivering, anticipatory eagerness was apparent in every part of her person. Even her hair moved.

Her mail this morning consisted of two receipts, three minor bills, an invitation to a charity committee-meeting and a Harrods' catalogue. Among Lionel's letters was one in his son's handwriting. He took this to his study, unopened, to read it there.

"Dear Father," it began, "I am writing to give you good news before you read it in your newspaper. I am engaged to be married to Caroline Chetwynd-Skopwith, my Colonel's daughter. We have known each other for some time, and I am certain that we are ideally suited. Caro is an only child, and I was not at all certain that the Colonel would approve of the connection. I was delighted to find that he gave us his blessing as heartily as anyone could ask. 'Mims', as Caroline rather delightfully calls her mother, was also perfectly sweet about it. There is to be a photograph of Caro in *Country Life* next month. You will be able to see for yourself that your future daughter-in-law is a good-looker.

"Her father met me in a very candid way about the practical issues. His brother has no children, and as Caro is an only child, she will come in for Skopwith in due course. The Colonel when he heard—I think he knew already—that I, too, was an only child was anxious about the future. He

asked me very pointedly if I was determined to keep Bloomdale on (when the time comes). Skopwith is a definite 'first'
in all his plans for us. If Caro and I were to have a boy,
there will be no problem; but he was disappointed himself in
this respect, and naturally wishes to anticipate a run of bad
luck in the family. In other words, he expected me to show
my hand so that he might arrange with his brother what
precautions to take. The idea of Skopwith ever being disposed
of—you understand—could not be entertained by either of
them. I spoke up at once, and said that as Bloomdale had
been bought by you only because it suited you, being reasonably close to London, and suitable for entertaining, I would
have no hesitation in selling it when the time came. It might
—who knows?—be considered then more prudent to let it.
But that is a detail.

"The Colonel was greatly relieved by my attitude, so much
so that it quite reassured me about the propriety of deciding
the matter on the spot without first consulting you, as I would
have wished. Caro has a little income of her own; the Colonel
will add to it when we marry, and I did not require his hint
that she will be well-to-do by any reasonable reckoning when
her parents and uncle pass on.

"There are—this will interest you—perhaps you are aware
of them—splendid pictures at Skopwith. The Van Dyck is
magnificent. The family has never allowed strangers into
the house; for this reason the collection is very little known.
Normally the Colonel is extremely reserved, but he expanded
at once—I suppose he welcomed an opportunity to discover
what sort of person he was letting into the family. We found
we were in agreement on every subject. He is very much surprised at the disappointing speed of my promotion, and he
promised to let a word fall in the right quarter. Mims (as she
insists I call her) took me aside after dinner. She was in the
secret, she told me, and almost as anxious as Caro—because
the Colonel is so rigid in his views and the sort of publicity
which our family has received is anathema to him. These
very old families outside the peerage are the proudest, I have

discovered. They intermarry with their own set, support in each generation the same school and college and regiment, and so far as is possible try to preserve an unchanging pattern down the years. Fortunately Mims had the good sense to play you up like anything. If only you had gone to Winchester there would have been less trouble; Harrow is a fine old school, of course, but it provides no guarantee and some lamentable examples. Winchester has blotted its copy-book too, but usually, the Colonel told me, through scholarship boys.

"I haven't told you much about Caro. You will approve of her, I know. She has quite a brain. That intimidated me a little at first. I can't get her to interest herself in stamps, but we have many tastes in common. And she has a wonderful sense of humour. I told her the story about Julia and the soup. I thought she would never stop laughing. We have dined out on it ever since. Should you drop a line to the Colonel? We plan for June in the Guards' Chapel. The reception will probably be at St. James's Palace. Tell Mother. I hope you are keeping fit. I've taken up golf again, but have been out of luck in making up games.

Yours affectionately,
Gerald."

"A wonderful sense of humour," Lionel murmured aloud.

He had read his son's letter through methodically. Eleanor would have raced ahead, gone back, and taken longer in the end, as well as getting many matters muddled. Gerald was indeed absurd; for that reason, Lionel felt a special tenderness for him.

He read his son's letter a second time, and fell to thinking of the bride. Nowadays of course there would be no trouble about a divorce; but what damage would be done in the interval! The blinded girl's eyes opened at last might look asquint at the world for the rest of her life. Gerald would receive a death-blow to his *amour propre*. To be discarded by a girl from the third best family in the border counties, and to be divorced not for any peccadillo—against that breeding was no insulator—but because she just couldn't stand him—it might be more than he could bear. He wasn't sensitive. God knows a wart-hog couldn't have discussed his nuptial arrangements with less feeling, but he was insanely vain—proud, he would have said—mistaking vanity for the nobler quality. This was the sort of revelation that could drive him to suicide.

While he thought over the matter, Lionel's mind reverted to the subject of the breakfast-table conversation—Runty's cursed autobiography. Suppose Providence in His inscrutable wisdom had thrown in Gerald's way a really nice girl, one capable of turning that unappetising chap into a pleasant fellow—there was always this miraculous possibility; girls did marry—yes, and love—the most unlikely people : suppose this had happened and everything was in readiness—the parents pacified, relations informed, settlements drawn up— and Runty's book came out with bizarre revelations of his year-long affair with the bridegroom's mother; it might well be like a petrol bomb hurled in their midst. It might not wreck the marriage, but it would certainly break the last connecting link between Gerald and his family. He loved Gerald without reason, and was touched by the knowledge that, until now, he was the only human influence in his son's life. At school the boy never formed a single friendship. "This is a rum sort of house," he used to say to visitors; but what if it produced this rum sort of boy? And if now, at forty, with a prospect of happiness before him at last, that egregious old egotist Runty Radish were to blight it with his boastings and obscenities—Lionel would never forgive himself. He had stood idly by while Eleanor led Runty round on a string. They parted, she alleged, when Runty fitted himself out with false teeth; but there was, no doubt, a mass of material to draw on before that.

Dignity : Lionel had a commonplace book in which he used to write down things that pleased him, either because he found them amusing or wise or in accord with his own experience; he had copied down a remark of Chesterton's: "The two things that a healthy person hates most between heaven and hell are a woman who is not dignified and a man who is." It seemed to have been written with his wife and son in mind. Eleanor's dignity was at risk. She had an inimitable way of wreathing amours in a golden haze, decarnalising them, blowing them up in iridescent bubbles, letting gauze fall between herself and tumescent reality. If Runty could be trusted to play the game, he might be indiscreet and yet leave Eleanor's reputation with some protective cover still; but he was not to be trusted. He made a parade of his unswerving devotion to truth, which amounted only to shamelessness in his own case and a ruthless disregard of the feelings of others. True he was the friend of the oppressed everywhere—blacks, Jews, Arabs, homosexuals, sex-offenders, anarchists—and his secretary had *carte blanche* to give his name to any protest anywhere provided it was against established authority; but where individuals were concerned he acted on the assumption that they were as devoid of feeling as himself. And if anyone infringed his legal rights, he called in a lawyer at once and pursued the offender tenaciously.

"Of all our friends I like Runty least, and that is saying something," Lionel had been wont to remark before this business blew up. And now he realised how well-founded was the claim. What was exasperating was Runty's impregnability. With such an international reputation in the modern world he was immune from scandal. Money, where large sums were at stake, didn't interest him; he had always been able to do whatever he liked; and the threat of damages was a matter of indifference to him. It might interest his publishers, though. Perhaps, after all, he should drop a warning line to them, it might have an effect, even at this late hour. Runty had probably inspired his publishers with his overweening arrogance. John Jackson, lick-spittle that he was, would be so bemused by his capture of the great man—who published his less-paying books with a decent firm—that he might need a broadside to wake him up to the risks involved in taking on the old reprobate and his scandal-sheet. Lionel moved to his desk and took out his pen. If he didn't write now, his resolution would cool.

"Sir," he began. "I see in today's issue of *The Times* that you propose to publish personal recollections of Sir Romney Radish. This is to inform you that Sir Romney has not sought permission to include any matters that refer to me or my family, and I shall take such steps to protect their privacy and mine as I shall be advised if he chooses to act on any assumption to the contrary."

"That should put a dint in the fatuous self-complacency of Mr Jackson," he told himself. "If only I could hint that his hoped-for, played-for, paid-for chances of making the Honours List may be at risk, that would do the trick. I wonder who else is involved? Runty was so indefatigable he may have hunted round the Royal Enclosure in his time. Now, who could tell me?"

Chapter II

THE LAIRD OF SMOGG, framed in the doorway, staring out to sea, would have made an impressive figure if he hadn't been scratching the seat of his trousers—meditatively, however, for he was sober—and on these occasions his faculties were engaged in sorting out realities from fantasies in the bemused muddle of his mind.

"I see that Runty is going to publish a book," Pamela said. She was sitting in a deck-chair in front of the cottage. Her husband made no reply, but continued to scratch himself, shifting slightly the point of maximum contact, and to gaze across the bay, or "lough", as he called it.

"I'd be fascinated to see it," Pamela added.

"Oh, shut up," said her lord.

She did.

It was a marvel to their ever-decreasing circle of friends that Pamela stayed with Angus. She was very rich; her father owned a bank—it was inaccurately said—in the States. Angus was her third husband, so that her fidelity could not be attributed simply to inanition. He, too, had married; how often, like everything else about him, was vague. His unions had been regular and irregular, and sometimes terminated with technical imprecision. The present marriage was unique for both spouses. They had turned Catholic in Assisi after a prolonged drinking bout in Rome, and had been married by a priest; the bride in white; there was a reception afterwards in the Argentinian Embassy. The choice of venue was never satisfactorily explained.

His wife's reference to the publication of a book antagonised Angus; he was by way of being a writer, and the prolonged gestation of his current work was doing nothing to improve his temper. It was not tactful to refer to other people's books in his presence unless there was a story of failure attached to them. But the remark took lodgement somewhere in his confused brain; and as he was thinking in fact about nothing, forced its way into the front of his consciousness.

"Runty, did you say?"

"Right," Pamela responded, brightening under attention, "Runty Radish."

"Oh, him! What's the book about?"

"It says here that Haymakers are going to publish Sir Romney Radish's autobiography. It is in two volumes; the first is about his personal life. The other will deal with his crowded career."

"If you had told me that in the first place, you would have saved us both a great deal of time. I didn't think that old exhibitionist had two volumes left in him. He's written out. I saw him on television when I was in London. He looked as if he had been taken out of a refrigerator for the occasion."

"I wonder if he will put me in."

"Put *you* in; why should he?"

"I just thought he might."

"You only met him once."

"Right."

There was a sphinx-look on his wife's face which Angus recognised and particularly resented. It came there when something pleased her and was being kept from him.

"I thought you only met him for a moment at some sort of conference for limitation of atomic weapons, or some crap of that kind."

"I didn't say 'a moment'. Horace was with the U.S. deputation. Right? Runty came on his own. He made a splendid speech and received an ovation from all the representatives of the Third World; but, of course, he was given no support by us or the European countries. The Soviet representative went out of his way to compliment him. He looked as pleased as a child. It was very moving."

"I still don't see why that should bring you into his memoirs."

"It was a very important conference. It led to nothing, of course,—they never do—but there was a great deal of attention paid to Runty's speech. It was published afterwards in *Encounter*."

"Well, if it gives you any satisfaction to read that Horace Cannon was accompanied by his wife—'charming wife' perhaps he will say—I don't grudge it to you."

Pamela did not take the special look off her face, and her husband interpreted this as a challenge.

"Well! Would it?"

"Would what, dear?"

"Would it give you any satisfaction to read your name in a list of those present on that occasion?"

"I don't think so. Everyone knows I was married to Horace Cannon, and naturally I accompanied him to Antananarivo."

"Why Antananarivo?"

"Conferences are always held at inconvenient and out-of-the-way places. It helps security."

"You speak about the man as if you had known him all your life. I shouldn't have heard that he was called Runty if you hadn't told me."

"He doesn't call himself that, and only a very few use the name to his face. He told me to call him Bunny when I wrote to him; but, somehow, I got into the habit of calling him by the other name."

"It certainly suits him."

"That's being rude, honey. The word is used affectionately, because he is short. It's partly due to the enormous size of his head. He would need to have been over six feet to carry that off. It's magnificent."

"I don't see anything particularly magnificent about his head."

"You haven't a plastic sense, dear. And then, his hair is like a lion's mane."

"A pretty moth-eaten lion."

Angus was being petty; he resented the reference to hair as he was himself quite bald, except for a fringe at the back, between his ears.

"Runty is a great man. Right? I don't like to hear you talk about him in a mean way."

"I dispute that. Personally I'd say he is a perfect example of the jack-of-all-trades. He's on every committee simply because he can't write any more. That last book of his was sheer bull."

"I think it is very moving to see a man of giant intellect happily writing for children."

"If you ask me, the reason is because he is in his second childhood. When are those people coming?"

"They said they'd be here about eight."

"I'm hungry."

"Fix yourself another drink and get me one."

Angus was about to do this anyway. Fixing the drinks, he continued to brood. He used to be rather pleased when Pamela dropped the name 'Radish'. Fame had kept him at bay for a long time, and he had not yet had time to become *blasé* about celebrities. Now he was one himself—in a small way. Here in Ireland, where he had come to live, he expected to be a lion, but the people—especially the literary people—never seemed to read anything except the works of a small group of their contemporaries upon which they lavished exaggerated praise or insensate abuse, according to whim. In London, at El Vino"s, for example, or on a quiet day at the Savage, he was definitely somebody. But it had been hard going in Dublin so far. His title, selected at random—he had spotted Smogg on a map and it gave him inspiration—was a talking point. It added a touch of romance to his confused personality.

But if anybody brought up the subject of his Lairdship a warning light in Angus's eye usually advised them to drop it. In his cups he was apt to challenge onlookers to admit that they didn't believe in the authenticity of his claim to be

Laird of Smogg. Occasionally his bluff was called—he was not a man of action—but as a rule he could depend on intimidating his listeners. Sometimes he pointed to Smogg on the map of the Hebrides, which hung in the hall of his Dublin flat, and said, "Sheep. Thousands of them."

That was all anyone ever heard of the island. Angus had never been there. American friends of his wife sometimes mispronounced the name.

"Smug, damn it, not Smog," he would shout at them, his eyes blood-shot.

He had been born in Australia, and came to London to work on newspapers, wrote several novels, rather sentimental in character and enlivened by reference to faeces and pubic hair. Further than that he would not be prepared to compete in the race for realism; and it looked as if he would never obtain notoriety with his pen, when he dashed off *In the Spring a Young Man's Fancy*, six months before the Profumo scandal. The coincidence brought him fame overnight. The battle for the paperback rights could be heard all over London, W.C.2. Since then he had not held his readers; but he was prolific with articles, usually deeply critical of contemporary *mores*. For these he was more than adequately paid, as he wrote them almost mechanically, and usually after a binge.

He met Pamela on a lecture tour in the States. Love for Scotland, she said, activated her seeking him out. When he angrily admitted that a week-end in Glasgow was the limit of his acquaintance with Macbeth's country, she found other grounds for sustaining her preference. She had always wanted to marry a genius. A genius with a Scottish title was better than a clerk in the embassy; but rapture began to recede after she printed "the Laird of Smogg and Lady MacDonnell" on their first invitation cards only to be told that she was to call herself plain Mrs MacDonnell.

"But why?"

"Mine is a courtesy title."

"What does that mean exactly?"

"You won't find it in reference books."

"Why don't you call up the editors?"

"It's no use. I give up. I can't explain. Americans never understand nuance."

"I mean to say, you are either the Laird of Smogg or you are not. I can't see any reason for a mystery."

"There isn't one. These titles are granted by acclaim."

"Like the election of a tribal chief?"

"Exactly."

The Laird was fretful, not only because he was hungry and not feeling well—he never felt well—but because the approaching visitors unnerved him. The MacDonnells had taken a cottage on the shores of Dingle Bay for three months, and put a notice to that effect in a daily newspaper. Such is not the custom in Ireland—a fact of which Angus, who was an avid reader of newspapers, was well aware; but he was not averse to forging his own customs.

On public occasions he wore a kilt, though as a rule his style of dress was formal. In the past he had taken to shepherd's plaids, sandals, etc. Now a Glengarry, worn in the evening (to conceal his baldness), was his only departure from sartorial orthodoxy. He was formal in manner, too, and rebuked levity at his table if its targets were inside his area of approval. He wrote to Ministers of State and offered them gratuitous advice; his comments on current affairs appeared regularly in the letter columns of the best newspapers in England as well as Ireland.

So far nobody in Kerry appeared to have read the advertisement of the MacDonnell's arrival at Dingle; then a postcard came inviting them to cocktails at Killarney Castle. This celebrated ruin had been taken for a year by an American, whose family and their families filled it. A plain and uninteresting group, they had sparsely diluted their company with locals, chosen, it seemed, at random or because of professional contacts. Angus very nearly made a scene when he saw what he had been let in for; but his displeasure was assuaged by the timely appearance of a resident land-owner and his wife, who made themselves civil.

Mrs McElligot's interest in the Hebrides might have caused trouble, but Pamela skilfully steered her out of earshot, and the husband conversed about Angus's book. By a happy chance Aloysius McElligot had only recently read it, having bought the paperback edition for his last plane journey. He was able to remember the names of the characters. Angus was pleased, and invited them to dinner.

But now he had misgivings. These occasions always ended badly somehow, even when he did his very best to be genial. In fact the success of a dinner or luncheon was frequently in inverse ratio to the effort expended in preparing for it. When he "threw himself" into a party, working up excess adrenalin in the process, a point of no return was reached inevitably, past which he tried to go with the aid of neat gin—always fatally; and genuine disappointment as much as chronic aggressiveness accounted for the savagery with which he abused those whom he had set out so blithely to please. On this occasion the portents were gloomy. He was fretting over the Runty Radish business. Instinct informed him that the topic was rich in prospective mischief. Pamela went on looking as if she had laid her first egg and was expecting a diploma from an agricultural instructor. Then, he suffered unease about the newspaper announcement of their arrival at Kerry. Swine that they were, his Dublin acquaintances were probably laughing at it behind his back.

To crown his misgivings was the wan fact that so far nobody had called although they had been in residence for a fortnight, and Angus had become a habitué of the saloon bars of all the hotels and public houses within walking distance. He aired his views in each, regardless of the company. In one pub the only person to listen was a deaf pedlar. He kept on saluting, which was nice.

Inevitably the visitors arrived late. This put Angus's nerves in a jangle, and he greeted them with considerable *froideur.* Pamela always gushed, and this confirmed their tentative opinion, already formed, that "the wife was the pleasanter of the pair".

Aloysius McElligot had an intuitive understanding of his fellow men. He summed Angus up at once—a man is much easier to evaluate on his home ground than when he is encountered abroad—and decided to "go easy" and, so far as possible, avoid a duologue. He kept close to the women, and admired Pamela's black silk pyjamas. He then admired the view from the cottage windows, and congratulated Angus on his perspicacity in renting such a delightful holiday home. Going to the single book-shelf, he took down a copy of *In the Spring a Young Man's Fancy.* Squeezing it appreciatively between his hands, as a Rugby player will a new ball before he kicks it, he went across the room calling out the title to draw his wife's attention to its comforting presence. The like of the sherry, which Angus poured out with meagre enthusiasm, he declared was not to be got in all the establishments for the sale of wine and spirits in Killarney. He was cut short when he started to praise the furniture by Angus's abruptly rejecting any responsibility for his hired house's appointments.

The poor man could not have worked harder, and if Angus thawed only gradually, his wife (who, unlike himself, had been cheered by the day's events) excelled herself. She swore eternal friendship with the McElligots, and got each in turn to promise that so long as the MacDonnells retained a Dublin residence, there, and only there, would they stay on future visits to the capital. Nor was their mutual junketing to be confined to that—Pamela insisted that they must come and stay with them in America. Angus seemed to concur in these spacious arrangements. He believed in a copious intake of friends; one could never allow sufficiently for wastage.

All would have been well if Pamela hadn't drunk far too much and taken Iris McElligot into her close confidence. What was she to do, she enquired of her new friend, leaning towards her and confirming Iris's opinion that she had nothing on underneath : she had had this tempestuous affair

33

with Runty—"you know Romney Radish"—and he was going to put it all in a book?

"*The* Romney Radish?"

"Right."

Iris was impressed. She had never indulged even in a flirtation in twenty years of marriage, and excelled in good-naturedly resisting tipsy overtures; but she admired women who did splendid dangerous things, out of her ken; she had settled for a quiet life with good solid Aloysius. The wide-eyed gaze (she, too, had drunk more than her quota) that she turned on Pamela was full of surprised affectionate encouragement. She was grateful for the vicarious thrill. What fun to meet someone really exciting for a change, and to find her, with all the world to choose from, offering devoted friendship! What a piece of luck they had accepted the dreary Americans' invitation. It just showed you: never despair: seize every opportunity. She could have hugged Pamela.

Aloysius, attracted to the exciting sounds, looked over towards the sofa, on whose broken springs the women were bouncing in a crisis of confidence. Decent man, he was pleased to see his Iris happy; and he was amiably curious about the cause of her innocent excitement.

"I think you are very mean, the pair of you, not to let us into the secret. Aren't they, Angus?"

His host never liked to be interrupted—he was in the middle of explaining the scheme he had outlined to the Minister for Finance to exempt writers from death duties—and he refused to look in the direction indicated.

"I'll bloody well threaten to leave the country if he doesn't sit up and pay attention. I could live on Smogg for nothing."

"It must be nice there. Lonely I'd have thought, in winter especially."

"Balls."

"I've never been there."

34

"Neither has Angus," Pamela called, giggling, from the sofa.

"She's pulling your leg," Mr McElligot observed, lowering his voice. He was alarmed by his host's reaction, and feared he designed to hit his wife with the empty bottle he was flourishing. But instead he slumped in a chair.

"I am fated to live in exile. How would you like to be born in bloody Australia and then be thrown into Fleet Street at twenty years of age? How was I to settle on Smogg with a mother and two whores to support before I had a penny to my name? To be an artist and to come from Australia is like being a pock-marked beauty-queen. You are beaten before you begin. And yet I persevered. My books were ignored: did you ever read *The Death of Pan* or *Gideon's Armour* or *Amanda's Artillery*? No, you didn't. Don't apologise. I dare say you never even heard of them. I don't care. It doesn't matter a ferret's fart to me. I dare say a monument will be erected to me in bloody Melbourne when I'm not there to see it. When I wrote *In the Spring a Young Man's Fancy*—they couldn't ignore me then. The world would have laughed at them. They crawled. It was obscene. Wouldn't I come and lecture? How long was it since I'd been back home? Smogg is my home. I'm a MacDonnell, not a bloody Australian bushman. It gave me a little satisfaction to write and tell them that. And now I've come to Ireland. Don't deceive yourself. I have no desire to put down any roots here. Frankly, I don't like what I have seen of the people. They are a hopelessly ignorant incestuous lot of born amateurs, if you ask me. But it suits me; and so long as it suits me, I'll stay. But I'll die on Smogg. I've plans drawn for a house there. Pam knows it. She knows my heart is set on it, that I'm living in bloody exile, and she mocks me in front of friends."

He buried his face in his hands, Mr McElligot cast an anxious glance in his own wife's direction; but she was too enthralled by the drama to notice any signals from him.

"Ah, poor dear. Be *nice* to him," she nudged Pamela, who wasn't attending.

"Oh, he'll get over it," she said.

"Tell us about this Radish man," Mr McElligot said to distract attention from Angus whom he supposed would like time to recover.

Pamela had been growing in self-esteem all evening. Angus was all very well; he had admittedly found fame with a book. That had won him her hand. But she was tired of being snubbed, and supplying orchestral accompaniments to his solos when guests were around. She was a somebody in her own estimation. She had married the best-looking boy in her Sophomore year. All right, he was half-way to being a fairy. That half didn't show. Anyhow, Horace Cannon was going places when she married him. If Kennedy had lived he might have been shifted somewhere interesting, for a change. Horace was pretty dull; but he looked well. He was a natty dresser. Other women used to look at him appreciatively. She would have got along with Horace if Angus hadn't turned up. She went to a lecture he gave on the corruption of modern society. She bought one of his books on display and asked him to autograph it. He wrote a long message on the fly-leaf, having first asked her name. That emboldened her to invite him to a party. Horace couldn't go. It all began that evening. Angus had a way not only of getting drunker than anyone else in a short time but of making whoever he was with as drunk as himself. She only sobered up when Horace's lawyers served the divorce papers on her.

She had been attracted by what Angus stood for rather than by the man himself. In appearance he was rather a mess. But she had had a unique experience with Romney Radish. He met her at the Antananarivo conference. They fell into conversation. He invited her out for an evening walk, pointed out all the stars and then, in the middle of a description of the voyage of Icarus, he pulled her behind a tropical plant and tore her blouse off, panting like a thirsty poodle. It was a disagreeable experience at the time, but it gave Pamela the confidence she required. Henceforth she need not think she had no appeal for men with brains. Sir Romney Radish, the Soviet representative had said—and all the black delegates present clapped when he said it—was the greatest brain on earth.

They hadn't an opportunity to make contact again on that occasion. Rather imperiously he had ordered her not to sleep during the rest of the conference in her husband's room. He would find accommodation for her, he said. But Pamela couldn't screw up the courage to serve a ukase on Horace, just like that. Nor was she quite certain she wanted to. Radish might forget her when he went away, and it would be difficult to explain her conduct to her husband. She liked travelling round with Horace, and Washington parties. She wasn't impetuous and then, although it was a compliment to be practically raped by Romney Radish, physically he was definitely an acquired taste, if one could ever acquire it.

The experience made her think twice as much of Horace afterwards; which went to show the truth of the proverb. A few kisses, tasting of curry, was all she had the opportunity of getting from Sir Romney after their first interview; but he said he would look her up. He frequently came to America, he said. She invited him to stay. He sent her a postcard from Dacca. Her long letter, in which she was satisfied she made herself interesting, drew a short type-written reply, with a message scribbled in ink at the bottom. She sent a card at Christmas. None came back. But it had been an instructive experience.

And now she decided to talk about it. Hell! Why shouldn't she? Why was Angus always the one to show off? These were really nice people. Iris was a dear. It didn't matter what Angus might say. Soon everyone in the literate world would be hearing about that night on the scratchy sand in Madagascar. The printed version, no doubt, would make it all sound more lyrical than it seemed at the time.

"I don't think I ought to tell you about Runty," Pamela began. "Runty, by the way, is one of those names that is used behind a person's back by people who know him very well. He asked me to call him Bunny. He had lots and lots of names to choose from. Romney is a little formal; one can't blame him for not using that, although it is his first name. Someone the family didn't like fell into Romney marsh and was drowned. Runty's parents called their next child Romney in thanksgiving. That is what he says. You ought to meet him. He's rather terrifying at first. He stares at one with *such* a quizzical expression in his eyes. But there's nothing to be afraid of. People say that where women are concerned he can't keep his hands to himself. But I think that is envy talking. Nobody he has ever looked at says it about him, I bet. He is a very passionate man. But I think that is very natural in a genius. We should make allowances. Tolstoy . . . But what was I saying?"

"You want to tell us how Runty laid you," her husband broke in.

The MacElligots glanced at him in alarm. A broken man apparently, a few moments ago; now, he sounded full of fight.

"You've no cause of complaint if I do. We weren't married then. I had never met you. I was married to Horace, who will have the right to complain. Right? Not you. You were conducting your own affairs at the time. *He* says."

The last remark, addressed with an ironic emphasis to the two guests, caused them to wilt. They were being dragged into this thing; but Iris ignored her husband's glances at the door. Her curiosity was aroused. Come what may, she would see it through. Life was uneventful as a rule. She had taken too much to drink, Aloysius McElligott decided, when Pamela lay back and addressed the ceiling.

"How shall I ever forget the marvel of the moon, the mysterious rustle in the sleeping forest, the sea beating on the shore, so much more slowly than my heart, cries of strange birds, and that cry (which he would interpret as he pleased) but which came when I put my hand on something in the sand, and it moved. We are adults. We are friends. We can talk about these things among ourselves. Angus tells me of his adventures. You, I daresay, have heard about each other's *tours de force*."

Mr McElligot was puzzled. He had the appearance of a man looking round in a strange place for his hat.

"Whatever Runty may try to convey in his memoirs to the contrary, I am telling you here and now, as between friends, because we are friends, and adults, he had me only once. 'Every woman,' I told him, 'owes that much to genius. But I don't love you. I am flattered—why pretend? I am kind of proud you picked me out of all the women. What woman wouldn't be? But don't get ideas about me. I belong to Horace Cannon,' I said. It sounded sort of funny bringing out the two names, but I thought he mightn't know who I was talking about if I just said 'Horace', like I'd do to you. We spent one night together. No more. I went away then, cut the cable, never answered his letters. I burnt them. I didn't like to think of prurient eyes gloating over them after I'd passed on, and seeing how frustration could reduce a great man to such—utter self-humiliation. My God! Get me another drink somebody. I've talked too much."

The McElligots exchanged glances. Theirs was not the right to turn to the decanter with Angus in the room. He had looked fatuous while his wife was making her revelations. A relief, as he might so easily have become violent. But he seemed to be rather proud of her, and took a proprietary interest in her confessions.

"Well, this *has* been an exciting evening. We haven't noticed the time flying," Iris said, getting up.

"Sit down," said the host. Aloysius stood up to cover his wife's withdrawal. He looked at his watch and said, "It's time for breakfast."

"We never go to bed here," Pamela said. She was sitting up and yawning.

"We have another late night ahead of us," Iris explained, standing her ground.

"I don't know why you've got to run away just when my wife starts to open up her soul. You can tell me about yourself, Iris. Come on. You must have gone behind the bushes in your time. We are all adults here, as Pamela has observed. Suppose we undress. My wife has a better figure than any I've observed locally. I'll say that for her. Show them those shots I took of you, Pamela. Go on. This is the time for full disclosure."

"We must really be getting along," Iris said, moving towards the door. Her husband, remembering he hadn't brought his hat, closed the ranks. They stood like dogs waiting to be let out.

Angus looked angry again, pulled the door open. "Go if you want to."

"We'd love to have stayed longer. We've had such an exciting evening." Iris put a foot on the gravel.

"A grand evening. Thank you, Pamela. Good-bye Angus. We must fix up another very soon." Aloysius pushed his wife in front of him moving towards safety.

They got into their car. Iris lowered the window and waved. Her husband attended to the driving. She saw their hosts wander out, tumblers in hand, staring after them, not waving. The track uphill from the bungalow took a twist at the top, bringing the house into full view for the last time before another turn led out of the gate into the public road. Husband and wife stood side by side, staring, looking huge in the light that poured out from the door-way.

Suddenly the taller figure seized the smaller; for a moment they grappled; then, silently, locked together, they rolled out of sight down the bank. Out on the road, Aloysius stopped the car.

"Did you see that?"

"Is he going to kill her?"

"Well, if he wants to, I won't prevent him."

"Shouldn't we do something? Suppose he *does* kill her?"

"I dare say she's used to it. Why did she marry him in the first place? Not for his blue eyes. He's as ugly as sin."

"It was an evening to remember. I did think she was asking for trouble when she told us about that Radish man. What husband would stand for that?"

"He looked as pleased as Punch."

"Well, I'm glad we are just plain ordinary. When all's said and done, it is the most comfortable way to be. Sometimes it seems so dull: but after an experience like that one's grateful. I wonder are we right not to tell the Guards? He looked quite capable of killing her."

Aloysius drove on.

Chapter III

LIONEL FELT ILL-AT-EASE in other men's clubs; waiting for Runty in the hall of the Athenaeum, he sighed each time the door opened and members and their guests entered, talking, and passed up the stairs. Runty, he remembered, was never in time for appointments. He knew too many people. His progress down the street was an obstacle race. Even now he was probably engaged in conversation on the steps. Five minutes later he appeared in the door-way, looking, as always, like a perennial schoolboy. He wore the sort of tweed schoolboys wore when they went first into long trousers. He was hatless, and moved as if he had been running. There was something schoolboyish, too, about the expression on his lined old face—a larky look.

"There you are, Nelly. I'm sorry if I'm late. I was nabbed by someone coming in. Let's find our table. I don't suppose you want to stand around in the bar."

Nobody had ever called Lionel "Nelly", but it brought back to him the days when Runty haunted Bloomdale. He had invented the name, and it annoyed Lionel. He did it, Eleanor explained, to everyone—gave them names—to pay them back for calling him Runty. But his nick-names never caught on. They were never happily chosen. Lionel had forgotten Runty's habits. That decisiveness about not going to the bar, for example. He didn't drink, and resented the time wasted by others in the ceremony.

"What are you having? I'll take a slice of roast beef, as raw as you can make it, and a glass of milk," he added to the wine waiter, who approached at the same time, then—turning to his guest—"Order anything you like. I never eat very much at luncheon. It puts me to sleep in the afternoon,

I find." Lionel was naturally co-operative; with anyone else he would have allowed himself to be discouraged from eating an adequate meal, while resolving not to let himself in for the same experience again; but these few seconds in Runty's company brought memories back; and he determined not to be bullied as he used to be when as a newly-married man he indulged his wife's bizarre inclinations, happy to think she was happy. Runty threatened her happiness now. He had a sort of charm. There was no denying that. It was the way he smiled : inviting one to join in the fun. The fun was all in his mind. He was without any visual sense; the normal diet of the Desert Fathers was Lucullian in comparison with Runty's; his only source of pleasure was in his brain. It was like a Swiss watch. Hearing it tick was a reward in itself. As a gossip, however, he was Olympian. He began at once about a scientist at the next table. "That angelic look after thirty is the unfailing indication of a concentrated womaniser," he explained. Lionel demurred. He didn't want to listen to Runty's gossip. Not today. His letter to the publishers had been met first by silence; a telephone call from Runty inviting him to lunch had followed.

He ran on agreeably and maliciously; Lionel found himself surrendering. He had forgotten what an attractive voice the fellow had. He had a fatal genius for intimacy. It was almost impossible to believe Runty didn't love one. But every now and then an unexpected prick revealed a pin concealed in the velvet surface. "He's as treacherous as a weasel," Lionel reminded himself. He was enjoying his lunch, having defied his host and ordered the very best the club's menu offered and a glass of champagne.

"I'm sticking to champagne," he said when Runty, pouring himself out water, offered to fill his tumbler. One always went with pockets empty and without a cheque-book when Runty suggested entertainment—he had learnt very early in their previous acquaintance. Really, the man was an enigma. Three fortunes given away to charity, but he would stick a woman for a taxi.

They were at the end of the meal; Runty was looking surreptitiously at his watch. Was he planning to escape? It would be just like him; satisfied that he had established an *entente*. Now, if Lionel were to take any steps or make any fuss when the beastly book came out, he would simulate wide-eyed astonishment; hadn't they dealt with all that? Lionel had seemed perfectly happy about it when they met at the club. Why was he going back on it now? Really, some people were very tiresome! And anyhow, it was too late to do anything about it when the book was actually published. In the second edition—if there was one—he would see what could be done. Meanwhile . . .

"About your book," Lionel began.

"Ah, yes. Is there anything else you would care for, by the way. I never eat any pudding myself."

"I'll have a cigar, if I may."

"Oh! Of course." Runty signalled the waiter. "A little Dutch one, I suppose, at this time of day."

"I can only smoke a good cigar."

The waiter, who knew Sir Romney's hopeful look, smiled and fetched the Havanas.

"By all means. I was only thinking of time. I'm sure, like myself, you have a hundred and one different things to do this afternoon."

"I'm in no hurry and, anyhow, I want to talk to you about the book."

"I must get the publisher to send you a copy."

"I'll buy it. Never give books away to people who can afford to buy them. It is inculcating a bad habit. I'm not, I hope, unreasonably apprehensive, but I would like to see any reference you are making to my family. Rumour has it that you are going to be indiscreet. That's your affair; but I don't want anyone belonging to me to bark their shins in the process."

"You wrote to the publishers. I wish you hadn't, Nelly. You know what publishers are. They got the wind up. Why didn't you get in touch with me?"

"Because I believe you are incorrigible."

"Oh, come. I thought we were old friends."

"Of course; but you would be the first to say that I would be a fool to rely on that."

"It's true. I never allow personal relationships to interfere when there's a principle involved. I broke with Olive when she baptised our first child, you will remember. But there are no principles at stake here. I had a problem : the book will cover my whole life. I couldn't impose any form on it unless I separated my various activities and kept the personal side in a compartment to itself. The publisher isn't very happy about the arrangement; he thinks everyone will rush for the first volume and there will be a falling off when the other one comes out; but, after all, my work in the world is what matters. My private life is of no greater significance than anyone else's."

"You are too modest. Not everyone has had your opportunities or was so ready to take advantage of them."

"I've had a pleasant life."

"Full of interest. Your book ought to be highly entertaining."

"You are very kind; but I always said you were by far the *nicest* of my friends. I wish I'd put that in, by the way. You injected me with your own diffidence. I should have overcome it. I'm afraid the book is in print, otherwise I'd have added a footnote."

"I'd much rather you didn't."

"A footnote might be a mistake, I admit. It would have a trumped-up appearance."

"I'm not talking about myself, Runty."

"I notice you've fallen into the habit of using that tiresome name. Nobody does. I'm Bunny to anyone that matters, and Romney to the rest."

"I am sorry. And, by the way, nobody has ever called me Nelly except yourself."

"I always thought—"

"Not a soul."

"I'm sorry about that. I rather like Nelly."

"I find it, in some way, diminishing."

"I hope I didn't use it in the book. I'd no idea—"

"If you did, I'll forgive you. What I am concerned about —I need hardly tell you—is how you deal with Eleanor. We have a son. I am anxious for her reputation on her account and on his."

Radish smiled his boyish smile. "I hope you don't think a friendship with me is injurious to anyone's reputation. I don't get that impression here today, for instance."

Ever since they had taken their places at table they had been interrupted by passers-by, who stopped to draw Runty's attention to themselves. With those he knew he was inclined to be puckish; to others, whose identity escaped him, he was scrupulously polite. In a room in which there was a popular historian, a poet, three scientists, four civil servants, a politician, an actor, a foreign correspondent, a subscriber to good causes, a retired novelist, and the editor of a top newspaper, Radish was undoubtedly a great man.

"Your fame makes it worse."

"I don't follow."

"People nowadays are much more open about things than they were, I know. I am not sure, on balance, whether it is a change for the better. There was a great deal to be said for keeping skeletons in cupboards. There is a time for everything: Eleanor will be sixty on her next birthday, you are an octogenarian; I can't think either of you has anything to gain by an intimate account of that friendship at this date. I know my son will resent it. In fact, I wouldn't put it past him to take the matter up with you if he finds I haven't. Naturally, he will expect me to. My honour is involved. Or so it will seem to him. In fact mine was rather an ignominious role; and I can't see myself emerging with any credit from your disclosures."

"There you underrate yourself. At the time—remember it was nearly forty years ago—you showed yourself to be eminently civilised. There were others who made protestations of the widest liberality, but when they thought one was trespassing on *their* territory they reverted with alarming speed to a state of nature. Do your remember Edelweiss? He threatened to take an action against me on account of Violet."

"I never heard."

"Oh, yes. Indeed he did. Very unpleasant it was. And she, poor dear, found herself shipwrecked in the process. I have never spoken to him since."

"If you repeat any scandal about Eleanor, she will take an action against the publisher. My son is about to get married. He won't think the time well-chosen for ill-natured gossip about his mother."

"I'll be perfectly straight with you, Nelly."

"Please don't call me Nelly."

"I beg your pardon. I can't cure old habits. As you must be well aware my friendship with Eleanor played a significant part in my life. Catherine had divorced me, but still hoped for a reconciliation. The cause of the rift was a very trifling incident, a midsummer-night's dream; we might well have come together again. We were made for each other in so many ways. And, then, there were the three children. But after I met Eleanor, it was clear that the breach was too wide. Catherine went back to New Zealand, and I made up my mind that I had to part with the children."

"If I had known that it was to cause such mischief I'd never have allowed you to come so often to Bloomdale. Eleanor said you were very lonely. She laid great stress on that at the time. She also convinced me that Catherine had treated you badly. I'm afraid, after so many years, I can't remember the details. This will make unpleasant reading. It will look as if I conspired to prevent you from mending a broken marriage."

"Don't worry. You remain in the background. A benign presence. I'm cross with myself for that. You have never been done justice to in the memoirs of the period. Without you there wouldn't have been any Bloomdale."

47

"Let's stick to you and Eleanor. We've been on the subject for some time, and I'm still very much in the dark. You do refer to my wife, I gather. I would like to see the references before you publish the book."

"I'm afraid that is out of the question."

"Very well, I'll tell my solicitors to write to the publishers and demand it."

"They can't do that, dear boy."

"They can. Nobody can prevent them. The publisher must be made to understand I'm not bluffing."

"Let me speak very plainly."

"I wish you would."

"My friendship with Eleanor is well-known. If I didn't refer to it, readers would draw their own conclusions. Instead of suppressing the incident I would only have given wings to some new crop of rumours. The truth never hurts. I do make it plain—this won't hurt you, Lionel. You are too sensible—I do make it plain that Eleanor and I were lovers for something over a year. But no longer. I make that quite clear. She never enjoyed the physical side of our relationship; after I had my teeth out she refused to resume it. It caused me deep unhappiness at the time. But, to put your mind at ease, I don't use your names. I invented pseudonyms."

"I still consider you are behaving like a cad."

"Nelly, dear! Nobody talks of cads nowadays. You might as well say I was a bounder."

"So you are."

"That sort of language is prehistoric."

"It should be revived. Men like you should give an example."

"So I do. I always did. I was thirty years before my time. All this Women's Lib fuss was commonplace with me before they even got the vote. I've always treated women as if they were men."

"So far as my wife is concerned, I don't think that is good enough."

48

"Oh, dear! I never thought you could be so difficult. You, Nelly, of all people."

"I advise you to withdraw the book and let me vet the chapter in dispute."

"I can't. I'm sorry. I can't."

"Very well. I told you what I'll do."

"I wish I could persuade you to be sensible."

"I've made up my mind. Now I must be going. You have all those engagements to keep."

Runty always looked for a lift; today he asked his guest to drive him to the Museum. They were standing on the steps of the club, when an old woman came past the Duke of York's pillar and crossed over towards the Haymarket. She looked up at them; her face darkened, but she passed by without giving any other sign of recognition.

"Not one of your admirers," Lionel remarked before he had seen Runty's face. It had turned livid.

"Are you feeling all right?"

"Perfectly."

Lionel suppressed his curiosity. After a few moments of silence Runty volunteered, "That was Helen. I haven't seen her for fifty years."

"She may not have recognised you."

"Of course she did."

Helen was the name of Runty's first wife. Runty said no more; but the incident served the purpose of breaking the tension between the two old friends. Runty began to gossip again. He had quite revived when the Museum was reached.

"Don't make an ass of yourself, dear boy," he said as he sprang out. Then he walked briskly through the gloomy pillars.

Lionel drove straight to his solicitors. They must act at once. He had let people like Runty run their rigs through too much of his life. From now on he would hold fast to what was good in the little that was left.

Chapter IV

THERE IS NO member of the family nowadays in the great publishing house of Haymakers. The shares are owned by a multi-millionaire whose fortune was made from fish and chip shops in northern towns. Sir Clement Trotter does not interfere with the running of the firm. He is a genial fellow, who enjoys his money. Some of it gets spent on the turf, where he has the reputation of being a good loser. Publishing satisfies another side of his nature. He has deep respect for books. They represent an aspect of life that he would like to have had time to explore. So long as John Jackson showed a reasonable profit on the investment, Trotter will give him his head. When it seems to be to the benefit of the firm he is prepared to inject more capital. For instance, the competition for the Radish memoirs was intense. The author's agent made it clear that the old man was not encumbered by any detritus of loyalty. This was his last major book. He wanted to clean up. The staid firm which had published his learned works and the pleasantly old-fashioned house which brought out his later novels and tales couldn't hope to compete. Clement Trotter gave his Managing Director an open cheque. Haymakers secured the manuscript.

John Jackson was understandably proud of his success; but he was not a happy man. The advantage of having a substantial background of wealth was offset by working in its shadow. Sometimes he regretted the old days, even with their ups and downs, their panics and uncertainties. There was nobody to answer to except oneself.

His present frame of mind was that of the leader of a bomb-disposal squad. There was only one alternative to success, and the penalty for relaxation was oblivion. Because of this, Jackson passed from what seemed like an unhealthy passion for his owner—if a day passed without some communication he panicked—to a morbid detestation of him. This led to very complicated states of mind. If, for instance, he picked up a newspaper and saw a picture of an immaculately dressed Sir Clement at Ascot, a cloud passed across the sun. If the caption said his horse was narrowly beaten, a savage pleasure immediately lit up the gloom; this was followed fast by the sickening realisation that he couldn't afford such pleasures. Failure for Sir Clement meant failure for him. An anxious, ill-tempered, disillusioned, critical Sir Clement spelled doom. And, therefore, he had to write and condole with him on his bad luck. He had to pretend that Sir Clement's affairs were his constant preoccupation. And at the same time, of course, he had to keep Haymakers in the front, running it for the ignorant tycoon.

So far as the Radish business went, Jackson had no reason to be uneasy. Had he failed to secure the book, Sir Clement might well have spoiled his day by asking why such a *coup* had been lost by Haymakers, and if John had pleaded lack of money would have pointed out that the money was there. John had anticipated this. But he was worried. Too many clouds had begun to gather on the eve of publication. His morning had been spoiled by a letter from Lionel Hartley's solicitors; and what comfort the afternoon might have brought was forfeited by the threatened arrival of Sir Romney Radish.

Waiting for him, John was unable to concentrate. The old man had sounded mischievous on the telephone; he was quite unscrupulous and unpredictable; until the visit was over all other work was impossible, and this was a nuisance. Idly, he picked up the proof-copy, wondering what changes Radish would try to compel him to agree to. His face registered aversion as he flicked—for the umpteenth time—through the dog-eared pages.

*　　*　　*

51

At this time I was living in virtuous poverty in a room over a public-house in the Wapping district. There was no need for this. Without calling on my guardian, I was entitled to £500 a year under my grandfather's will—a useful sum in 1913. But I was persuaded that pure thought was not possible in the presence of any luxury. My room was scrupulously clean. I washed the floor every morning and the walls gleamed with fresh whitewash. I slept on an iron bed. A wash-basin, a chamber pot, a table and a chair, and a chest of drawers I bought for half-a-crown was all my furniture. But I had rented the whole attic storey for my books, which I paid a young woman to keep dusted. I was proud of my library.

At night I walked ten miles before going to bed. Otherwise I spent all my time reading or writing. At this period I was bewitched by metaphysics. Later on I came to the conclusion that they were an intellectual luxury—an elaborate, unprofitable game, sublime tomfoolery. The only justifiable use of brains such as mine, I decided then —after I married Olive—was in the mitigation of human suffering or the addition to human knowledge. Experience taught me finally that the only activities worthy of praise are creating objects of beauty and making people laugh.

In 1913 I still had far to go. I had discovered Kierkegaard and was annotating him. I was planning, under the guise of fiction, a devastating send-up of Bergson. I had in hand an essay on Spinoza. I was busy. And I was twenty-two.

Women, as I explained in the first chapter, had played no part in my life. After Nanny Evans was sent away— my mother thought she was spoiling me and I had developed a Welsh accent—I had nothing to do with anyone of her sex; an intensely religious boy and very shy, I was not the sort who would develop ideas about the housemaids, who were, apart from my mother, the only woman I saw. On account of my delicacy and also—I heard afterwards—because of my elder brothers' histories

I was not sent to Eton. Instead I had a series of tutors. They never stayed long. Suddenly my father would take a dislike to whoever was in residence, and out he would go.

My elder brothers resemble my father, who looked— Whistler was often heard to say—"like a bison out of business". I look very like George Philips, a frequent visitor at our house, and a brilliant musician. He was small and exquisite. Rather like pictures of Pope. I have certainly inherited his head; on neither side of my family was there any record of talent or, in many cases, even literacy. They couldn't help their eminence. They found themselves sitting on a coal mine. My father had a capacity for doing nothing which I have never seen excelled. He would have been quite happy grazing in a field, had he acquired a taste for grass. I cannot believe an intellect like mine came from the Radishes. My mother's family had more pretensions to intellect. There was Jewish blood in the background. And there was some mystery about her grandmother. It was said that she had an affair with Talleyrand in his old age in London. He was a cripple by that time, but who knows? That old intriguer had survived by miracles : he may have had one left over—a phoenix flame. If so, I hope he has been satisfied with the long term result. I am.

With an uncomplimentary noise, Jackson threw down the book and buried his face in his hands. What a bore it seemed, and if anything were to go wrong, Sir Clement would want to know why had he been asked to cough up a quarter of a million. Nothing must go wrong. The contract contained a most carefully-drawn clause the effect of which was to make doubly certain that the author would be responsible in the event of libel actions. The agent had tried to insist on the usual clause, but Jackson held out. Spectacular damages and a court case, perhaps an appeal as well, might be costly enough; but there was also the danger of an injunction, holding up the book. These were the normal risks of publishing, but they were aggravated in the present case. Like all universally loved men, Radish had powerful and vindictive enemies. He had lived such a varied life and passed through so many phases, it was difficult to chart his career. As he had given contradictory opinions on every subject, he had annoyed everybody at one time or another; and spite is more enduring than gratitude and more prone to realise itself in action. But, beyond these considerations, Radish himself had contributed to the climate of apprehension. In several interviews he had said that his revelations would shock; he might hurt old friends and disappoint admirers. It was clear that he was using the occasion to disburden himself of a lifetime's accretion of obligation and grievance.

Then there was the manuscript itself, vetted by lawyers and others, none of whom could give Jackson the sort of clearance he required. So much depended on how people might react, they said. To be completely safe the book would have to be cut so drastically that it would have fallen flat. In any event, the author was not prepared to sacrifice his Rousseau image. He had set out "to tell all". On the title page he had written:

> O monstrous world. Take note, take note, O world!
> To be direct and honest is not safe.

Radish hadn't taken to his publisher; he didn't find his charm convincing. It was a plastic version of the real thing, as he could demonstrate if it pleased him to. It did not. He was feeling guilty about his desertion of the firm with which he had had such pleasant relations over his fiction. This was the only part of his huge output by which he set any store. Fondest of all his recollections was a perceptive notice in *Homes and Gardens* in which the amiable critic saw the point of his modern moralities. "The Aesop of the Atomic Age" that reviewer had called him. He intended to write a letter of thanks, but refrained: it would look as if he found such discernment a novelty.

54

This smiling parasite hadn't read one of his books, and yet lied to his face about them, and gushed in a way that was despicable. Only the vulgarity of notoriety and the prospect of pelf impressed a fellow like this. (Why had he let the agent pass dear Charles Matheson over? The memoirs would have given him the fillip he needed at a time when he found himself outdistanced by the tycoon-backed publishers, and his list was beginning to look tired.) It was only when he was with John Jackson that Radish nourished these regrets. Away from him arithmetic triumphed. The computer that his intellect was rejected a sentimental diet.

Jackson was quick to notice that his patron was out of sorts. He thought of something that might improve his humour. "Excuse me for one minute, Sir Romney, I have something that may please you." He fluttered out. Radish, looking after him balefully, spotted the proofs. He snatched them up, turned over the pages with the purposeful haste of someone looking up a telephone number, and stiffened with the concentration of a game dog when he found what he was in search of; but the hand holding the book was trembling.

"To return to Helen." How carefree he had felt on the morning when he composed that pregnant sentence! Now it read like the interjection of prosecuting counsel. How typical of Helen to be alive when it suited everyone that she should be dead! But she had always been a nuisance—his first and greatest mistake—the thought of her, childless, married to that intellectual recluse in Germany, brooding over her fancied wrongs, used to haunt him. She was the only thing in life he was afraid of, because until he met her he had never known what it was to be hated.

The reason he gave in his memoirs for parting with Helen was a clash of principle on breast-feeding. He had refused to countenance the practice on aesthetic grounds (amusing when one thought of his pioneering work for compulsory breast-feeding in later days, demonstrations outside Queen Charlotte's hospital, a march past the strip-tease clubs in

Soho), but that was not the whole truth or—even by a generous computation—half.

What turned her finally against him (she said dreadful things) was when he went to New Zealand and set up house with Catherine. He lived in solid bourgeois comfort then.

But that was the gloomy ending. It began as romance—the purest romance of his whole life. How vivid it was still, that life of complete asceticism and perfect cerebration, the days spent in study and making notes for his philosophical essays, the nightly walks through the mean streets, oblivious to his surroundings, lost in abstract speculation—then that winter evening when he found himself in an unfamiliar street staring at a photograph, in a show-case outside an obscure theatre. *Hedda Gabler* was the play. It was booked for a week The company described itself as the *Westminster Play Study Group*. There was an air of high-minded failure about the whole enterprise. The theatre itself looked as if it were longing to be adapted to some more cheerful purpose. The cast, judging from the photographs, were destined by nature for a select vestry, or foreign mission work. But out of the surrounding gloom stared those amazing eyes. They were all one saw of her face. Helen Westby her name was. She was playing Hedda.

He stood transfigured by the eyes—for how long he didn't know, because he only became aware of himself when a brewer's dray threatened to run him down.

The eyes followed him down the street, kept him from sleep, shone up from the pages of his beloved books when he arose as usual at six o'clock to start the studies of the day. It was impossible to work, to think, to eat. He found himself drawn back irresistibly to the theatre and, as one mesmerised, buying tickets for the remaining performances.

Theatre was a new experience; pantomime and, later, visits to Irving at the Lyceum, and Tree at His Majesty's, with his grandparents, was all he had known in childhood. No contrast could have been greater than those prosperous evenings and the sequence of static Ibsen performances to

56

three-quarter empty houses in which there seemed always to be someone with a tubercular cough. But he had eyes and ears only for Hedda. Oblivious to her marked Lancashire accent and her railway signal gestures, her eyes held him enthralled, and she seemed in that draughty, dirty, deserted playhouse like Faust's vision of Helen.

That he loved her to madness was only part of his intoxication; now he knew the excitement of a successful explorer; he had discovered a new Duse.

The pattern of his life was established—the satisfaction of a passion—desire on this occasion, more usually vanity—combined with the moral force of a mission. Helen Westby must take the place she was entitled to on the world stage.

Thus he saw his purpose when he sent in his card. He did not add the flowers appropriate to these occasions. Helen must take or reject him as he was—his life dedicated to truth. He had made no provision in it for women or for love. If these were to be added, they must not imperil the grand framework. He had ten books to write before he was thirty.

He smiled now when he remembered the tussle with his conscience before he used a card which made clear who he was. She must love him for himself; but he was little more than a boy and desperately anxious not to fall at the first hurdle. He was not sure that cerebral distinction was enough to impress a woman. He had no small task. He was always arguing, and very positive in assertion. His mother made no secret that she found him a bore. And he was puny in build. Hitherto his prominent forehead had provided the only reassurance he needed, but now he bethought him of his receding chin and skinny hams. He knew a great deal of poetry by heart, never having any difficulty in memorising what interested him. Would she be pleased if he recited to her? His voice was rather high, but he could modulate it. They might be very happy reading aloud together. But hardly at the first visit. Should he kiss her hand? He wished he had a worldly friend to consult.

It was too late now; he was invited to her dressing-room.

She had taken off grease-paint to reveal a pasty complexion. It was at once disillusioning and reassuring, like all the other events of that evening. After initial shyness she agreed to come out; he had not supplied himself with the wherewithal to give her supper in a restaurant. He acted as if he expected assistance from a genie. Radish smiled again as he read.

A man of the world would have had his arrangements made, a table booked, his own apartment in order for a post-prandial visit. Not I. It would have seemed cold-blooded and calculating to me then to have looked beyond the moment of meeting. Pioneer of artificial birth-control and a tireless advocate of eugenics, I have perpetuated myself half a dozen times because of this fastidiousness. I will not anticipate where the heart is the compass. I speak of myself in youth. In later years I had to march with the times.

She had looked touchingly shabby when dressed to go out, and accepted without protest the idea of going back to the flat and making-do with lettuce and hard-boiled eggs.

Observing his preparations, she took over when they were at the kitchen stove and made delicious omelettes. They sat on the bed and ate them. Gradually he overcame his shyness; tentatively he put an arm around her waist : she let it remain. He completed the encirclement. They fell over in an embrace. The warmth of her body was delicious; the relief relaxing beyond belief; he had not slept the previous night; he felt himself slipping effortlessly into oblivion. When he woke up, he was alone. There was a note on the table. "Thank you for pleasant evening. Helen." At the bottom, as if by after-thought, she had written an address. He took comfort in that.

If only he had left it there! But he searched her out in her squalid lodgings. She had run away from home, she said—a narrow-minded, widowed mother in Bolton. When he invited her to his lodgings, she moved in without demur. There was no reason that he could see why his noble programme should be interrupted. He had removed the temptation to wander abroad by domesticating Venus.

As far as Helen's career was concerned, he planned to translate the Greek tragedies for her, and she could play the leading roles. His Greek was above average—as everything about him was—and it would be a pleasant change.

But he had not made allowances for Helen's disposition. He had seen her only as part of a divine plan. Radish winced as his eyes ran over his account of the sequel.

Our first night together seems touching in retrospect; but at the time was embarrassing and, to me, profoundly discouraging. Helen advised me to see a doctor. However, that wasn't necessary, I was relieved to discover. On the whole we were very happy, but my absorption in philosophy—there were nights when I couldn't sleep, so active was my brain—was incompatible with Helen's demands on my virility. Very early I was learning the lesson, which later experience supplemented, that an exalted view of human destiny and the most advanced opinions could be accompanied in a woman by an animalism that would shock the average strumpet. My weight went down to eight stone. I feigned illness. My work made no progress. I found difficulty in concentrating. When I should have been reading Spinoza, I would turn to old numbers of the *Strand Magazine*. We were on the edge of a crisis; then Helen found she was going to have a baby. I think the shock of this disclosure was the determining cause of my turning away from metaphysics to natural science.

"I am terribly sorry for keeping you so long, Sir Romney. Our lift seems to have gone out of order. I thought this might please you."

With a playfulness that he reserved for suitable occasions, Jackson produced a parcel and insisted on Radish opening it. Inside was the first copy of *My Thousand and One Days*. The effect was disappointing. Instead of his face lighting up,

Radish looked petulant. He had already approved the cover; but that did not prevent him from pointing out several blemishes. Jackson dipped into his bag of comforts and brought out a proof copy of a puff in the Sunday newspaper which was going to serialise the book. It compared Radish, to his advantage, with Plato, Darwin, George Eliot and Max Beerbohm.

He pushed the cutting aside. "I'm not happy about the extracts they've chosen. I want you to take it up with them at once. I'll decide what they are going to print."

Jackson was aware of his failure with his author; but he laid the blame where it belonged. Like other famous men, Radish was an exacting curmudgeon when you had to deal with him in business. The serialisation had been arranged through his own agent. He had bargained, and closed with the highest offer. A contract had been signed. Naturally the newspaper had carefully chosen the extracts most likely to please their readers. Radish had confined these to three Sundays, ending a week before publication day. They concentrated on episodes in his love life, and undoubtedly left the impression of the Casanova rather than the Plato of the age. Readers would not want to hear why he forsook metaphysics for natural science or why he abandoned that for history and politics, nor yet his ambition to be remembered as a writer of stories for children.

"I'm afraid they won't re-open that. Your agent tried to strike a balance; but it wasn't on."

"Then he shouldn't have committed me."

"You gave him a free hand."

"Who said so?"

"So I understood."

"You shouldn't have taken anything for granted. I am on the telephone."

"You were in Greece."

"The use of the telephone is not forbidden to visitors to Greece."

"But I thought this was all over and done with."

"If you did you don't know your man."

The publisher shrugged and smiled hopelessly. For a moment he had been tempted to let fly the verbal equivalent of a kidney punch.

"I'm old. I have nothing to gain. I'm indifferent to money. I've all the fame I require. My reputation will rest ultimately on my small but exquisite contribution to fiction. The references to Plato don't take me in for an instant. That is merely an example of the empty vulgarity of the age, and an inevitable outcome of semi-literacy. Who of all people who are impressed by them have read Plato? Have you? No. Of course you haven't, or Darwin or Bacon. Yet you flourish these names in my face. I insisted on the best terms for my book because I am a perfectionist. Dealing with sharpers I am determined to outsharp them. Why, do you think, I gave the book to your firm?"

"Because Haymakers has a reputation—"

"Nonsense. Because you offered the largest advance. I'd have much preferred to give it to Charles Matheson, a very dear friend of mine. Forgive me if I talk in this strain. It is the privilege of age and serves to clear the air. I realise that a book like mine, written by someone like me, is bound to create controversy. That goes without saying. But I am not at all inclined to let that controversy upset my personal life. I don't mind what happens to the newspapers; and I am more than a match for any of the self-righteous and conceited interviewers on television. I enjoy my jousts with them. They are supremely comic figures; the great clowns of our time. We have no Grocks or Chaplins now in the entertainment industry. They are all in the service of what is called 'the media'."

"Forgive me for interrupting; but I don't quite see what this has to do with your book. Your agent arranged the serialisation. It has nothing to do with us. The publicity you speak about will assist sales."

John Jackson looked huffed. What had he done to entitle

the old monster, looking like Mephistopheles in retirement, to sit there lecturing him?

Romney sprung to his feet. "I feel you are in a hurry. I beg your pardon. I shouldn't waste your time over my little book when you have matters of greater moment to attend to."

"I am more than ready to discuss your book, Sir Romney. I hope we have given it all the care it deserves. I am only drawing your attention to the fact that we are not responsible for serialisation. And, by the way, Mr Lionel Hartley's solicitors have been at us again about the references to Mrs Hartley. Someone must have shown them the proofs. They are threatening libel proceedings. We are not unduly worried about that in the light of your assurance. But, if you like, I'll get in touch with the Editor. Perhaps it would help if you saw someone, even higher up. Lord Stoat, for instance."

"Stoat doesn't like me."

"I'm sure you only imagine that."

"He has conducted virulent campaigns against me in his time. My children's books are never reviewed in his beastly newspaper. That is deliberate."

On this inconclusive note Radish left the publisher's office. How buoyant they both had been when the book was in preparation! How jubilant Jackson had been at his luck in securing the most coveted manuscript in the market! Now they depressed and irritated each other. The book had become a source only of worry.

A subject for a sermon. John Jackson was the first to recover. Thanks to his acumen his firm was covered against libel. If Radish was having second thoughts about his own lack of reticence and decent feeling, that was his business. What got John down was the old man's arrogance. Whenever it came to the crunch he asserted himself like the most reactionary old Tory. When it suited him he preached equality and fraternity, but nobody had ever managed so shrewdly to get the best of all worlds. If now he had walked into unpleasantness, he richly deserved it.

On second thoughts, would he be wise to hold up the advance on publication day? If there was a libel action it might be very difficult to get Radish to cough up. He had a reputation for being very close when it was a matter of a private debt.

Sir Clement Trotter, in an armchair at the Royal Automobile Club, was undergoing what was for him an unusual ordeal. He was looking at a book. His manner of smoking his cigar nicely accompanied Sir Clement's perusal. Sometimes he puffed away; at others he held his smoke. At these moments he saw squalls ahead; when the smoke coiled upwards he was running before the wind. Sir Clement, it could be seen, was a man accustomed to reading balance-sheets. The lawn-mower movements of his eyebrows alone indicated this.

John Jackson had supplied his Chairman with a copy of the index. This greatly facilitated his work. It was the first of the books published by his firm that he had read before it appeared. Not that he read a great many at any time; he was not a reader, being one of those who believe that the brain should not be distracted from its principal employment. At night, if he was not recreating himself, he liked to sit back, smoke, listen to a little music or watch television, his mind rehearsing the events of the day. In this manner he got his inspirations and hunches. The Radish memoirs, being a scoop for Haymakers, interested him. He had increased his investment, and this was the way he always demonstrated interest. As with any other investment, he relied on his instincts or intuitions to send up flares. He couldn't give any explanation for it.

His friendly, bluff manner misled John Jackson, who knew his employer didn't read, and had never had pre-publication trouble with him before. When the Chairman casually asked for a proof-copy, glanced at it, and then asked for a copy of the index, John was surprised and uneasy. He put the request down to a whim; there was no reason to believe that the Chairman had misgivings, but all the same he would have preferred it if he hadn't gone "poking his nose" into John's side of the business. He might come up with some damn-fool questions at the eleventh hour.

In the bar of the R.A.C. Sir Clement met Lord Stoat. They greeted each other affectionately, their paths never having crossed in business.

"I see you have Runty's memoirs there," Lord Stoat said. "We are publishing all the cream."

"Have your legal men raised any points?"

"No. I'm sure not. If they had I'd have heard about it. Why do you ask?"

"I'm a bit worried. I can't explain exactly. I don't like the old man. There's something inhuman about him, for all his preaching universal love. He struck a hard bargain with both of us."

"We were ready to pay. We couldn't let any of the others get it."

"Quite so. I was glad to see it in our list. It was a feather in our Manager's cap. But I've decided to give it the once over myself. Who is Leonard Blue?"

"The name seems to ring a bell. Was he one of the sex murderers between the wars?"

"According to what I was reading here before I met you, he lives near Rye and he has a blue-stocking wife who had affairs with every critic and artist in England."

"Let's look him up in *Who's Who*."

"He's not there," Stoat announced, a few minutes later.

"That's surprising. According to the book he is a diploma-tist, and his wife is a celebrated hostess."

"Some of these chaps like to keep out of reference books."

"Leonard Blue strikes me as the sort of man who appears in *Who's Who* automatically. Let's ask Gumble over there. He's sure to know."

Gumble had the reputation of being the most cultured among the regular drinkers in the club's premises. He responded with affability to the question, made wild shots in the air, as the amateur oracle will, but decided finally that the name defeated him. Dejected a little by his failure—he would have liked to keep up his reputation, with Stoat especially—he continued to puzzle over the question. When the two captains of industry were leaving, he darted forward and suggested that the name was not the real one. "Leonard Blue may be still alive." It was all Trotter needed. He clapped Gumble on the back. But when he had spread his napkin on his stomach his glee evaporated. However pleasing to his vanity to have his hunch justified, the next consideration was alarming: if Radish had substituted a name it would be no cover to anyone in the know. Worse, the fact that such a shameless old sinner—for that was Sir Clement's opinion of the great man—thought it expedient to cover his tracks suggested the presence of libellous matter as certainly as green scum on still water advertises the presence of frogs. He opened his mind to Lord Stoat; if the worst happened both of them would be sued. The book could be withdrawn, but the publicity of newspaper serialisation would attract exemplary damages.

"Have you paid him an advance?" Stoat enquired.

"Yes, two-thirds."

"I'd hold on to the rest."

"I shall."

The two men parted after luncheon, not waiting for a chat over coffee. Trotter took himself off to a quiet corner of the reading room, Stoat hurried back to the *Sunday Echo*, in whose offices it would be as if a tidal wave had swept down Fleet Street and broken there.

Clement read every reference to the Blue family; and by the time he had completed his research he had taken in the plan of the book. Next he turned to "Radish" and read "Helen", "Catherine", "Olive," "Grace", "Vera", described respectively as the first, second, third, fourth and fifth wife of the author. In any case where he saw "death of" in the index, he ticked off the name. He ignored references to celebrities; they were accustomed to abuse and inured to exposure; there was little fear of danger from them. It was from the obscure that hostile action was to be expected. "Jones, Molly", for instance, was not to be passed over lightly. What had he said about her? "My secretary for many years." Could that be libellous by innuendo? One would have to see what had been the fate of other holders of the office. Radish had married one. Old, much-married, distinguished men not unusually ended up with their secretaries; the hand that taps the typewriter comes into its own when the one that rocked the cradle loses its grip. Sir Clement knew these things. He knew a great deal about the world, but very little about the corner of it in which Radish moved before he became a universal carrier of sweetness and light. There were people who knew it, though, chaps like Gumble. Trotter rang the bell and asked the servant who answered it if Mr Gumble were still, by any chance, in the bar. He intended to offer him £50 to read the proofs then and there.

But Mr Gumble wasn't. He had left and had not yet returned. There were sabbatical hours. So Sir Clement went to his lawyer. He acted always in this independent way. If he was assured there was no cause for alarm, John Jackson would never know about the investigation, but if there were, the Chairman, fully armed, would descend on him. And life would become threatening and awful.

Sir Clement patronised an efficient law firm. One partner specialised in libel. He would take the proof home that evening and discuss it with Counsel next day. Then, having forseen and provided, as the world's greatest generals have done, Sir Clement retired and slept. There was nothing more he could do. He would husband his resources. He must be at his best on the day.

In the *Sunday Echo*, the same steps were being taken. But there an underlying panic was apparent. Jobs were in hazard. John Jackson, not as yet having heard from his Chairman, went about his business with a light heart. The sales staff reported a huge demand for the book. John, euphoric, wrote a rather coy letter to Radish, whom he addressed as "Romney", wondering if he would consider a fiction offering for the spring list. After the letter was posted, he regretted it : the old man was capable of snubbing him, even in the hour of victory.

Chapter V

A TALL AND eccentric-looking person, suggesting a tortoise walking erect, was parading outside Runty's house in Eaton Square when the owner returned. His manner as he came forward was excitable, and Runty looked anxiously up the street. He had once been assaulted by a member of a League for the Improvement of Public Morals, and it had been an undignified as well as a painful experience.

"Sir Romney, I am Angus MacDonnell. I want a word with you."

"I'm afraid I don't know you."

"You don't keep abreast with contemporary fiction. I might have guessed as much from efforts of your own I've come across."

"I haven't time at the moment for a symposium. I don't usually conduct them on my door-step. I must ask you to let me open my door, Mr O'Donnell."

"*MacDonnell*. Perhaps you have heard of me as the Laird of Smogg."

"I'm afraid not. If you will allow me to pass, I'll undertake to look you up in Debrett."

"You'd be wasting your time."

"Peacefully."

"I've been trying to get you on the telephone. I've rung here and at your house in Wales. You're avoiding me. You are a coward, Radish. I intend to expose you."

"So! You're the mysterious telephone caller; usually in an advanced state of intoxication, I understand. Let me inform you I don't intend to allow you to continue with this persecution. If you don't go away this instant or if you ring up again, I'll hand the matter over to the police."

"Whose brutal methods you exposed in a recent article, I seem to recall. No, Radish, the game's up. You won't threaten me. I'm acting in a perfectly legal manner. I could punch your head. But I won't. Your age protects you. But you mustn't play on my good nature."

"For the last time, will you stand aside?"

"No."

"Very well. I'll send for the police."

"By all means. Have you a whistle? If not, I'll assist you."

Angus put two fingers in his mouth, and a sound like a call to lunch at a factory split the air. The birds in the air were silenced. Two dogs trotted up and rubbed themselves against the legs of Radish's trousers.

"I'll appeal to the bystanders," Sir Romney said.

But the little scene, although it had not gone undetected, was being watched from a distance. No blows were being struck; and it was assumed by everyone that the great man had planned whatever was going forward as a preliminary in a larger campaign, particulars of which would be disclosed in due course to the press. Had he stepped forward and cried for help, there would have been a response, one can hardly doubt; but his dilemma didn't really justify such an extremity. Clearly he was not in danger. When he frequented clubs, members accosted him in similar fashion, admittedly with some amiable excuse, and held him up to his aggravation. But he didn't expect to meet the perils of clubland on his own doorstep.

"If you ask your solicitor to communicate with mine, a meeting can be arranged if they decide the matter calls for one. The firm is George Hatch and Co., Lincoln's Inn."

"There are some matters that are too delicate for lawyers. I'm concerned with a wife's reputation. Now, I hope you understand why I have been trying to get in touch with you."

"I haven't the pleasure of Mrs MacDonnell's acquaintance, I'm afraid."

"When you knew her she was Pamela Cannon."

69

"I can't recall the name. I'm afraid you are making some mistake."

"Were you ever in Antananarivo, Radish?"

"Let me see. I was once, several years ago, at a disarmament conference."

"Has the penny dropped?"

"I beg your pardon."

"My wife's husband was on the American delegation."

"If you say so. I remember the Soviet representatives; and there were some very good friends of mine from Africa at the conference. But I don't remember any Mr Cannon. I find as I grow older that Americans all tend to seem alike. I think it is the way they speak. Underneath the polysyllabic abstractions of their irrepressible jargon, I have never been able to discover more than two or three commonplaces."

"My mother came from North Carolina."

"I beg your pardon."

"You needn't apologise."

The inconclusive discussion had lowered the temperature. The stranger's manner was violent; but it was probably misleading. Radish in his time had encountered many of this type, usually failures in various branches of the arts; perhaps it would be well to hear what he had to say rather than to have him continue his campaign, so difficult to deal with effectively in the present state of the law once the man was in possession of his telephone number. There was a time when Kingsley Martin was forever ringing him up. It never occurred to him then to look for police protection. This fellow was probably a faddist and a bore. He could be bought off, most likely, with a subscription.

The reference to Antananarivo struck no chord. He could remember the very generous reception his speech received on that occasion, but otherwise it had been much like any other conference. On an average he had attended six a year for half a century, not to mention miscellaneous discussion groups, lectures and, of course, entertainments innumerable, wreathed in memory in a fog of verbiage, and echoes of hand-clapping and distant rumbles of conversations with earnest and, for the most part, plain-visaged people. There had been oases in the desert of discussion—night clubs, moonlight bathes, desert drives, girls of all nationalities, tours of red-light districts, and even . . . one must experience everything. He was not ashamed. An American diplomat and his wife on any of these occasions would have been as memorable as a rose on a floral wallpaper in a lodging house.

"If you would care to come in, I'll be able to spare you a few minutes; but I must tell you"—he looked at his watch—"that I have an appointment at four o'clock, which I mustn't be late for. What a bore," he added, to lend a touch of verisimilitude to the precautionary fib.

Angus widened his shoulders as he followed his wizened host through the door, an adjustment to the shift in the situation. He was coming in by invitation. Radish led the way into a small book-lined room. Angus's eye passed over the titles automatically, and searched in vain for any sign of a cupboard. Please God, the old buffer would ring for a servant to bring down refreshments. But that reference to a meeting in quarter of an hour and something about the appearance of the room discouraged cheerful expectation. The rather formal way the old man sat in his chair, which forbade Angus to relax in the more comfortable one he occupied, imposed a certain formality on the meeting.

"Please smoke," Radish said when Angus produced a packet of cigarettes.

"Thank you, I don't," he added when the packet was thrust at him.

"Now, perhaps you'd tell me what is on your mind."

"Well, it's a little bit embarrassing. If Pamela was still Mrs Cannon that would be one thing; but now I'm talking about my wife."

"If it embarrasses you, why not keep it to yourself? I got an impression of eagerness and even urgency. But that may have been a misconception on my part."

"It is urgent, but still it's embarrassing."

71

"One might say the same of several surgical operations."

"You've hit it. It is about your memoirs."

"Ah!"

"I would like to see the proofs. I may not be able to permit you to publish the book without some alterations."

"Do you take this line with all memoir-writers? By what right do you claim to act as a self-appointed Lord Chamberlain? There is no censorship of books in this country, you must understand."

"Less irony please. It is lost on me. I have used that weapon too often to allow myself to be intimidated by it. I am here on behalf of my wife, and on my own behalf as an interested party. I want to know what you are saying about Pamela in your book. It is a more straightforward way to behave than to let you publish and then take you to court. I am only concerned with my wife's reputation."

"You are suffering from a delusion. My dear Mr MacDonnell, let me assure you, I have no recollection whatever of meeting your wife, and so I can positively assure you that she is not mentioned in my book. Are you satisfied?"

"My wife has a very distinct impression of meeting you. You raped her."

"I beg your pardon."

"So well you may. You raped her on uncomfortable sand in Antananarivo."

"This is pure fantasy. I never raped a woman in my life. I never had any need to. I don't pride myself on the fact. I can very well understand in certain circumstances the urge. With some men it could well be irresistible. But I am not one of them. I will take you into confidence to this extent, Mr MacDonnell—I would be grateful if you didn't publish the fact—I very much doubt that I would be capable of raping any woman. Apart from my diminutive stature, I need co-operation in my sexual partners. I am instinctively collaborative, not imperious. I do not mean to suggest that I didn't take the initiative—I usually did—but a man as much in the public eye as I am inevitably encounters a fair muster of volunteers. But in no circumstances have I ever forced anyone. I must assure you on that score. You need have no misgivings about Mrs MacDonnell. So far as I am concerned she is still *virgo intacta*."

"That won't wash with me, Radish. It won't wash with me. *So far as you are concerned* may sound very well in summer in Eaton Square, but not in Antananarivo, Radish, not in Madagascar; not under a tropical sky, Radish, when the amorous bird of night is on the wing, the scent of mimosa all round, and jacaranda, kaffirboom and tulip-tree. After a day when the sun throbbed like a fever, Radish, in your midnight revels by the forest side, loaded with wine, flame in the loins, the stars ablaze, a woman at your side, the sea calling—how was it with her then, Radish? How was it with her then?"

"I never drink, and I have no such picture in my mind. You take an exaggerated view of the scenic properties of Madagascar."

"Let me see the proofs, Radish. Let me see the proofs."

"I haven't got a copy here."

"Don't be evasive."

"I am not being evasive, and I must ask you to leave if you adopt that hectoring tone. I have no objection whatever to your calling my publishers, Mr Jackson of Haymakers. I'll telephone him and ask him to let you read the proofs in his office. I can't allow you to take them away."

"Why not?"

"Because it is not the practice to circulate proofs of a book which is about to be published. The objections must be clear to you. You are a writer yourself, I thought I heard you say."

"Oh come, Radish. Don't pretend you haven't heard of me."

"I'm not pretending. It would be most discourteous. I feel very apologetic about my ignorance. You must put it down to my advanced age; and I have to confess to a block where contemporary fiction is concerned. I read Trollope nowadays

73

and I've gone back to George Eliot. How inconsistent we are, Mr MacDonnell. I am regarded as being in the vanguard of contemporary thought, and yet I fall back on Victorian novelists when I read for pleasure. How do you explain it?"

"For one thing, I don't believe you are in the vanguard of anything. You've arrived at the stage when journalists have got round to your work. You've become a name. You're public property. You are like Guinness or Aspirin or Coca Cola; you are accepted without examination. But who reads you that matters a damn?"

"I'm on the course of prescribed reading in every American university."

"Does that give you any satisfaction? If it comes to that I'm on the modern English course in the University of Santiago. I got a letter yesterday from a student there. Would you like to see it?"

"Thank you. No. I, too, get letters of that description. Do answer it, by the way. We owe that to the younger generation."

"I should jolly well say I did answer it. By return post. He wanted a photograph of me and my autograph. You know it has been one of my beliefs for a very long time now that the future of western civilisation lies in Latin America."

"We must talk about that another time. I was interested in what you said just now, and not offended by it, not in the least. At the moment I am best known for my opinions on the great questions of the hour. But I quite agree with you, that is a very ephemeral distinction. My scientific work has been superseded. That is inevitable. But I have made some discoveries. In metaphysics I only claim to have re-interpreted some of the philosophers for my own generation. People have been kind enough to say that in doing so I made a small contribution to the common stock. But we may waive that on the score of partiality. I will agree with you Mr MacDonnell that in fifty years my name will count for little or nothing in the areas in which it is now distinguished, but by then, I

74

hope, I will be found in my proper niche. I lay any claim I may have to immortality to my fiction, especially my fables. Lord Snow told me at dinner recently that he puts me well above Kingsley and any English writer in that line. Maeterlinck was the nearest, and even he seems sugary now. My art is pared down to the bone. 'Little ivory figures,' Snow called the fables. It is a pity he hasn't done more in criticism. That was his forte. I think the novels. . . . Well . . . I like Charles."

While Radish was talking a mood of self-induced geniality lit up his features. The charm that he had been able to summon at will, ever since middle-age, was overwhelmingly in evidence. He turned a face of such sparkling benignness towards Angus that a vision of champagne floated before him. An instant. And it was gone. The face turned away again, and Radish recalled himself to the importunate presence of the Laird of Smogg.

"Now I'm afraid I must bestir myself. The enemy"—he looked at his watch again—"won't be appeased. I've enjoyed our talk, Mr MacDonnell. It was very kind of you to call. I appreciate it. And I hope that you are satisfied there was no ground for your anxiety."

"I want to see those proofs."

"Very well. Call on Jackson. Tell him I sent you."

"He may try to fob me off."

"Don't let him."

"I can't sit there for a week reading through the whole bloody tome."

"You must please yourself. It was not my idea. I asked you to accept my word."

"How can I? You raped my wife, and you ask me to believe you've forgotten it. I'm not a fool. And what is more, I owe something to my own reputation. You may not have heard of me, Radish, but I don't mind telling you that any competent critic—I'm not talking about figures of dough set up by the Fleet Street establishment—any critic who counts will tell you that in comparison with *In the Spring a Young*

75

Man's Fancy your puerile little pieces look like lark droppings."

"Why a lark, Mr MacDonnell?"

"Take any bird you like. The smaller the better. A wren if that pleases you."

"I must take a note of your book. I shall be interested to read it. I'll tell Lord Snow about it. But I'll warn him that you would resent any praise from him."

"I don't mind if he praises me. I was only trying to cure you of the delusion that a compliment from that old cod carried any weight with me."

"We have had a therapeutic session. I hope I have also convinced you that you or, perhaps, Mrs MacDonnell is also suffering from a delusion. By the way, what age is your wife?"

"I resent that question."

"I asked clinically. She may be passing through that period when fantasies of this kind do take hold. I'd have a word with her doctor, if I were you. One of my wives, when she was in the same phase, imagined that she was being pursued with seductive intent by the Duke of Connaught. He was well over ninety at the time. I only mention this. Don't misunderstand me. And don't worry. It passes. But it can be a very distressing period. Fortunately my other wives were always on one side or other of the bourn when we lived together. Grace was the unhappy exception. Forgive me for hurrying you away like this. I did enjoy our talk. I think we succeeded in clearing the air."

Angus found himself being shepherded towards the door, all power to resist paralysed by the confusion of this new idea. He had come out armed with a powerful grievance. He was prepared for opposition; but he did not expect to encounter an effective diversion.

"But my wife hasn't come to it yet," the sufficient answer when it occurred to him, was spoken to a door which, he noticed, could have done with a fresh coat of paint.

"He's a stingy devil," Angus told himself. "I can see him

hoarding paper and string. There's no juice in him. Never was! I'm sure he lives on nuts. I couldn't bring a dog into my house and not offer him a drink: but he's chock full of arrogance, indulges himself in his meanness, wallows in it. I'd be ashamed to behave like that. When I assumed my title I took on its obligations, and I discharge them. That old taproot thinks his long line of distinguished ancestors gives him his right of way through the elementary decencies. He must have known my tongue was hanging out."

Brooding, discontented, feeling he had been outwitted, Angus took himself to the Savage Club, where he was refused admission. He wanted to think. There was of course the possibility that Pamela was entering the biological minefield. It didn't happen with a bang. There would be a gradual accumulation of warning signs. She was forever dropping Radish's name on the score of one meeting at a conference. Not until the night with the McElligots—when she was as tight as a tick—did she come out with this revelation of a passage between them. Could it be that she was imagining things? He had better avail himself of the offer and call on the publisher.

John Jackson had heard of Angus, and welcomed him civilly, as he did anyone with book-generating possibilities, accepting his assurance that he came with the author's approval. Soured by his recent encounter with the old man, who was proving difficult, ungrateful, and disappointingly unglamorous, he saw Angus as an ally. Any enemy of Radish's was today a friend of his. If Angus had kept cool, he would have left the office with the proofs, but something in his manner, reminiscent of a dog looking for a buried bone, alerted Jackson to his risk.

"I'm afraid I can't put the proofs at your disposal."

"And why not, pray?"

The Laird of Smogg had taken over, and, as always, fatally.

"Because you have no right to them."

"I told you Sir Romney authorised it."

"Not to us."

"You don't take my word."

"Sir Romney—as I think we agreed—can be difficult."

"Oh, Hell! I've travelled all the way from Ireland, Mr Jackson. You can't treat me like this."

"I have to. There are other people, people with much more right than you have to see the proofs that I have refused them to—the Hartleys, for instance. An excerpt about them will be featured in this Sunday's *Echo*, and even they have not been informed of its contents."

"Hartleys? The Go-Between?"

"I beg your pardon."

"The writer man?"

"We are at cross-purposes. L. P. Hartley, if that is who you are referring to, is dead. I was referring to Eleanor Hartley, and her husband. Radish calls her 'Priscilla Blue'."

"Oh! Mere socialites. Of no significance."

"But very much interested in these memoirs."

When Angus was gone, something in his eye at the moment of departure, as in a golfer's who has driven beyond his wonted length, came back to disturb John Jackson's equanimity. He shook off the impression of unease. After all it wasn't as if he were dealing with just anybody. One could trust a man of MacDonnell's standing to know how to behave. Such was the insane counsel Mr Jackson gave himself.

Chapter VI

THE MEMOIRS WERE not out of the minds of the
Hartleys at Bloomdale. Eleanor felt a weight on her spirits.
Life was inevitably less exciting than it used to be; were it
otherwise she couldn't have stood the pace: but nowadays
instead of bearers of good tidings, visitors to Bloomdale were
apt to be historical in their approach. Would she be kind
enough to tell them what D. H. Lawrence was like? What
Augustus John did? What Huxley said? She enjoyed these
visits, and liked to get the even more frequent letters, some of
them from the most out-of-the-way places. But it was not the
same as being the epicentre of the creative volcano. And in
her soul there were embers still aglow. A very gentle fanning
could still set them on fire. It rarely came. Of the great days
of Bloomdale, the only survivors were old faithful queers,
who talked more gently than had been their wont, but still
enjoyed the baring of claws. They would get huge enjoyment
out of the revelations in the Radish book, provided their
names appeared even once in the index. Eleanor admitted
to herself that she, too, would get a vicarious thrill. It would
bring down the research students in hordes; what would she
say to them? "It wasn't me" or, if Runty had behaved like
a rotter, admit it and tell the truth about him. They would
be afraid to print it. Runty always got away with murder
and seemed to be proof against attack himself. Routine
denunciations by Mrs Grundy only added to his reputation.
But Lionel would suffer. With age, she had come to appreciate more fully his extraordinary tolerance.

Now the old wounds would be opened by this strange man
whom only her vanity had allowed her to admit as a lover.
Many times she had taken up a pen to write to him and

appeal to his sense of decency (if he had one). But each time the pen stuck on the page like a reluctant donkey, refusing to move. How could she say it? It ought not to have to be said. She had been to blame in letting so much pass unchallenged in other books, hints for the most part; but there were definite assertions in some cases, and if she had objected, the writers were entitled to say that they were telling the truth. And nowadays to talk of bad taste, or to take any of the old stances only made one look absurd. So she let it go, again and again. But why did she always rush to read these books and look for her name in the index with the same sort of thrill with which she heard her bedroom door-handle creak in the great days of Bloomdale? One protested as a matter of course, and consented because it seemed fussy to make a row; and it was fun, and it hurt nobody. But it was hurting Lionel now.

One morning a strange-looking man appeared quite early and asked to see Mr Hartley. The matter was urgent, he said, and private. He gave his name as Angus MacDonnell. Mr Hartley would know of him, he said. In this he was too sanguine.

"I've seen him on the telly," the maid said who answered the bell. She spoke as an ally. Lionel was not in the mood for callers. He went in search of Eleanor. He found her arranging flowers.

"There is a man called MacDonnell downstairs. He wants to see me. Ever heard of him?"

"MacDonnell? MacDonnell? You don't know his Christian name?"

"Angus."

"Ah. That ought to be the man who wrote *In the Spring a Young Man's Fancy*. I've seen him on television. So have you."

"I remember. Tall. Looks like a demented younger brother of General de Gaulle."

"Pop-eyed."

"That's him."

"I wonder what he wants."

"Says it's private and urgent. Sounds like a demand for a subscription."

"Perhaps you'd better see him. You might fob him off with a pound, he'd stick me for a cheque."

"I'll tackle him. You'd better stay here until the coast is clear."

So matters had been arranged between this understanding pair on many similar occasions. If the caller was sympathetic or persistent, Lionel usually found himself laid under tribute eventually.

Eleanor did not find Angus any more prepossessing in the flesh than on the box. For one thing he was sweating copiously; his eyes behind their glasses were blood-shot, and a persistent tremble in his large frame suggested that he might begin to melt at any moment. Her eyes lit on his bag.

"I'm afraid my husband is very busy this morning. This time of day is never good for him; but can I do anything for you, Mr MacDonnell?"

"I have come from Sir Romney Radish's publishers. I had hoped to discuss it with your husband."

"Oh, have you the book? Do let me see it. I was just about to ring up our bookseller to order a copy when you arrived."

"I had better explain myself. May I sit down?"

"Please do."

"Do you know who I am, Mrs Hartley?"

"I think I recognise you. You're the author."

Angus, on tip-toe for insult, bowed, mollified.

"You haven't seen any advance proofs of this book, I suppose."

"No."

"Neither have I; but I have had a glance and it was enough to give me a shrewd idea of what we may expect. That is why I want to see your husband. The first instalment is due for publication in the *Echo* next Sunday. It must be prevented *at any cost*, Mrs Hartley."

Eleanor blushed. (She had forgotten the sensation.) The

manner of the announcement, the glare that the thickness of his glasses magnified, the amalgam he presented of sweat and twitch and over-emphatic gesture made her feel as if she were indecently exposed. Involuntarily she looked across the room at her reflection in the glass on a painting of cattle in a Dutch landscape, adding to her confusion.

"Why? Is it libellous?"

"I hope so."

"I don't understand."

"From what I have gathered"—and here Angus was taking his risk—"the revelations may reflect on the credit of your family."

Eleanor blushed again. She wanted above all else that this absurd person should go away and stop embarrassing her. She was certainly not going to go through the offending passages with him. What business was it of his? This was sheer impertinence.

"I think you had better see my husband," she said. "If you wouldn't mind waiting, I'll tell him why you are here."

She found Lionel in his lair, a small book-lined room, overlooking the river. "This awful man. You had better see him. I think he is slightly mad."

The contrast between the man she had left and her husband—dapper, clean-shaven, his skin as fresh and sweet-smelling as an apple, with his amiable intelligent eyes—was a reproof to her; and this increased when she saw her photograph on his desk.

"I'm sorry," she said, kissing his receded hair-line. He patted her hand. "We couldn't be better off."

It was true; and the picture of Lionel, whom she really loved and thanked God for every time she thought about it, sent her back heartened to fetch the grotesque reminder of the follies of her over-indulged youth.

But Angus was only part of the trouble she had brought— and still might bring—on Lionel. "This is what I've done. I'm sorry," she seemed to say, looking like a child who has broken a window, as she showed the visitor in.

Angus had the darting eye of a captured animal. It took in the room, the quiet-looking, neat, smiling man, the books, the window and the view, the cabinet in the corner (especially the cabinet in the corner) to which his eye travelled when Lionel inquired what he could do for him.

"You have come a long way. Perhaps you would like a drink."

It was so different from the interview with Radish. Angus responded to the well-bred amiability; not realising that it was only there so long as advantage was not taken of it. He felt better after a large whisky and the prospect of another. Lionel had kept him company in sherry, "going easy", Angus noticed. He always noticed drinking habits.

Lionel invited him to open his mind, and sat back in his chair, his head against the window curtain, in the shade, while Angus, in the full light, gave vent to his feelings. His indignation against Radish was apparently solely on account of the liberty he had taken with Mrs Hartley. "I was only able to get a glance. But I am informed on excellent authority that this chapter will be featured in the *Sunday Echo*. Mrs Hartley is identified as a Priscilla Blue. Surely that will fool nobody. The material is scurrilous and scandalous."

"You weren't aware of this," was the remark with which Angus broke the short silence that followed. He had expected to meet a face as warlike as his own, and was disappointed when Lionel seemed to have let his attention stray to a boat-party on the river.

"Nice to be young," he said, and then, apologetically, "I heard about the book, of course, but this is the first time I've met anyone who seems to know what is in it. There is going to be another volume. That is a lot to have to buy, isn't it? With the price of everything. Book prices are simply bounding up. What are they asking for it?"

"I don't know. I came here from Ireland to see if we could arrange for concerted action. The instalment in the *Echo* on Sunday will be taken out of the chapter you're mentioned in. That's for sure. We have no time to waste."

"What, if I may ask, is your interest in this?"

"The feeling of outrage of any decent person, in the first place, at such treatment of any woman. And as well as that, I don't mind admitting to you, I've suffered in the same way; but in my case Radish has been cowardly. He knew I would strike back; he tried to cover his tracks. In your case, he relied on your legendary good temper."

Lionel's face did not display any gratification.

"I don't really see why you should bother yourself on my account. If you have been offended you should see your solicitor. He will advise you about your rights. You must assume that I am able to look after myself. I don't really see the advantage of any teaming-up operation. Besides you remarked that the offensive extracts concern someone called Priscilla Blue. Why should anyone identify her with my wife? Did you gather that there were precise references to me or my wife by name?"

"If I were you I'd resent this subterfuge more than if the man had had the courage to use real names. Everyone will see through it. She is one of the most celebrated figures on the literary scene."

"I must say I prefer the camouflage. I'm amused by your assumption that Romney is referring to us. I wouldn't, had our positions been reversed, have called on you and told you to your face that I recognised you and your wife under pseudonyms. Were we friends, it would be different. I would be concerned for a friend, I hope."

"I trust you don't resent my action."

"By no means; and then I understand from you that you have had cause for offence. I hope it won't appear in the newspaper. In a book, I always think—because there's not the same concentration—one feels less exposed."

"May I take you into my confidence?"

Angus leaned forward, his blood-shot eyes, as they stared through thick lenses, looked more than ever like frantic fish in an aquarium. At the same time he waved aloft an empty tumbler.

"Please help yourself." While Angus was acting on the invitation, Lionel continued in his mild manner. "I'm not sure that it is ever wise to give confidences unnecessarily. Sometimes one must; but I make it a working rule not to park out my secrets. One loses track of them, and they are apt to turn up again, altered out of recognition. Don't tell me anything, Mr MacDonnell, that you don't feel you have to. Of course, if I can be of any help, that's another matter."

"I had hoped we could get together."

"And I've told you I'd rather not. But thank you very much for the suggestion. It was most kind of you."

"You may feel differently when you hear what I have to say. How would you like it if Radish had raped your wife?"

"I shouldn't like it. I can tell you frankly. But I consider it most unlikely. There are very few full-grown women who couldn't defend themselves against the worst Romney could do in that line. Or so I should have thought."

"He raped Pamela."

"That does surprise me. I'm shocked to hear it. Romney is a very old friend of ours. I've never known him to be otherwise than an extremely civilised person. And then—is Mrs MacDonnell very *petite*?"

"By no means."

"Then I am even more surprised. If you had ever seen him trying to play tennis you would see what I mean. He could hardly serve from the back line. I don't suppose he weighs more than eight stone."

"You must allow for the force of lust; then there is the shock of unexpectedness. A sudden leap in the dark—savage country—no one within call. By the time Pamela had asked herself what had hit her, her assailant had come and gone, I daresay. I've never asked my wife for details, you understand."

"Perfectly."

"But she has given me the general picture." Angus laughed ironically. "He raped my wife in Madagascar. I suppose he thought he would be safe so far away from base as that. I'm going to make Radish pay through the nose for it. The girl he attacked, thinking her the snobbish wife of some petty U.S. official, who would be delighted by the attention, is now married to someone who knows exactly the value of Radish's attentions. He has the Laird of Smogg to deal with now."

"The Laird of Smogg? What has he to do with it?"

"I am the Laird of Smogg. It's a courtesy title in our family."

"I once passed Smogg in a yacht. We went for a trip round the Hebrides. I remember the island. The name sticks, like the one beside it. Eigg, I think it is called. Is there a Laird of Eigg?"

"We don't recognise him because he doesn't recognise us."

"That seems fair; but it is rather a pity. I don't suppose there are a great many people to know on the island. Do you live there all the time, or only in the summer?"

"The old house was destroyed."

"Oh, dear! I was going to say that if I lived in the Hebrides, I wouldn't mind what Romney said about me."

"In my case it's not what he's written, it's what he did. In your case the boot is on the other leg. He did very little apparently. I don't know how Mrs Hartley put up with him for so long."

"I'd rather we kept off the subject, Mr MacDonnell. In fact, I don't think I should keep you any longer. I know you have a long way to go and a great deal to do. You must not waste any more of your valuable time with me. I've listened to what you had to say with the greatest interest."

"You are not prepared to act then?"

"I'm afraid not. I find the whole subject distasteful. I'm not even prepared to discuss it. By the way—you will forgive me for saying this—you are not, I may take it, going to mention our conversation in any newspaper. I have seen you at your request, but this wasn't an interview."

"Mr Hartley, I am amazed, sir, that you could possibly

put such a construction on my visit. I am, I hope, modest about my position; unfashionably so, it hasn't helped; but I should have thought you would have known that I would hardly be looking for gossip-paragraphs. I approached you because I considered we were both in the same case, victims of this senile megalomaniac's lust for notoriety."

"Please"—Lionel looked genuinely upset—"Don't misunderstand me. But nowadays everybody is writing for the newspapers. Cabinet Ministers and Generals have their reminiscences in readiness to shoot out the very moment they retire. Nobody has either dignity or shame. An adulterer is interviewed in the bosom of his family."

"Quite so. I lament these things as much as you do; but it does not give me any solace. I am a writer of some standing, I hope, not a hack reporter."

"Please. Please. You must forgive me. I am a little on edge today, not myself. If I haven't said very much, Mr Mac-Donnell, I must not leave you under the impression that I am not greatly concerned. I am much obliged to you for drawing my attention to the matter. I was misled by an assurance given to me by both the publisher and the editor that neither my name nor my wife's nor this house were once mentioned. Romney did say he was using pseudonyms, but I didn't pay sufficient attention. I didn't think it was the practice in writing biographies; surely it defeats their purpose."

"If the people were not clearly identifiable. In that case it adds sauce."

"I must say it has disappointed me very much in Romney. I cannot understand how any man could treat old friends in such a scurvy way."

"Nothing from that quarter surprises me. By the way I noticed you said 'Romney'. Surely 'Runty' is what his friends called him?"

"Only *to* his friends."

"I must be going. If I am to have no help in stopping this book, I have no time to waste. Good morning. Thank you, I'll find my own way out."

Angus had been snubbed. Wherever he turned, he was met with ingratitude. No wonder he adopted a hostile attitude to the world. It was a bloody world, full of bloody people. This epicene old money-bag, even after these shocking revelations, still seemed somehow to stay on Radish's side and against him. It was intolerable.

He strode out, waving aside Lionel's hostly gesture. Whisky kept Angus close to tears always. Was it fanciful to see liquor in the moisture which dimmed his eyes whenever he thought about the loneliness of his struggle? Even Pamela couldn't help. Her sympathy went so far; but when real understanding was required, all she could do was to offer to do something—go to bed or make a cup of tea or get up a party. She had no imaginative resources. She couldn't penetrate his soul.

He could understand Mrs Hartley's embarrassment. She was not prepared to discuss her predicament with him, and pushed him over to her husband. He had put up a convincing show of geniality; but it was on the surface, underneath he was loyal only to his clique, and resented a newcomer, even one inspired by a genuine impulse of fellow-feeling.

Angus's feet rang out on the stone floor of the hall; the front door slammed behind him. Eleanor, standing beside her husband, her head on his shoulder, watched the departing caller.

"I think he meant well," Lionel said. "Did you ever meet anyone who sweated quite so much? I wonder if it has anything to do with the amount of whisky he drinks. He soaks it up. I wonder how he manages to write. Perhaps the atmosphere in Ireland absorbs moisture."

"What had he to say?"

"He has a grudge against Runty, says he raped his wife. I can't believe it, unless she is a midget. But he seems to have a bee in his bonnet on the point, and he wanted me to join forces with him. I'm afraid he thought I'd be a useful stalking horse. My dear, I might as well tell you, Runty has done his worst and used different names. It won't take anyone who matters in. The lawyers should have insisted on seeing the book instead of accepting the undertaking. I didn't feel happy about it. I'm going to ring them up now and see what can be done. But we are getting very near the deadline."

"Darling, how can you even look at me? I'm awful, quite awful. Don't say I'm not. I know I am."

"I'm upset only on Gerald's account. I assured him that he had nothing to worry about."

"You matter to me much more than Gerald does. I'm not sure that he doesn't ask for it by being such a prig."

"Parents shouldn't have children if they want to lead undisciplined lives."

"Don't make me feel worse than I do."

"I blame myself, not you. It reminds me of dear Tom.

> And I Tiresias have foresuffered all
> Enacted on this same divan or bed;
> I who have sat by Thebes below the wall
> And walked among the lowest of the dead."

"You were so much more worthwhile than any of them, but you spoiled me. You let me take you for granted as well as the help you were prepared to give to sillies that any other husband would have thrown out of the house, I didn't deserve you; but I have you now, and they are all gone and forgotten."

Did Lionel smile? She was never quite sure. He was such a deep one.

"We may have forgotten them; but they have not forgotten us."

"Oh, that beastly Runty! I could smack his self-satisfied little face."

"What a pity we can't resort to fisticuffs. But at sixty-eight I can't beat Runty up when he's over eighty and practically a dwarf. I don't feel like assaulting Stoat. He owes me nothing, and I can't hold him personally responsible for the general decline in newspaper standards. He is cashing in on it with everyone else. The publisher chap is only doing his job. I suppose if justice were to be done I ought to beat you."

"You should have done that long ago, dear. I can't see what it would achieve now."

"I'll ring up the lawyers."

He dialled the too familiar number.

The partner in charge of Lionel's business was an experienced man. The accusation of negligence which he heard in silence gave him time to think. His proficiency in handling his clients' affairs was second only to his expertness in looking after his own. Lawyers needed this skill; theirs is a risky profession : their mistakes do not get buried, but live on to haunt their sleep. The later life of Macbeth resembled in many respects that of a solicitor in large practice. There is a Banquo in the waiting room of most busy offices. As such the usually undemanding Lionel sounded to his adviser's listening ear.

In moments of stress telephone lines shorten, the speakers come very close. They can hear breathing; silences speak. These phenomena attended the end of Lionel's complaint, not that his manner had been hectoring or threatening, but it had been plain and firm. He was making it quite clear that he had asked for professional help and had not got what he would be asked in due course to pay for. Confidence; that was the note Mr Mayberry had to strike first. Reassurance might follow; and if that had to be jettisoned, a watertight excuse must be at hand. And only then could aggrievance raise its head. The interview must end with the client abashed and apologetic.

Mr Mayberry grimaced at the ceiling. "If you don't mind holding on for a few seconds, I'll read you the letters from the publishers and from the editor. One moment please."

Breathing more heavily, he spoke again after a slightly longer delay than he had promised.

"This is our letter to the publishers.

Dear Sirs,

We are informed that you intend to publish shortly two volumes of memoirs by Sir Romney Radish. We act for Mr and Mrs Lionel Hartley of Bloomdale, Farse-on-the-Water, Bucks. Our clients have been given to understand that they appear in the memoirs. In order to avoid controversy, and in the best interests of all concerned, we must ask you to let us see these references, and for that purpose will you oblige us with the manuscript for perusal. For our part we undertake to return it with the least possible delay together with our comments.

"The letter to the editor of the *Sunday Echo* was in much the same terms. To the first we received a reply by return.

Dear Sirs,

With reference to your letter of yesterday's date. In view of the shortness of the time we have not sent you the two volumes, but instead we enclose the index to the first. We do this to shorten your labour. You will see that neither of your clients nor their residence is mentioned once by Sir Romney in his first volume. If you do not accept our assurance about the second volume, we will be pleased to send you the proofs at an early date.

Yours faithfully,

"Lord Stoat himself rang me up about the extracts in the *Sunday Echo*. He said that he had insisted on seeing them when he heard that we had written on your behalf and he begged me to assure you personally that neither you nor Mrs Hartley is mentioned."

"And you didn't ask to see the extracts."

"I had already seen the index. And when Lord Stoat—"

"Don't go on. Did you see the name Priscilla Blue in the index?"

"Let me see. I have it before me. Yes. Priscilla Blue appears in an inclusive entry between pages 87 and 120. A Leonard Blue is mentioned once, on page 87."

"If you had taken the precaution to read the proofs you would have recognised us at once. As our family solicitor you are aware that my wife has figured in other memoirs. It was unavoidable; we entertained a great many people who write that sort of thing. Sir Romney was a friend of ours. You must have known that."

"I have learnt not to pay too much attention to rumours."

"But you must pay some. Surely it was an elementary precaution."

"I had the assurance of Duck and Lime, who are above reproach in the profession. Lord Stoat, I should have thought—"

"But they both harped on this business about names. Surely that in itself was suspicious."

"Not in the least. If the author had written a novel one would have looked behind the fictitious names; there is no precedent for this."

"I am still of opinion you should have looked for yourself and not accepted assurances."

"I perused the index."

"You were taken in."

"I certainly agree there has been sharp practice. I'm going to take the matter up with Duck and Lime. If necessary I'll raise it with the Incorporated Law Society."

"But that won't be much help to me or to Mrs Hartley. I advise you to get busy. It is not too late to prevent publication on Sunday. After all, they can get another extract out of the wretched book. As to the publishers, can't you apply for an injunction straight away?"

"That will give maximum publicity to any scandal. I'd like to see the offending passages. I'll get on to Duck and Lime at once, and ring you up after lunch. Will you be at home?"

"I'll come up to London. I'll call at half past two, if that suits you."

When Lionel had finished telephoning, he sat down heavily, looking suddenly older. It was true; he blamed himself, his attempt at over-civilised living had ended in this. Just when he had come round the last bend in the river, and glimpsed the sea towards which he had steered his craft so skilfully, he was faced with rapids that had not been marked on his map. On these the boat would go to pieces. He was too tired to save it. All he had worked for was a few miles of calm sailing after a long tricky journey. He didn't care about himself; and Eleanor—whatever his responsibility towards her might have been—had herself to blame; but it was bad luck on Gerald, the boy who should not have been. Lionel thought about his own mother. He had adored her. She was quite as flighty as Eleanor. More so in some ways. Eleanor at least had used her own home as a base. His mother appeared only to vanish again; and his father consoled himself with a hard-faced woman, who conveyed increasingly as time went on the idea of penance rather than consolation.

He had grown up with a romantic picture of his mother, which nothing that he learned about her could injure. They had such happy times together. She was always fun. Laughter and colour and sound and scent—all his first precious enduring awareness of these were personified by his mother. She died young. That sanctified her. His father didn't marry his mistress. He was not an imaginative man; but he had a sense of the fitness of things. And when he grew up, Lionel understood him; they became friends.

He grew up with romantic illusions about women, derived from his mother, and a conviction that love was for giving not getting—Agape not Eros—an end in itself. He learned that from his father, who never said a word, but stood humbly beside the grave while the others who had known his wife, looking like a Greek chorus, disposed themselves among the surrounding cypresses. Silently, they slipped away,

93

each noting the others and doing sums in his head. It was the first time Lionel had ever taken his father's hand.

His only concern in this Runty business had been for Gerald. He was sure he had made everything safe until that madman appeared this morning—a sample of horror to come. He must go and see Gerald and convince him that he was anxious to save him from the consequences of his parents' indiscretion. He would not put it off any longer. At the best of times the decision to see Gerald required an effort of will, and he was not feeling up to it. If he delayed he would weaken; he must put through a telephone call at once. Waiting for Gerald to come to the telephone he struggled against a temptation to put down the receiver.

Gerald's voice, solemn and minatory, confirmed the wisdom of the impulse to ring off; but it was too late now.

"Is that you, old chap? I'm a little worried about something. I want to discuss it with you. Could you get off for the evening? Come and dine with me at Brooks's. I'll be there at half past seven."

Gerald agreed. He knew his father would not seek him out unless the matter was serious. He managed to convey by his tone that such short notice was unreasonable and inconvenient. He had a genius for putting whoever he was talking to in the wrong. After dinner tonight his tone would convey that the food hadn't come up to scratch. There was no pleasing him.

If the solicitors had made up for their negligence it would all be much easier. Even in that event Lionel decided he must warn Gerald about the matter. There might be unpleasant developments. Better have it all out now. But if there was no way of stopping Runty this would be the worst evening in Lionel's life.

Chapter VII

"IT WAS VERY good of you, old chap, to come up like that. I hope it didn't upset your plans."

Gerald looked suspiciously at his pink gin. "I had, as a matter of fact, arranged to take Caro out. But she was very good about it. She is a very plucky kid, and considering how right in every way her own upbringing has been, wonderful at making allowances. I suppose you want to see me about something to do with mother."

Lionel was not quite sure whether he was grateful for the directness of this. It saved time; but it cut through his defensive outworks and left Eleanor exposed to the first attack.

"Indirectly," Lionel said. "Indirectly," he repeated, as if the repetition lent covering fire. They left the bar and went into the dining room, which was almost empty. In a corner they would be able to talk it over. Gerald's attitude to his mother made Lionel feel guilty. "You shouldn't have done this to me," was what he conveyed. It was intolerable; Lionel put up with it as part of his punishment. Now he decided that he had been punished enough. There wasn't much of life left. He was going to enjoy it in his own way and cast off for ever this feeling of being a criminal out on a ticket of leave.

"Let me tell you what the worry is," Lionel began.

During this recitation, Gerald kept his eyes on his plate as if he did not want to contaminate the prawns before he had heard the worst.

"I saw the law chap this afternoon," Lionel continued, "and I made no bones about it. They let themselves be made fools of. There is a paragraph in the *Evening Standard* saying

95

that the sales of the *Echo* on Sunday are expected to go up
by 100,000. Stoat is not going to throw that away when his
lawyers have a letter from mine giving him a clearance."

"But, surely, if he knows there is going to be a libel action
he won't go on."

"There won't be. Runty has letters from your mother
which may well bear out some of the nonsense he has
written."

"But, my God, has no one right to privacy?"

"He calls her Priscilla Blue, married to a Leonard Blue.
I am informed that the account is rather scandalous."

"But that is a childish hoax. There are no such people, I
take it. Everyone will know who he means."

"Exactly. But truth is a defence in a libel action, and
between ourselves, old chap, is it not better to endure this
nine days' wonder than to go to court and have it all spelled
out and underlined and gloated over? I am mortified for
your mother's sake; and I think we should both bear in mind
that this is very hard on a woman. What a low hound Runty
is. Why did he do it? Not for money. Perhaps he had some
obscure desire to get even with women. Between ourselves, I
gather that he was no good at all. All smoke and no fire. I
suspected it. I could never understand what any woman saw
in him. Lots of brains of course; but that is irrelevant, I
should have thought, when one gets down to business. You
never heard of women chasing Einstein. Perhaps they did. I
am never surprised by anything I hear. Where have I been
all my life? How badly everyone seems to behave. I wish I
had known. It's rather a comfort in a way."

Gerald rapped the table with a fork. "I think I had better
see the solicitor."

"By all means. I shall ring him up and say I want you to,
otherwise he might make the excuse that he can't discuss
his clients' business with anyone else. They are very foxy,
these chaps. But I wish they had been more on their toes on
this occasion. I'm sure something could have been done if
they had moved at once."

"I may be able to shake them. Caro's family have influence if they choose to use it, and I should think they will in the present instance. That fat swine Trotter owns Haymakers. He bought it for prestige reasons. I'll let him know that his chances of improving on his miserable K.B.E. will be very slim indeed. The *Echo* is more difficult. We might have to move through the Palace."

"Gerald! You *have* become a power in the land."

"If you don't mind, this is hardly a moment for facetiousness. My whole life has been ruined by my mother. I thought that persecution would end when she passed sixty. But this is worse than anything. I don't enjoy speaking to you like this, Father; but it isn't the time to mince words. I've too much at stake. My mother is not going to wreck my marriage. What I've got to consider is how to move."

"Uncle Peter?"

"He seems to enjoy mother's notoriety. The last time I saw him he laughed at me. I haven't gone near him since. I've cut the Lapworth connection. I find them tiresome. No. I shan't go near mother's relations. The question is, shall I speak to the Colonel or to Mims? You must admit that it is hard on me to have to confide this sort of thing to my future father-in-law."

"But he must know all about you, Gerald. Your mother is **one** of the best-known women in England."

"Not in the Chetwynd-Skopwith circle. They are not interested in third-rate literary gossip."

"With all due respect, they can't be completely fossilised. They must make some contact with the world. They read, I presume. The men join the Army, go to clubs—they must talk about something. The North of England is not at the Pole."

"I can assure you that the difference between the atmosphere I was brought up in and life at Skopwith, where I spent last week-end, is as great as if there was a hundred years in time and ten thousand miles in distance between them. It was part of the depravity of Bloomdale that one

97

was brain-washed into thinking that the people mother collected round her were the norm. I wish you could come to Skopwith and see what it's like there. I admit they keep very much to themselves and the two other families on the border they dine with. Life is quiet. You mightn't like it. I do. I've found the sort of people I am at home with, and I'm damned if I'm going to let that woman spoil it for me now."

"Don't call your mother 'that woman'."

Gerald turned to his plate and carved the grouse with deliberation. His father watched him with awe.

Nobody could be so unattractive as Gerald looked just then. Instead of feeling antipathy, Lionel was overcome with remorse. That Gerald was so satisfied with the horror he was, added to his pathos. Who could have seen this resulting from the undiscipline in Bloomdale? Gerald must be proof that environment is more important than heredity. Eleanor was behaving perfectly when he was begotten. Or was she? Did he represent some momentary aberration on their honeymoon? She had left him at a circus, he remembered, and gone in search of her bag. Was she long enough away for . . . The idea was absurd, indecent. But it would explain Gerald. The meal was finished in silence.

If Gerald's friendless condition explained his father's affectionate concern for his welfare, it was not one of his grievances against the world. He was always critical, frequently outraged, but never inclined to self-pity. His conceit forbade it. No one, he would have argued, with such consistently high standards could hope for cheap popularity; and, then, he was forever telling upstarts off, putting them in their place: what, he might have asked, did he need friends for? Now that he had Caro all to himself he felt complete within if permanently assailed from without. So long as he avoided a quarrel with Cecil Harkness he could boast of a friend. It was a unique relationship. Cecil, ten years older than Gerald, was a bachelor with a flat in Maida

Vale, which nobody had ever seen. The amount and source of his income was a mystery. He had been to the best educational establishments, had outraged officers and men in one of the best regiments, and spent all his latter days glaring out of the window of one of the best clubs.

No man, we are too often told, is an island. Cecil, in the club window, might be cited as the exception; but to his fellow members he seemed more like a volcano, and was treated with the same respect.

For many years he confined his glare to the scene from the club window, then someone, with the motive that inspires a timid householder to purchase a savage dog, suggested putting "old Cecil" on the committee. Ever since, even when his eye was on the street, his ear was cocked for even the breath of an alleged infringement of club rules on the premises.

His zeal had a limited appeal; speculation about his age became more frequent and pointed. Only Gerald recognised a fellow-spirit. For him that red face glowing in the window was a welcoming light. He never failed to greet Cecil, and nodded complacently when Cecil gave a short bark in return.

One day they were sitting opposite one another, Cecil was glaring out of the window, Gerald into the room where their club-mates were conversing or reading newspapers. By chance their eyes met, and Gerald involuntarily spoke his thought aloud: "Would you like a game of chess?"

In thirty years, Cecil had never been asked to join in anything by anybody—the effect on him was extraordinary. He refused at once, automatically; but his eyes, which too frequently protruded, receded and revealed a commotion within.

"Did you say you wanted a game?" he said.

Pedantry—Gerald's bane—compelled him to repeat his question exactly.

"Well, I'm very busy just now. But if you still feel inclined for a game, I'll join you in half an hour."

"I'll be in the card room."

Cecil got up, walked half-way towards the door, and returned to where Gerald was sitting.

"I could manage it in quarter of an hour."

"Splendid."

Then Cecil went to the lavatory, where Gerald joined him.

By tacit agreement they proceeded thence to the card room. Their games became a feature of the club, part of the furniture. Cecil was the first person Gerald ever defeated, as Gerald was the first to ask Cecil to play.

Each became very precious to the other; as they agreed on all points, spoke mostly in monosyllables, and never met outside the club, their friendship was not much at risk. Cecil never consulted Gerald about anything, but sometimes the younger man sought to profit from the experience of the other, setting store unwisely by his jealous advice.

Gerald happened to drop into this club to pass away the time before he met the lawyer by appointment, and found Cecil in his usual seat. Gerald proposed a game. He played even more ineptly than usual and Cecil won with a queen, a bishop, a rook, two castles, and three pawns in hand.

Cecil, naturally, was reluctant to attribute the slaughter to his opponent's loss of form. He crowed a little. Gerald was not prepared to let that pass.

"I can't concentrate. I'm in terrible trouble, old man."

Cecil Harkness did not encourage confidences; he dreaded encroachment, involvement.

"I'm sure you're exaggerating," he said.

"I wish I were."

Without encouragement, Gerald told his problem; and his friend, once it became clear that there was no money involved, was prepared to listen.

"If you take my advice you'll just say to this lawyer fellow, 'I'm taking this up with the Law Society.' That will scare the daylights out of him."

"Really?"

"I speak from experience. Let him think he is going to

have to pay up out of his own pocket, and he'll scuttle.
That's all these fellows understand."

Gerald repeated the phrase to himself several times; and
only when he was sure he had got it right took leave of his
friend.

He entered the office of his father's lawyers with more
arrogance than he would have assumed in the mess, betray-
ing the unsureness everyone feels who has to battle in
unfamiliar territory.

This was not the firm Gerald employed when he needed
legal advice. He went to a man whom he could bully. Meek
Mr Edwards had grown to hate Gerald's formula, always to
preface his question with the assertion that it was one that
would give the solicitor "no trouble at all". That left him in
a cleft stick : if he disagreed he appeared incompetent, if
he answered at once he was precluded from making a
reasonable charge. But Mr Edwards, a small man in a small
way, with a family, nourishing impossible hopes of getting
eventually the paying end of the Hartley estate, could not
afford to make Gerald the obvious reply when he made his
inevitable gambit. In these opulent chambers, Gerald could
not lord it as was his wont.

Mortimer Mayberry, who had learned that he was in the
outer office, left him to cool his heels there. The solicitor,
conscious of having handled the case wretchedly, was fighting
with his back to the wall, and he was determined to make use
of every tactical advantage. He had seen Gerald quite
recently in connection with his wedding arrangements. Like
Lionel, he had wondered where this long prig could have
come from, and antedated Eleanor's fall from grace by
eighteen months.

Gerald was brusque when he came in. His best chance he
knew was to fire first. Lionel, even when he was aware of his
lawyer's mistake, tempered the wind a little. Not so his son.

"I've come to see you about this mess your firm has got
my family into. I understand that you have authorised the

publication of material which you must know is offensive to us as well as being highly libellous. I am here today on my own account. As you know I'm marrying one of the Chetwynd-Skopwiths—by the way is the settlement ready? I hope there has been no mix-up over that."

Mr Mayberry had decided to skate over his own mistake and to stand on the ground that it was irrelevant as Radish had letters to support his case. The Hartleys would be foolish to court publicity. In a sense Gerald had made it easier by being so rude. He decided to end this interview at once. He stood up. Gerald did not take the hint. Mr Mayberry sat down again, looking ugly.

"What are my future in-laws going to say when they read the *Sunday Echo*?"

"How can I say? I don't know your future in-laws."

"Do you imagine it will give them any pleasure?"

"That all depends. They might find it diverting."

"You don't know the Chetwynd-Skopwiths."

"I haven't had that pleasure."

"Well, let me tell you, they will be surprised when they hear how your firm has managed this business. Nobody comes out of it with credit, Mr Mayberry. Nobody."

"You had better be very careful what you say about my firm's handling of the case, Major Hartley. We have nothing to apologise for. You seem to make the not uncommon mistake of confusing a solicitor with a blackmailer's assistant. It is not our duty to make empty threats in order to satisfy clients' whims. You are in the wrong office. Which reminds me that I have a very important consultation at three, and it is now five minutes past."

"I am not going to be put out before we agree on a course of action."

"The only course of action I'll agree to is that you remove yourself from here at once."

"I'm damned if I will. I insist that you try to make good the damage you have done by your negligence and incompetence."

"Repeat that outside, sir. Repeat it only once, and I'll summon you to answer for it. You'll pay for those words. I'm a good-tempered man. I have a regard for your father. But I—"

"I'm taking this further. You haven't heard the last of me."

Now was the time to deliver the *coup de grâce*. Gerald searched in his angry mind for the phrase he had memorised so carefully. Something to do with the Law Society. But what? He knew nothing about the Law Society. Could Harkness have meant the Lord Chancellor? That made sense. Anyhow it was worth trying.

"I think matters have got to a stage when I shall have to report them to the Lord Chancellor," he ventured, and then waited for the explosion.

Mr Mayberry smiled evilly.

"So far as this firm is concerned, Major Hartley, you may report them to the Privy Council if you are so inclined. You are not a client of ours. We have the highest regard for your father and your trustees. Were it not for them, I would tell you exactly what I think of your extraordinary performance this afternoon."

"You'll regret these words, sir. I'll report them to the— the Law Society."

Mr Mayberry rose.

"You're going to have a busy time. I wish you God speed. But I really must ask to be left alone to attend to the business of my clients."

Gerald decided to withdraw, to regroup his scattered forces. The Lord Chancellor had been a misfire and the Law Society called into action too late. In the same position, the Duke of Marlborough would have disengaged from the battle.

His "Good afternoon to you" and the noise of the door as he slammed it were his last shots. He went away regretting his handling of the matter. He shouldn't have come without getting legal advice. Damn Cecil.

By the irony of coincidence his taxi on its way to St James's Street went past the Palace. As he looked up at the windows, from which no friend beckoned, he felt less confident than last night when the magic of the Chetwynd-Skopwith name seemed powerful enough to enlist the sort of aid that rocked dynasties. Lord Stoat might not after all be summoned to the Chamberlain's office. Trotter, if he paid up again, would probably get his peerage. When it came to the point people didn't put themselves out very far for one. Righteous indignation tended as a rule to be an end in itself or at best a letter to *The Times*.

No doubt there would be several of them after the revelations; some complaining, others finding eccentric excuses for the lowest form of blackguardism. Gerald decided to hold his peace. But Cecil Harkness would be an old man before he played another game of chess. There would be nothing to keep him out of the club window in the long days ahead.

Chapter VIII

SINCE HIS HASTY journey from Ireland, Angus had
had no rest, neither had he had time to find a place to stay
in London. "I'll put up at the club," had been his last words
to Pamela when, looking anxious, she had seen him off. He
spent the first night in a doss-house near the station, treason-
ably describing itself as the Queen's Arms, as a temporary
expedient; and the journey from Bloomdale to London was
not long enough for him to decide upon whom to light with
an eye to lodging. Pamela kept him short of ready cash;
and he had no intention of paying the ruinous rates in hotels.
The fare was a sufficient sacrifice to make for what he now
saw as a disinterested campaign on behalf of Mrs Hartley.
Her husband's stark ingratitude did not deter him; his
concern on Pamela's account played on his mind only with
a chequered flame. He could not quite sort out the essential
grievance: was it that Pamela had spent a night with
Radish? Or that Radish was ignoring her? Or that Radish
was making sly references to her? One moment the gravamen
of the charge lay in one of these; then it switched to another.
The over-all effect was to keep him at a pitch of dangerous
excitement. He found himself quarrelling with everyone,
nearly coming to blows with ticket-inspectors on the train,
for example.

It would have been pleasant to have taken a taxi at the
station, to have arrived at a friendly house, bathed, and
rested before going on with his campaign. Had he gone to
Fleet Street or certain parts of Chelsea later in the day he
would have seen familiar faces, have hailed and been hailed,
at bar counters, but where was there anyone who would
invite him for the night? To whom could he hint at such a

possibility? He had no club now since the trouble over the annual subscription with the Savage. Pamela had a cousin somewhere, but they hadn't kept in touch. It was a stark indictment of contemporary depravity that a man's passion for asserting the truth and denouncing fallings-off from traditional standards should leave him, after ten years residence, friendless in London. Was that too drastic a word to apply to his condition? He didn't think so; and yet he yearned for love. Dog-tired, he stepped into a taxi, and only then realised he had nowhere to go.

"The *Sunday Echo* in Fleet Street," he said when the driver expressed irritation while drivers behind sounded impatient horns. When he arrived at the newspaper office and looked around the massive premises, so invulnerable and majestic-seeming in comparison to his complaint, he had his first misgivings. Nobody was bothering about him. He stood with his bag in his hand, crumpled and unshaven, and he might have stood there until closing-time without anyone coming up to him to ask him what his business was. The impersonality, the indifference of the scene, gave him a poignant sense of his own position. He was tempted to go back to Ireland and leave Radish to God.

The appearance of a sleek-looking person, smoking a cigar, and receiving salutations from any staff in view, as he made his way across the marble hall to the lift, acted on Angus like the spider in the tale of Robert Bruce. The contrast between this (most probably ungifted) favourite of fortune and himself, the deference paid to that other and the indifference to his own committed genius, aroused the lion, never asleep for long in Angus. He thought for a moment of rushing across the hall and engaging the attention of this influential person. If he did, he would harangue him; and the indifference all around would change to hostility. The experience of years told him this; people on the whole seemed to be incapable of being fired with one's own indignation; they took it as an attack on themselves; they became unfriendly—in some cases violent—one's utter loneliness on earth, poised lifelong between the extremes of neglect and dislike, was brought tragically home. Tears came to his eyes.

A porter watching him went to a desk and made an observation to a clerk; on instructions received, he approached Angus and asked, civilly enough, what could he do for him.

"I have come to see the editor."

"Have you an appointment?"

"No. I crossed from Ireland yesterday."

The porter glanced quickly at Angus's bag and then asked his name. Discouraging though his appearance was, he could still be of importance to the *Echo*. "They come in all sizes," the porter had observed of journalists through the years. Habits of drunkenness, outward appearances of extreme distress, were not to be read as conclusive proofs of unworthiness. This man might well be a columnist of note. What worried the porter was the reference to Ireland and the leather bag.

"Go over to the desk, they will look after you."

Straightening himself, he did as he was told. There was a note of arrogance in his manner as he made his request. The editor's secretary was summoned to the telephone. She said to send Mr MacDonnell up. He was getting somewhere now. But what was he going to say? Should he complain on behalf of Mrs Hartley? Or lay the charge of rape? And if the latter, he weighed the prospects of the editor's agreeing to publish alongside the first instalment of Radish's memoirs a paragraph to say

THE LAIRD OF SMOGG BETTER KNOWN AS ANGUS MACDONNELL AUTHOR OF *IN THE SPRING A YOUNG MAN'S FANCY* ACCUSES SIR ROMNEY RADISH OF RAPE. SEE FULL STORY INSIDE.

Slight, he decided. Was it then wise to mention the rape charge? Might it not make the editor suspect malice? And so far from adding weight to his plea that all references to the Hartleys be cut out, militate against the impression of a disinterested crusade? He must appeal to the editor on the highest possible ground. In doing so the only relevance of the rape was to remind him that there was another side to Radish. The editor might be too much taken up with the public image of the Messiah and be over-tolerant of pecca-dilloes before the onset of sainthood. He might cite Augustine, even Saint Paul. It was tricky.

Confusion of this kind, arising from chronic inability to identify the issue in dispute, was one of the contributory causes of Angus's explosive temper. His automatic answer to a sniper's bullet was a discharge of heavy artillery, and not always in the general direction of the provocative shot. He was aware of this tendency in himself, but unable to remedy it. His first approach was often civil enough; he didn't choose to be embroiled in conflict; but if his overture were not accepted at once at its face value he could never wait for a situation to develop, he went into action at once.

Seedy-looking, and unshaven though he might be, there was a world of self-importance in his manner; and the editor's secretary covered up her vagueness as to his identity. They spoke, to some extent, at cross-purposes. Her task was to save her employer from the importunate. When she heard what his business was she could decide whether to fob him off—as she had to do to somebody every quarter of an hour —on someone less august, perhaps an ordinary reporter. This would certainly have been the case if he had opened with a rape charge. He didn't. He introduced himself as having come straight from Lionel Hartley to see the editor about the Radish articles. This was a very urgent topic. The telephone had been busy with it. But so competent a secretary as Miss Trigger knew that at these times one needs to be on guard.

"What precisely is your connection with the matter?"

"I am deeply involved—my wife, for one thing—but I don't propose to go into that aspect of the matter. It will arise later, in its own place. What I am here about is the references to Mrs Hartley. I told her husband this morning that I would support him in any action he proposes to take. I shall put down a question in the House."

Miss Trigger now had the information she required: this was a Member of Parliament. Left, she decided—very left. That combination of arrogance and unkemptness was unmistakable. The editor would be annoyed by the visit; but she had to use her judgement; if she said he was too busy and hurt this unsavoury person's feelings it might have unpleasant consequences. She decided to hold Angus while she discussed the matter with her employer.

He put away a new iron with which he was taking practice golf swings when Miss Trigger came in. She had a way of catching him out, which made him rather afraid of her.

"Mr Angus MacDonnell, the M.P., is outside. He has been sent by Mr Lionel Hartley to discuss the Radish articles with you. He is threatening to put a question down in the House of Commons."

Admirably succinct, it succeeded at once in undermining the editor's confidence. He couldn't remember any M.P. with that name. And he should. It was familiar. He was beginning to forget proper names, and this was highly dangerous in a newspaper man. Next thing, he'd be forgetting who was dead.

"I'll have to see him I suppose. Perhaps he doesn't know that Stoat has taken the matter over. I tell you what. We don't want him raising a rumpus in parliament. Say I'll be delighted to talk to him, but I really think he is wasting time. He should see the Chairman. Ring up Lord Stoat's secretary and get him off our hands."

Miss Trigger approved. The editor waited a moment after the door closed before he picked up the iron again.

Angus was mollified. Instead of being sent down—his glare when Miss Trigger closed the door instead of calling him in anticipated this—he was being sent up.

Lord Stoat's secretary was thrown off balance. She, too, recognised the name but couldn't place it. The threat of a question in the House, however, left no time for speculation.

She promised then and there to fix an appointment for Angus at four o'clock.

Slim calves might have won Miss Fairfax her place in Lord Stoat's office; they would not have kept her in it. She was in fact a middle-aged, single-minded woman supporting a nephew. After she made the appointment, she proceeded to look Angus MacDonnell up so as to have a dossier on her employer's desk before the interview. He was not in the list of members of Parliament. But there was an Angus MacDonnell in *Who's Who*, who was born in Australia, wrote a novel which she remembered the name of because Tennyson had anticipated it. The entry began "MacDonnell, Angus, Laird of Smogg". His address was in Dublin and he did not appear to have any Scottish property. She turned to *Debrett*. He was nowhere there: then she put a query to the editor of the gossip column of the *Echo*.

Angus, in a state of slight euphoria—he had not expected anything when he told the taxi-driver to bring him to the *Echo*—went down Fleet Street buoyantly. It was now lunch time; there was no getting in anywhere; and his bag was a nuisance. If he had anywhere to go to dump it, he could brush himself up in readiness for an interview which he believed intuitively would be a turning point in his life. Less than an hour ago, he had been close to despair; chronic frustration seemed to be his lot, and he had been tempted to throw up the campaign and find a pub.

On what needle-points destiny turns! The perception of one girl had transformed the scene. For years he had wished to be alone with Stoat, or any other newspaper magnate, and give him a taste of his quality. Hitherto he had relied on editors, men of comparative straw, preoccupied with their own concerns, unable, and very often unfit, to take long or comprehensive views. The more he thought about it (by this time he was at Charing Cross), the more significant did this opportunity appear. Was it not a pity to waste the valuable time discussing Radish and the Hartleys? What did Hartley mean to him? They had shown neither appreciation nor gratitude for his concern on their behalf. And what was the point of telling Stoat that Radish had raped Pamela at Antananarivo? He wouldn't be interested. Were Radish in his prime it might be an opportune base from which to launch a general attack on the mischievous mountebank; but it seemed, somehow, irrelevant when he was all of eighty-three, the event took place twenty years ago, and the details were muddled. Besides, it might boomerang. Who could tell? Nowadays a rumour of this kind might be exactly what Radish needed. His appeal was to the young. No youthful excess but was greeted with a congratulatory telegram : what if he was to become an egg-headed sex symbol? It could happen. The old were always anxious to prove themselves by endurance tests, and in the confusion it might well appear that he had passed his fitness test as an octogenarian. God only knew what capital he would make out of it.

If that were so, Angus decided, he must plan the interview carefully. The secretary would announce his presence; Lord Stoat would be seated behind a desk, probably smoking a cigar, and would invite him to sit in front of him; or, more encouragingly, Stoat would say "Do you use these?" opening a cigar-case, and lead him to a pair of comfortable arm-chairs. In either case he must not allow the initiative to be wrested from him. After a civil, but not obsequious, acknow-ledgement of the great man's kindness in giving him an interview at short notice, he must launch himself at once into a larger theme; pornography, the right to privacy, Northern Ireland, under-ocean fuel—something which could let Stoat grasp at once the mettle of the man he had encountered by a lucky chance. This also had the advantage that it would get over the difficulty of the question in the House. He had let that slip out, and if anyone were tiresome enough to press him upon it, he was going to say that he intended to use an M.P. to do this little service for him. The nice girl in the *Echo*, he could see, had jumped to conclusions. That wasn't his fault; but it might be a stumbling block in the way to accord, if misinterpreted.

If Stoat were sufficiently impressed—and Angus could picture him so engrossed that his cigar hung suspended and forgotten in mid-air, an arrangement about the Radish episode would be come to at once—a matter of ringing for a secretary and dictating a minute to the editor. The larger result would be an appointment. "I'd like to see you in charge of the *Echo*'s interests in Ireland" or, better still, "Why don't you come back to London? We need you here." It might well be that with Stoat's support he could stand for Parliament. (Who represents the Hebrides? He must look it up.)

Walking rapidly, talking to himself, Angus was brought back to the sterner aspect of reality by an expletive. He had stepped out in front of a taxi. To stop the flow of abuse, he opened the door and got in.

"Drive me to Romney Radish's house in Eaton Square," he said.

Grumbling to himself, the driver accepted the order. Angus was leading a charmed life. The idea of going to Eaton Square was spontaneous. He had nowhere else to go. Given time to consider he might, after the favourable turn in his affairs, have settled for some hotel; but he had to shut the man up, and once again his good angel had provided a way. This was inspiration. Some force greater than himself was at work. He must allow it to carry him forward. He was only fifty-six. Disraeli suffered early rebuffs, and became Prime Minister when he was sixty-four. Churchill was even older. Admittedly their preceding years had been more colourful than Angus's, but neither of them had had to start off in Australia and, then, they had the incalculable advantage of having been born at the right time. In his own case he suffered from being at least a century before his time in some matters and as long after it in others. He would have been a world figure had he been born in Italy at the time of the Risorgimento, he was sure. Destiny plays us tricks; but Angus, though often despairing, had never abandoned wholly the conviction that he was being preserved for great things. Without that stimulus he would never have been booked for a talk with Lord Stoat or on his way to call on Romney Radish.

The taxi-driver and Angus did not see eye to eye about the appropriate fare; the altercation on Radish's doorstep, when the driver tossed the tip of fourpence out of the window, was deflating. He felt abandoned. The door looked impregnable, impersonal, and unwelcoming. A knock or a ring on the bell would hardly, he felt, be sufficient to open it. His bag undermined his status as an afternoon caller. He was feeling hungry and thirsty. The driver's ribaldry had ruffled him. The moment had passed. He needed to be wafted on the zephyr. Ideally, Runty should have been standing at the open door, welcoming.

A woman, who had been an interested spectator of the recent *fracas* and had overheard the driver's derisive references to both Angus and Radish, came forward.

"If you are looking for Sir Romney, he isn't seeing anyone. He is resting before the meeting in Trafalgar Square."

Angus turned defensively to see what sort of person had volunteered to advise him. A glance was sufficient. Shabbily-dressed, no longer young, with the apologetic expression of one who habitually drinks and smokes too much and eats too little, she belonged in the great army of failure. Such a one could not help him. He shrugged, and cursed himself inwardly for not having got rid of his bag. It would intimidate the servant when he answered the bell. A purely psychological matter; but the presence of any form of luggage presages embarrassing consequences—the caller intends to stay or has something to sell. Even the gesture of feeling in a pocket arouses apprehension in a listener and an impulse to rush for cover.

The woman's run-down appearance, which disqualified her at once in Angus's eyes, reminded him that he hadn't shaved and the coffee stain on his shirt required attention. Impulse was all very well, but he mustn't push his luck too far. A minimal cooperation was required. Here he was, and he must make the best of it. And, anyhow, Runty in pictures was always surrounded by the scruffiest crowd imaginable. It would not do in the Stoat office. There, Angus must look like Cabinet material and rely exclusively on persuasive address.

There was nothing for it; he rang the bell. The door was opened by an African in a white coat. He had the look of one already primed; his eyes engaged elsewhere, as if he were about to make an announcement on television. His prepared expression discouraged communication and restricted its range.

"Is Sir Romney at home?"

"I'm sorry, sah. Sah Romney is resting. He has very important engagement this evening."

Angus was disagreeably aware that his progress was under surveillance from the pavement. He assumed his most authoritative voice, the one he used with Dublin writers.

"Will you please tell Sir Romney, the Laird of Smogg wishes to see him before the meeting. He has something of vital importance to communicate. There may very well be a demonstration against him in Trafalgar Square. I promised Lord Stoat, whom I am meeting again at four o'clock, that I would see your employer first. The outlook is threatening. I foresee a police charge. Lord Stoat is rather anxious."

"I did not catch your name, sah?"

"The Laird of Smogg."

"Will you wait a moment, please."

He left the door open but did not invite Angus in. An omission he repaired as soon as the servant went upstairs. He was acting as much for the benefit of the woman outside as for the servant and himself, for he never forgot what was due to his own dignity.

From upstairs, he thought he could hear the murmur of voices. Then a door shut discouragingly. Soon afterwards the African re-appeared. Staring at a point an inch above Angus's head he said "Sah Romney very sorry. Must rest before meeting. He said not to worry. He will ring up Lord Stoat himself. Promise."

He stood firmly in the hall, opening the door very wide, disclosing all that was happening within to the lingering watcher in the street. She was making no effort to conceal her curiosity, and her presence cramped Angus's style. He must make an effective exit, and put her in her place.

"Tell Sir Romney I shall convey his remark to Lord Stoat personally this afternoon. If Sir Romney has second thoughts he can ring me up at Lord Stoat's office. I shall be there from four o'clock on."

"Very well, Sah."

The fellow's immovable expression was the sort of thing that drove Angus into the rages that he afterwards regretted. He would have liked to bring his bag down on the curly head. But he turned away with dignity, and pretended not to see the woman on the curb.

"I told you. You were only wasting your time."

"Is there a taxi-rank here?"

"I don't know. I was never here before. I'd go to the corner if I were you."

Angus nodded, and then proceeded in the direction she indicated, pretending to be unaware of her attendance at his elbow.

"If you were going in my direction we might share a taxi. My feet are nearly falling off me."

"I'm in a hurry, I'm afraid. I came with a very urgent message for Sir Romney from a friend of mine in Fleet Street. That African, I'm afraid, didn't convey the message properly. I may have to go to Scotland Yard."

"I've nothing to do. I'll go along with you as far as there."

"I'm afraid, madam, you have the advantage of me."

"I never laid eyes on you until today. But I felt sorry for you. You'd come a long way, I could see, and I knew why they wouldn't let you in. If you'd known Radish as long as I have you'd have left your bag at the station."

"You've worked for him?"

"I wouldn't say that exactly. We were friends at one time. But I haven't laid eyes on him for close on thirty years."

Angus gave another look at his self-elected companion. In profile there was undoubtedly the ruin of good looks; a nose that was delicately modelled, the eye he could see was well placed under a slender brow. The deep lines in her face, the fallen ends to her mouth, defective teeth, powder and rouge carelessly applied—these were what one saw at once. She was like a picture at an auction in need of repair; only a trained eye could see what the ravages of time had hidden. Her hands were well-shaped, red from rough usage. Her too juvenile dress was unintentionally pathetic. There was something pathetic, too, about her shoes. They told of much walking.

"You haven't got a cigarette on you, by any chance? I've used up my last."

They were standing at the street corner now. He noticed the wolfish way she pulled at the cigarette and the trembling of her hand as she lit it. So did his own. What a day it had been! When the visit to Runty proved an anti-climax, this new possibility presented itself before he had had time even to lose his temper. She was a skeleton from his cupboard—a child could see that—but there was something disarming about her, not only her slight Irish accent. He might improve their acquaintance without being stuck for more than a cigarette and a cup of coffee. There was nothing predatory about her manner. As she was all too obviously super-annuated, there was nothing to fear in the way of involvement. He must exercise discretion about where they were seen together. She didn't fit in with his afternoon plan, but she would fill a gap.

"Where are you staying?" she said.

"I crossed over at a moment's notice. I dare say I can get a bedroom in one of my clubs."

"If you would like to freshen up you could come to my

place. I haven't much to offer, but we could have a cup of tea."

He frowned.

"Oh, I only suggest it because I thought it might be better than going to a hotel or somewhere before you had a chance to clean yourself up."

She thought she had given offence and her quickness to reassure appealed to him. He had frowned because she gave no indication of having been impressed by his reference to clubs.

"Thank you. I would be glad to take advantage of your offer. I have been rushing about since dawn. It isn't too far away, I hope. I must be with Lord Stoat at four o'clock in Fleet Street."

"I'm almost opposite to Lords, the cricket ground."

Angus frowned again. The artless woman shouldn't have thought he needed assistance on that. His irritation was momentary. St John's Wood was a surprisingly respectable address. He had had a vision of a long drive through squalid streets.

A taxi came up then. Rita, as she told Angus to call her, took charge. They spoke very little on the way. He was regrouping his forces; the woman took her task seriously and directed the driver at every turn. The taxi came to rest outside a dairy.

"Here we are."

Angus, looking puzzled and cheated, clambered out. Rita was fumbling in her purse for money. In situations of this kind his reactions were always slow. But he became conscious of what she was doing in time to prevent it. Somehow the way in which she rummaged, like a caged bird picking seed, gave him a cameo of her poverty and touched his congested heart.

Rita put a key into the door beside the shop and led him upstairs.

"I am very lucky," she explained, "friends of mine let me have a room. I'm nominally the caretaker. I keep an eye on the place and help them in the dairy at odd hours."

They went up two flights of stairs, then Rita unlocked the door of a partitioned room, rather like a stage-set for a kitchen-sink drama.

"You can wash in there." She pointed to what looked like a cupboard. "While I make tea."

Inside he had to bend to look into a small mirror. What he saw alarmed him. He was not given to examining himself in detail, and assumed that a general impression of a personality painted in with broad strokes was his. Perhaps it was the tininess of the apartment and the mirror, throwing him grotesquely out of scale, that made the bloodshot eyes in the unshaven face look like an escaped convict's. Was this the face that had been presented within the last few hours at Bloomdale, the *Evening Echo* and Romney Radish's? Surely the growth which had assumed the sharpness of pig bristles was not there until he met Rita, who didn't mind. No wonder she had passed over his reference to clubs. She saw him as a companion in misfortune, one who was turned away at doors, with no means and nowhere to go.

He shaved, injuring himself a little, but the minute spouts of blood, on which he put cotton-wool, were preferable to what they replaced. He washed his teeth under the cold tap, and was momentarily refreshed when he replaced them. The stain on his shirt responded to soap and water; but there was a damp patch in its place which would be there for some time. A tooth-brush helped him to restore comparative order to his hair fringe, not visible in the mirror.

Rita's friendly expression when he emerged reassured him.

"That's better," she said.

She had gone to trouble. Little lacy paper mats and a tea set that looked as if it had been intended for a doll's house were laid out on the table, and biscuits were spread on a plate.

"I'm letting the tea draw. And I'll make you some sandwiches. I've jam, or would you prefer cottage cheese?"

His hunger had passed the point of such fine discrimi-
nations. He would have eaten a dead cat. It took immense
control not to seize the whole plate of biscuits and wolf
them.

"I could boil you an egg if you like."

He assented.

"Would you be able to manage two?"

He would.

"My, you must have been hungry," she said, "poor
dear!"

Angus was essentially spontaneous. His reactions were
often violent and so quick that he was frequently deep in a
quarrel before he realised that no offence was intended;
but he could also respond to kindness, particularly when
it was unalloyed with any suspicion of patronage.

"A tart's bedroom," had been his assumption when Rita
opened the door. But now he realised that he had been too
hasty in his diagnosis. It was very lucky that he hadn't made
some casual, broad-minded reference to the state of the
market in her profession. She was—he now saw clearly—
an ageing woman hanging courageously on to a lower-
middle class respectability. The bottle was probably her
trouble.

The room was furnished after the manner of the poorer
auction rooms. There were knick-knacks everywhere, neither
useful nor pleasing. The sofa was covered in mouse-brown
rep. There were dried ferns in unlikely vases, in unsuitable
places. Figurines, fancy egg-cups, little tables that trembled
in sympathy with heavy traffic outside, two chairs, neither
comfortable nor strong, seemed to owe their presence to the
imperatives of convention. They were hardly to be sat upon.
But Rita perched on one; Angus subsided on to the sofa.

"I'm afraid the springs are gone in that. I'm always
planning to have it mended."

"I'm very comfortable."

"I've a drop of whisky."

Angus followed her glance towards a corner cupboard. A

large photograph of Radish stood on top. There was a pause, as after a distant explosion, while they observed it.

"You used to know him?"

"Yes. But it seems so long ago, like something that happened in another world. I was twenty-two."

Angus began a gallant demurrer, and then lost heart.

"I was quite good-looking in those days. It's hard to believe."

"Not in the least."

"You can't fool me. I have my own eyes. If I could only get my health again, I might be better. I'd need six months' holiday and an expensive job done to my teeth."

"I think your teeth . . . Your teeth look fine to me."

"I look like an old horse."

She glanced at herself in a pocket-mirror and grimaced. "How did you meet?"

"My father was a top trade-unionist. He was in Ireland with James Larkin. That's where I was born. Then he came to Liverpool. He lived for socialism; he was self-educated but what you would call a superior type of man. When I was a child he used to read to me; and I was better off in that way than the children I mixed with. Then I was an only child. In Liverpool we were surrounded by Irish families; there was a baby in every corner. I got a good education, and I had a job in the library. I was full of romantic ideas in those days, and I even tried to write poetry. Can you imagine *me* writing poetry?

"There was a club that my father was secretary of; famous people used to come and speak at it in the winter months. We had Laski and John Strachey; and then Radish agreed to speak. Before the meetings my father used to have the visiting speaker in to tea with us. I wanted him to give them dinner. We could afford it; but Dad had a principle about tea. He thought it was a betrayal to ape the ways of the governing class. I remember those teas. They were rather grim. Dad had no small talk and looked severe. Ma couldn't get over her shyness, and kept on offering food. The guest was never at ease, unless he liked girls. Then he concentrated on me.

"Radish made no effort to converse with the parents. He talked away to me, nineteen to the dozen; in a nice way, too; asked me all about myself.

"When tea was over there was still an hour to go before we had to leave for the meeting. Radish turned to my father and said, 'Your daughter tells me she has written things. Is there anywhere we could be alone together? I'd like her to read them to me.' I remember how poor Dad blushed with pleasure and Ma, of course, went on like a clucking hen. They left us together in the parlour, and what could I do but try to read out my stuff, feeling a perfect fool. Before long, although he kept as quiet as a mouse, I sensed that he wasn't listening. I looked up suddenly and I caught him staring at me, almost mesmerised he looked. 'Go on,' says he. 'You're not listening,' I said. 'You've a throat like Aphrodite.' 'I wish my neck was thinner.' 'It is quite perfect. Has no one ever told you? I must have you painted. I wish I could draw; I wouldn't do you justice.'

"He was staring at me so hard that I felt quite embarrassed; but he was perfectly at ease; then he stopped admiring me, and said he was interested in my work, but something in himself made it impossible for him not to criticise, and he had to admit that what I needed was a richer educational background to give me more ideas. I was glad my father couldn't hear him saying this, after all the money he had spent on me. At the time I knew that he was ambitious for me, and if I could do better than this library, he would not stand in my way. But what was the great Radish going to suggest? I was too old, in my estimation, to go back to studying.

" 'Listen, my dear,' he said,"—and here Rita broke into a not entirely inept imitation of Radish's accent and manner —" 'I am very pleased to have discovered such beauty and talent in Liverpool. To be quite frank I did not have very lively expectations of this evening. It has been a revelation.

We are friends, I think. I make friends very quickly. I know at once who belongs to my world and who is outside it. I only try to reach to the first. Tell me, have you a young man, a boy-friend?' 'Sort of,' I said. 'What precisely does *sort of* mean? Are you engaged to anyone?' 'Not really. There is someone; but it is all rather confused at the moment.' 'Very well, if you are not committed in any way, why not come and stay with me in my London flat? I'll be there next week-end. You know my age. I'm fifty-seven. I can't promise to come up to the standard you may expect from your Lotharios, but I think I should be able to make up for that in other ways. There's no task so beautiful as opening up a young mind to all the possibilities of this world of ours. Let me help you, my dear. I think you will find I can.'

"I didn't know where to look. He had rail-roaded me. I thought of my parents on the far side of the door and wondered what they imagined was going on. But my father idealised Romney Radish; and one of the articles of his creed was that anyone who put himself on the side of the workers must be morally a superior type. Besides he hadn't made a pass at me in the ordinary way. There was no suspicious silence, if the old pair were listening. He went burbling on. I was properly bothered, but he kept me fixed with those penetrating eyes of his and I had to say something. It was true I hadn't promised Peter definitely. He had a problem. I would have been mad with him, I must admit, if the boot had been on the other leg; and in the end what decided me, I'm afraid, was vanity. No matter how randy he was, it was flattering to have someone so famous pick on me, and not just to pass the time for the evening. He was actually inviting me to London. I blurted out something stupidly obvious about Lady Radish; as if he hadn't been over all that in his mind. He looked very solemn and told me that he and his wife were very happily married and had a perfect understanding. She never came to London but lived in the remotest part of Cornwall, out of the reach of trains, and liked it. I blustered again. Of course he could see I was on the hook. I knew the look on his face, like a doctor's listening to a stethoscope. I said I was entitled to some free time, and I could get away from the Library, come down to London on a Friday evening. He said he would write to me and give me precise instructions. Once that was settled, he switched off, and seemed to forget my poetry. He let my hand go and moved to the piano and began to play Chopin. Then he asked if I played; and he began to sing in such a funny high-pitched voice I had to blow my nose hard to prevent myself from bursting out laughing. I noticed this in Radish—he told me to call him Bunny, but I never could—that, for all his sophistication, where he himself was concerned he had no sense of the ridiculous. There was I, a working-class man's daughter, who knew very little about anything, and had met only men of my own class—except Peter, who was in our amateur opera society—and yet I wouldn't think of doing some of the things he did without shame. I think it came from his being so sure of himself. Anyone else, having collected me for a week-end, would have gone on looking spoony. Not him. I suppose he was pleased at having arranged everything so neatly, and was celebrating. Dad knocked at the door eventually, and said it was time to go. I couldn't take in any of the speeches—they always bore me anyway, even when Radish was talking my mind kept racing away. I was wondering what he had in mind exactly; and what it would be like. And I tried to keep out of my head the idea that it would feel very queer to be locked up in a house alone with someone who looked like my grandfather. At twenty-two, fifty-seven seems older than God. Am I boring you?"

Angus had moved on the sofa, and that led to a jangling of springs. So far from any trace of boredom his face at that moment resembled the mariner's at the discovery of the North-West passage.

"Go on," he said hoarsely. "Don't stop."

"A letter arrived. I have it here. I have all his letters. I'll show it to you if you like."

"Later. Later. Tell me everything that happened."

"He wrote a short letter asking me to thank my parents for their hospitality. Then he gave me train times (as if I couldn't have looked them up for myself). He was pernickety in these sort of ways. I was to go straight from the station to Ebury Street and ring three times. The door would then open and I was to proceed upstairs. The door of my room would be ajar.

"It was an off-putting letter in the circumstances, more like a plan for a bank-robbery than a tryst. I began to wonder what I was in for. Fifty-seven seemed to me to be such a legendary age (ten years older than my father) that I was prepared to believe anything. Perhaps Radish hadn't meant what I thought he meant. If so what had I let myself in for? I very nearly backed out; but curiosity overcame everything. I did as I was told. After three rings and a slight pause, there was a click and the door opened. The hall was reassuring; it could have been an Archbishop's house. I didn't know anything about furniture or pictures. But I got a solid feel. In this sort of situation in a film one would have had to pass through a bead curtain and someone would have beaten a gong. I went up two flights, a door was open on the landing. The room was lined with books, there was a large divan-bed in the corner. Someone had left a vase full of flowers on a table in the centre of the room and a book lay open under it, set out like the lesson for the day in a church. I was obviously intended to read it. The book was by Freud. The piece chosen for me was the case-history of a girl who had had trouble with her father. I was puzzled. And then the door opened and in came his nibs as naked as the day he was born.

"I stayed with him until Sunday. I had to go back by the evening train. He ordered a taxi and gave me five pounds to cover my fare. I never saw anyone else all the week-end. We lived on cold things and drank milk. He never wore a stitch. The house was centrally-heated, and I got used to his appearance after a time. It's odd how one does. A friend of mine found her mother dead at the bottom of the stairs. The police said the body must not be moved until after the inquest. My friend said it was extraordinary how, after a day, one got used to the corpse, and literally took it in one's stride."

"Did you ... ? What exactly ... ? Did you see him again?"

"Not for a few months. My engagement was still hanging in the air. My young man, as I told you, had a problem. I suppose my vanity was hurt at not hearing from Romney again. He sent me only one quite short letter, like one would write to anyone who had called with a pot of home-made jam when one was ill. I have it. I can show it to you. Well, anyway, for the hell of it, I wrote him quite a nice letter for Christmas, and enclosed a poem which I partially cogged out of anthologies in the library. I am telling you things I feel ashamed of now, but I suppose I was anxious to make an impression and a little nettled because he seemed to forget me so quickly. I got a reply by return asking me to meet him at Victoria Station at half-past two on the following Friday. He knew of a comfortable hotel on the line. He went into quite unnecessary details, and seemed to think I required a guarantee that the hotel should be all it should be, fires in the bedrooms, well-sprung beds, etc. We might have been tame old invalids going off to recuperate. Again I was in two minds; but I thought I ought to go, having already gone so far, and by now I knew exactly what to expect.

"He met me, and all went off as planned; he wrote me a rather longer letter this time explaining that Plato's ideal was, what he called 'a gradual progression from the imprisonment of the flesh to the freedom of the spirit'. He thought we were on that road; but, of course, it would take me longer as I was so much younger and less experienced. He was always asking me questions to try to find out about me, but I wouldn't tell him anything. He did ask me the first time if I was a virgin."

"And what did you say to that?"

"What I said is my business. Anyway, he seemed satisfied. I didn't know how to answer his letter. It seemed to me he was making a rather complicated apology for not being able to do very much. Considering his age, I was quite prepared to make allowances, and I couldn't see what Plato had to do with it. Platonic love meant one thing to me, and I couldn't see that he had done anything to set it up. It was only an excuse. I rather despised him. I suppose I was taking pride in the discovery that, for all his fame and brains, I could make him feel inadequate.

"Nothing happened after that until I read somewhere that he was going to the United States. Once again I wanted to find out if I had left an impression on him—I was vain, wasn't I?—and so I wrote a short letter to wish him luck. The newspaper said that he might stay in America and lecture on literature, now that he had taken up his fourth career as a creative writer. He wrote back a very pleasant letter, said he was delighted to hear from me, and suggested that we should meet at Chester for the week-end. He hadn't seen the town for years, and it was about half-way from home for both of us.

"So I met him in Chester. We knew one another better by this time, and it was the most satisfactory of our meetings. We saw very little of the city; he spent most of the time in bed, but he had books with him, and he read me quite a lot of poetry, chiefly by Donne. He asked me what I thought was the best passage in English prose. I didn't know what to say. I wasn't used to that sort of quizzing. He told me he liked a sermon of Newman's, and nothing would do him but to sit up in bed and read it out to me. I nearly died laughing thinking what anyone would say if they saw us and knew what we were up to.

"He looked so funny sitting in his skin, reading out, you know, all that about the shadows lengthening and the busy world being hushed and—it was quite beautiful really but I couldn't see how he would think of that sort of thing at such a moment. When I told him so he gave me quite a lecture and said it was a sin not to rejoice in a body like mine, and to think there was anything wrong in celebrating it. He didn't convince me, because although I suppose I was rather lax—it would be nothing nowadays, but we were not so easy-going then—I felt sinful. There was no pill in those days. The other business was inclined to turn me off—what was I saying?"

"You said that you didn't think a sermon was appropriate for pillow talk."

"That's right. But it was very typical of him. And to be quite truthful, I was glad enough when the week-end was over. He was beginning to bore me. After this session he wrote a lot to me—on the way to America, and again when he got there, asking me to join him, saying I had restored his youth and all that sort of thing. I'm sure you've heard it all before. It's funny how everyone is the same when they let their feelings run away with them. But I had made up my mind that I was going to marry Peter, and I had had enough of uncertainty, and the Radish business meant nothing at all now that I had got blasé about it. Also—have you noticed this yourself?—when he didn't write to me I was piqued and wanted to remind him that I existed; but once he started to implore me not to give him up, I was determined to put an end to the affair for ever. He gave up writing eventually, and he married a fourth or fifth wife—I could never keep count—out in California."

Angus was standing up at this point of the narrative. There was about him the air of a general making final dispositions.

"That was the last you heard of him?"

"Yes, but once when I was down-and-out—years later—I wrote to him. I didn't know where to turn. He sent me ten pounds and a book of stories for children he had written and copies of reviews from the newspapers comparing him to Hans Andersen and God knows who else. I wrote to him then another time; but he didn't answer. Then I felt ashamed to be bothering him. Honestly, I think he had forgotten me. But the other day I saw he was writing his memoirs, and I remembered I had those letters, so I thought he might like to have them. I didn't really expect him to give me money for them, but I thought he might see me once and have tea together, when I reminded him of the sprees we went on. I wrote to him, and he wrote back asking me to send him all the letters. 'I hope you are well.' *I hope you are well* indeed! What did he take me for? I wrote back to say I would call with the letters on the following afternoon. When I came the black boy said Radish wasn't in, but I could leave the envelope with him. Of course, I refused. I went back again today and I was told Sir Romney was resting, and would I mind sending the letters. Then you came and I felt sorry for you. I could see that you were on your uppers, and I wanted to tell you that there was nothing to be got in that quarter. But you wouldn't listen to me."

"I'm listening now. I don't know what gave you the impression I was 'on my uppers' as you put it. We haven't much time, but I must tell you about myself. I'm Angus MacDonnell the author. I'm also Laird of Smogg, if you are interested, but I don't use the title when I write. It so happens that Radish is using letters of a friend of mine to compromise her. I came over to London to see if I could prevent it. He was a friend of my wife at one time. He treated her very badly. I have an appointment at four o'clock, as I told you, with Lord Stoat. I want you to come along and bring the letters. If Radish refuses to see reason the *Sunday Echo* will announce next Sunday that it will print your story. Don't worry. I'll write it for you. We can settle the terms later. I should think the paper will pay handsomely. But I must convince Stoat that this isn't just blackmail. Put the wrong way our action could be misinterpreted. You see that."

"You mean, people might say I was trying to screw money out of the old man?"

"Precisely. You and I are only interested in justice."

"To be candid with you, I don't give a damn what he says about anyone else. They can look after themselves. And I'll be honest and admit that I was hoping he'd give me something for the letters. I saw a letter from Bernard Shaw fetched over £100 the other day. I could do with £100 at the moment, I don't mind telling you."

"If you want £100 I'll give it to you for the letters."

"You're kidding. Where would you get £100, my dear?"

"I thought I told you who I was. Consult *Who's Who* if you don't believe me."

"Oh, please, don't be offended. It was only seeing you there, and you so badly in need of a wash and brush up, and carrying your old bag, and being shown the door by his nibs—I thought you were pretty much in the same boat as myself. I didn't mean to make little of you."

Angus was always prepared to consider an unqualified apology, and the woman's good-nature was transparent; moreover, she was indispensable. Now there was something to use in the battle, real ammunition, not threats merely. He must use it with maximum effect; bring Radish down, overwhelm Stoat, forge indissoluble links with the Hartleys, and make Bloomdale his second home. He must use it so that the impact would be felt in Dublin as well as in London. They were provincial blind mice over there, in that little city—chauvinist, incestuous, inward-looking, and incorrigibly ill-bred. They must have their eyes opened for them, and understand that so long as he chose to live there and enjoy income-tax concessions he expected to be treated with the deference that was his due. In future he would only answer to his full title, he decided, and address his Irish acquaintances by their surnames only. Put a little of the old-fashioned boot in, in fact. It was high time.

"I don't feel disposed to argue. I must leave at once if I am to keep my appointment with Lord Stoat. You must decide: will you come with me? Or would you prefer to sell the letters now and let me use them as I think best? I have my cheque-book here."

The woman looked down at her poor shoes. "We have no time to waste," Angus urged. He would have liked a more glamorous companion; but matters had gone beyond the stage of consideration of appearance. Pride wouldn't allow him to press his cheque on her. He preferred not to recognise the fact that she was not sure it was good.

"And where are these letters?" he said, intending by his tone to put their relationship on a proper footing. She went to a drawer and took out a parcel. In everything she did there was humility. The world had beaten her into submission. She had no desire to be other than kind to this man, had no wish to dominate him; it was only that she saw him as one like herself who had gone down in the struggle. His bravado she hardly listened to. She understood it. He was trying to impress her to keep up his own spirits. Even his appointment with Lord Stoat (whoever he was): that, too, she saw as a fantasy. Possibly this lord was another Radish, who would also turn him away. She knew people like Angus, who were kept going by delusions. One of them had the idea that he would get the contract for the plumbing at the Ritz; it needed only a water shortage to bring about the happy event. That mentality went with a tendency to drink. Drink made other people timid, from anxiety to hide their little failing. If she took the cheque and it bounced, she wouldn't be able to get her letters back. She didn't like to express her doubts; she didn't want to hurt his feelings.

"I'll come along with you, if you don't think I'll disgrace you."

"We must go at once."

It was better than a refusal; he would show her what a mistake she had made when they met Stoat. But she delayed, trying to titivate herself. Angus was shaking with rage when he eventually pushed her out. He waved wildly at every taxi in sight, irrespective of the fact that they were occupied.

When the bedraggled pair arrived in Fleet Street, five minutes late, Angus led the way. Rita followed, like a captive in his procession. The secretary met them at the lift. "I'm so sorry, Mr MacDonnell," she began—her face telling the message before she had spoken it. "I was trying to get in touch with you, but I didn't have any address in London. I'm afraid Lord Stoat has not been able to keep his appointment. He was called away suddenly. He asked me to give you his sincerest apologies."

Rita, standing behind Angus, had imagined some such encounter. It was taking a form that didn't surprise her. Angus who had seen himself in one armchair, Stoat in another, a decanter on a table between them, staggered back. He was breathing so heavily, Rita was alarmed for him. She would have liked to have taken his hand and led him away to a pub. There she would comfort him. What did it matter? Radish or Lord Stoat—there was no difference between them; they were the favoured few locked up in success, Angus and she were free of the wide world of failure. By no means alone. No need to feel lonely since they had struck up with each other; no need to despair if he had the price of a drink.

She reached out a tentative hand. He brushed it away as a mother does when a child tries to coax her to come home when she is talking to strangers.

"I don't understand. I was present when the appointment was made."

"I know. But I'm afraid his lordship is more than usually busy at the moment. He had to cancel other engagements."

"When is he going to see me?"

"He didn't say. Perhaps you had better write and explain the matter. I do think that would be best. He's off to Paris next week; and then he will be going to America. He was very sorry, I know, not to be able to fit you in."

"Will you take a look at these."

Angus took the packet away from Rita, pulling it, as she

seemed reluctant. The secretary received it as if it were a damp baby.

"Those," Angus said, rather loudly, "were written by the Radish person to this lady, Miss—"

"Mrs Mooney, Rita Mooney," his companion filled in.

"Mrs Rita Mooney," Angus boomed to compensate for not knowing it and for the inadequacy of her support.

"If Lord Stoat were to see those, he might think twice about careering off to Paris."

"May I show them to him?"

"You are actually asking me to leave them here; is that it? Ho! Ho! Ho!"

"How else is Lord Stoat to see them?"

"Ho! Ho! Ho!"

They were at an impasse. Miss Fairfax gesticulated to signify helplessness; Angus simulated mockery; Rita, convinced that the game was up, appealed to him with her eyes to come away. She had kind eyes. But he was acting as much for her benefit as for Lord Stoat's secretary. He was not going to be put down when he held the winning trick. After a while, when he thought he had established mastery, he conceded.

"In fairness I think we should let this lady have a look at the letters, Mrs Mooney. Then she can decide for herself whether the matter is urgent."

Miss Fairfax acquiesced, if only because it gave her the time to think. Angus and Rita sat side by side in the office— they were not invited into the inner sanctum—while Miss Fairfax sat at her desk and read the letters carefully. When she took a note, Angus demurred, but not angrily, rather as if he were playing with a too-exuberant kitten.

For love letters they were singularly brief and dry; and it required a certain effort of imagination to reconcile the short but heartfelt appeals at the close with the businesslike tone of the earlier notes.

"You said they were written to you?" Miss Fairfax turned to Rita.

"That's a damned impertinent question."

Rita put a restraining hand on her companion's sleeve and nodded to Miss Fairfax. "Don't answer that, Mrs Mooney. This woman has absolutely no right to question your *bona fides*. I vouched for you."

Miss Fairfax was struggling with temper; but she had taught herself to be impersonal. What mattered was that she would do whatever was best for her employer. Rudeness, if necessary, within limits, might have to be endured in the process, and she was accustomed to nuisances.

She ignored the man. "These are your letters, then, Mrs Mooney? They are your property, I mean."

"I told you—"

"Because"—Miss Fairfax ignored Angus's interruption—"you know that while you could sell them, you can't publish them without Sir Romney's consent. You haven't got that, I suppose."

Rita looked at Angus. She was out of her depth. If only he would take it easy. He stepped forward, and assumed command.

"We can't get anywhere unless your employer condescends to talk to me. Let me explain the position—I can see that you have not been brought up to date—I am a friend of Mr and Mrs Lionel Hartley of Bloomdale, of whom you may have heard. On Sunday next you are proposing to publish very damaging matter about these friends of mine, whose hospitality the Radish man abused on several occasions. I've been in touch with your editor; his secretary agreed that the matter had now gone above editorial level. This will be a national scandal. A question will be put down in the House."

"By whom, Mr MacDonnell? I understand that you told Miss Trigger you were putting down a question. I can't find your name in the current list of M.P.s."

"I don't know who Miss Trigger is, but if she worked for me I'd fire her; she has taken a great deal on herself. I am seeing a friend in the House of Commons in the morning."

"The member, I presume, is whoever includes the island of Smogg in his constituency."

Angus, behind his bluster, had been puzzling out the reason for Lord Stoat's escape; he was too used to strategic withdrawals in the past not to see this as a case of tactical change of plan. Something had happened since this morning. The reference to Smogg and the tartness of the tone in which the lonely island was referred to made all clear. This woman had been looking him up. Very well. If that were the case, she knew that she was dealing with the author of *In the Spring a Young Man's Fancy*. The moment had come for a dignified withdrawal. There was nothing doing here. They were wasting their time. He rose in his loftiest manner, and turned to Rita.

"Come. We must stop fooling. Fortunately Lord Stoat does not own all the newspapers, and my name still counts for something in Fleet Street. We shan't take up any more of your valuable time Miss—"

He picked the letters up, concentrating on his companion, over whom he seemed to hold a protective cloak, and strode towards the door. Rita looked back, allowing herself to be hustled out, but still not wishing to leave behind an impression of ill-will. She lived by propitiation.

Miss Fairfax stood up also, not a hair out of place, neutral. She returned Rita's smile and moved mechanically towards the door.

"Thank you. We can see ourselves out," Angus said. He looked neither right nor left until he was in Fleet Street. Then he leaned against a lamp-post.

"That tiresome bitch will lose her job over this. Where can we go to now? Damn Stoat."

"Is there any sense in going anywhere, dear? Did you hear what the secretary said? I can't publish the letters unless Radish consents. And he isn't likely to, is he? I don't see what use they are except as keepsakes."

"You heard her say you could sell them. I'm sure they'd fetch at least a hundred pounds at Sotheby's."

"I don't want to do that, until I have to. I mean—I haven't much to hang on to."

"There's nothing to prevent me from writing a piece for you, describing the whole affair. We can make short quotations from the letters—they are pretty flat, anyhow. Perhaps it's just as well we can't use them. The story could make them sound more exciting than they are. The description of his Radishness making his appearance in his birthday suit, for instance. That will be enough to set off most of his own revelations about his friends. I think what we ought to do now is to get the story written, offer it to one of the Sundays, and show them the letters. If I stand over them, I think they'll be satisfied. I might be able to get a loan of a typewriter in the *Express*."

His name was sufficient—after a certain amount of delay, highly irritating in so far as it contrasted with the antici- patory picture he drew of their reception to Rita on the way—to secure him a typewriter. Rita sat quietly on a chair, looking like an unfetched parcel, and he hammered away at a story. This was his profession. He had lived as a journalist before he became a celebrity; and it was like old times to be tapping out the clichés.

"There." Rita was woken from her reverie to find several sheets of typescript on her lap. She looked up hesitantly as much as to say "Am I to read them?"

"That's supposed to be your own story." Her meekness would soon become highly irritating, he decided. He was beginning to raise his voice when he spoke to her. Not a quick reader at any time, she was flustered—it seemed a long time since she had had literary aspirations of her own. Sometimes she made little exclamations, like someone talking in her sleep, and sometimes she paused and looked up, asking herself a question. But then she saw Angus's minatory stare, and dived back again, and went faster. It was like eating breakfast in the presence of a jailer. And it took time. Her face did not register either pleasure or admiration. Angus grew impatient. "Well?"

She became apologetic at once. "I'm nearly finished. I don't know how you did it. I think it's wonderful."

What value had praise from such a source? He was impatient to get on. It was now nearly seven o'clock. "Haven't you finished it yet?"

"I'm sorry. Yes. Now. That's it. I'm sorry for having kept you waiting."

"Well?"

"Oh, it's awfully good. Marvellous. You'd almost think you had been there. Where did you get the idea that he was formed like a child?"

"Instinct."

"Oh, I see."

Before leaving, Angus sought out the young man who had lent him the typewriter and thanked him with elaborate courtesy for his kindness. It was the first time today that he had had the opportunity to play the part of the Laird of Smogg.

"That's all right, chum," the journalist said, failing to live up to the occasion, and showing no interest in the birth at which he had assisted.

"I wonder if he could help," Rita whispered as he turned away. Angus snorted. The same idea had occurred to him, but he wasn't going to risk a rebuff at that level yet.

"Why didn't you try it on someone there?" she said as they left the office. "It's every bit as good as other stories I've read in the *Sunday Express*. You must be terribly clever. I couldn't have done it without you to save my life. I'd have got all bogged down trying to describe my feelings."

He stood still to lecture her. "How can I get it into your head that much more is involved than selling your story to a newspaper? We could do that right away. I suppose I could get you £500."

"Oh, do!"

"I'm sorry. But that wasn't what we agreed upon. I'll get you money. Don't worry about money; but this is about something much more important. This is a battle between me and Radish and his publishers and the Stoat empire. I want to bring them all to their knees. I think the best thing to do now is to drop the carbon copy of this story into Radish's letterbox with a note to say it is about to appear. I'll offer to see him beforehand to discuss a settlement."

"Suppose he agrees not to publish; what happens then to my £500?"

"By then your letters will have become so valuable that I would hesitate to put a price on them."

Had she said "Are you sure?" as she wanted to, she would only have driven him into a rage, she knew; and anyhow he had enough on his mind as it was. Besides she didn't believe he had any idea what the letters were worth. For these reasons, and because she had grown fond of him as she would have of any stray that she had taken home, she held her peace.

A drizzle was falling outside the *Express* office, and taxis had become harder to get than Orders of Merit. After fruitlessly waving and yelling, Angus began to walk in what he thought was the direction of Eaton Square. In Trafalgar Square a small crowd of people was gathered. Youths were carrying banners calling on the Government to take the Army out of Northern Ireland. On the platform the speakers sat huddled under umbrellas. The Chairman who spoke in an accent that made his utterance imprecise called on "Sir Romney Radish to address the meeting".

Radish's appearance at that moment acted on Angus like a prod from a spur. When the routine clapping subsided, he booed so loudly that a policeman stepped forward, and hostile faces turned back and glared in his direction. Rita plucked at his sleeve; but he was too excited to notice.

Although he looked incredibly old and frail, the speaker's voice was as clear as a flute. He thanked the conveners of the meeting for having invited him to attend. As the sworn enemy of imperialism and colonialism, he was naturally interested in their manifestations in Ulster. In the name of all present he solemnly called on the Prime Minister to

remove the troops from Northern Ireland. Then he paused
as if to let the message pass along to Downing Street before
calling for three cheers for the freedom-fighters in Ireland.
"I am a man of peace and an apostle of non-violence, but I
recognise the truth of the adage that given sufficient provoca-
tion even the worm will turn. He has turned to some effect
in Northern Ireland. He has taken on the British Army. He
has attacked capitalism at the same time as he has fought
for liberty. Lives have been lost. It is very regrettable. Nobody regrets it more than I do. But I lay the responsibility for
those lives where it belongs, at the door of Downing Street,
at No. 10."

Cheers interrupted the speech. After the cheers, Angus
booed, supremely oblivious to the angry faces around him.
"Do be careful," Rita urged. He had forgotten her presence.

Then came the high point of Radish's speech. This was
for the headlines. He was offering a practical solution to the
troubles in Ireland. When the troops left they must be replaced by a peace-keeping force. This gave the Government
a wonderful opportunity: an army recruited from the Third
World was the obvious solution. It would be a major step
forward in race relations, and could be recognised as a land-
mark on the tortuous road towards universal peace and
brotherhood. Most of the audience were presumably Irish in
London, and this suggestion drew forth only a few scattered
cheers from those who operated on the cheerful principle
that anything said was to be applauded.

"I have a new vision of Ireland," the speaker went on.

"Bus and underground," said someone, and might have
raised a laugh, but unfortunately he was standing too close
to Angus, already suspect of treasonable motives.

"Shut your bloody mouth, you," a young man, evidently
in the building trade, said, moving closer. "Get him out of
here," someone else shouted, jostling Angus. Rita recognised
the signs of present trouble, and sensed that Angus would
make a Roman Holiday for the less dedicated, depressed by
rain and boredom, longing for a diversion. This time she

pulled at his sleeve with fierce determination. All around them she saw faces looming—some angry, some jeering, some menacing, others implacably neutral; none offering help. Pushing and jostling increased. Angus, still oblivious to his danger, watched his enemy bow to a final salvo of applause.

"Rapist," he yelled.

His voice was very loud, very clear, and elaborately "upper class". But to that audience the "R" sounded like a "P". They were listening to a calculated insult to the minority in Northern Ireland. Any obscenity attaching to Radish personally was preferable to calling him a papist at such a moment. A hand seized Angus by the collar and pulled him back. Others held his arms and started to hustle him out of the crowd. Rita looked round for the policeman who had taken an unfavourable view of Angus's first appearance. He was standing with another at a little distance, out of view of the scene. She ran towards them, sobbing.

"They're going to murder him."

If she hadn't been there, Angus might well have been killed. In his condition, at his age, he was a bad subject for a beating-up. Thanks to Rita, the two policemen arrived in time to rescue him. By then his clothes were torn; one eye was closed and he had lost his hat. In the circumstances he had come off lightly. "Come away, dear," Rita urged. At that moment, the admirers of Radish, carrying him shoulder-high, bore down upon them. The old goblin face was wrinkled into a smile of fatuous complacency. It was too much for the battered Angus. He pushed aside the policemen who were sheltering him, and raced towards the cavalcade.

"Cur! Swine! Pimp!" he roared.

He had the satisfaction of observing Runty look up to see whence the greeting came before a descending baton marked the spot.

Miss Fairfax prided herself on her efficiency. What other secretary would have gone to the trouble of compiling a

dossier on a caller with such thoroughness as she? Lord
Stoat knew more about Angus MacDonnell, if he chose to
read it, than the average historian knows about the Plant-
agenets. He might also have learned for the first time the
population of Smogg, the ecumenical nature of the commun-
ity's religious life, and that it belonged to a gentleman with
a pedigree going back almost to Solomon.

In spite of his lordly manner he would not refuse money,
and if the letters were worth having the *Echo* would pay.
She gave careful instructions on arriving at the office that
anyone calling who mentioned the Radish serial was to be
referred to her at once. When, during the afternoon, she was
told that there was a Mrs Heidl at the desk with something she had written about Sir Romney Radish that she
wanted to show to the editor, Miss Fairfax said the caller
was to be sent up to her. There might be a row with the
editor afterwards. He had taken the view long since that
Miss Fairfax was too officious; but she knew her rights. The
Radish matter had been taken over by her employer.

Trying to reconstruct the sequel on the sleepless nights that
followed, Miss Fairfax was haunted by Mrs Heidl's alarming
eyes. They seemed to constitute the whole of her face. Under
their baleful influence, she agreed to call that evening at
St Jarlath's—a home for distressed gentlewomen—at Putney
(and she had been looking forward particularly to a concert
on B.B.C. II).

At first she had resisted. Why should Mrs Heidl not
submit her contribution like everyone else? What was her
special source of information on the Radish story? The old
woman was stubborn and mysterious. Miss Fairfax must
come and judge for herself. When casually, but distinctly,
Mrs Heidl referred to Radish as "my husband", Miss Fairfax
smiled. Now she understood the situation. She was dealing
with a lunatic.

Mrs Heidl, observing the smile, dipped into her shabby
bag and fished out a faded photograph, an old-fashioned

sentimental post-card—lovers in a rose-wreathed arbour. The young man in the straw boater was indisputably Radish; the eyes of his companion had not changed.

Miss Fairfax went to Putney, and sweated for two hours in a dark, stuffy room, cluttered with paper and what looked like the contents of an obsolete theatrical wardrobe, draped over the crazy furniture. Over all hung a smell as of rotting hay.

Endlessly smoking cigarettes, with a fine disregard of the falling ash, Mrs Heidl, propped on pillows, concentrated on her red-eyed, coughing visitor's struggle with cramped handwriting and faded pencil. She gave up at last.

"Lord Stoat will have to read this himself."

"I shan't let it out of my hands."

"It will be perfectly safe."

"After all, I think it would be better if I were to see the editor of *The News of the World*."

"Oh, no! I am sure we will buy it."

"I want two thousand pounds. One now; the other when I deliver the manuscript."

Miss Fairfax had come prepared. That is how the *Echo* does things.

"I will give you a thousand now, if you will let me take away the manuscript."

"I've stated my terms. I must see the editor. I'll call tomorrow afternoon."

Miss Fairfax did not want to make any mistake this time. And the room was now so full of smoke that she would have paid the sum demanded if only to escape. She handed over the notes.

Chapter IX

LIONEL LOOKED FORWARD to breakfast; it pleased him to meet his wife again after what always seemed a month, because he slept badly. His was one of those affectionate natures that takes pleasure in the proximity of people they are fond of. Even when he was in his study he enjoyed her interruptions. When she didn't come, he gave up whatever he was engaged at and went in search of her. He waved when she passed the window on her way to the garden. What he liked particularly about Eleanor was her appearance of having put on everything for the first time, ten minutes before, especially for his benefit. She continued to contradict all that the psalms said so lugubriously about the human condition. Even her intense worldliness had a cytherean fragrance. At sixty, she retained a childish love of pleasure; and when her adventures hurt him, he consoled himself with Burke's dithyramb on Marie Antoinette: "Surely never lighted on this orb, which she hardly seemed to touch, a more delightful vision."

That hit her off exactly; that explained why he could never count her transgressions as sins. They had the weightlessness she gave to everything. He had never seen her in any of the disadvantageous situations that nature is so fertile in contriving at the expense of dignity. Other men possibly took pride in their brogue-wearing, down to earth, honest spouses; he did not envy them. If they had been spared his exquisite sufferings, they never knew the joy of giving a caged bird its freedom and protecting it for forty years against the cat. Forty years! It was quite incredible. Nothing changed. Still the week-end parties—the steady turn-over of new talent looking for his support, and the strange painful private game of guessing who would be next to have his name inscribed on Eleanor's roll, which by now must run close the Légion d'Honneur. Now it was this chap who looked as if he were wearing a wig. Eventually he would hear the truth about that. For there always came a time when the pain had gone and Eleanor spoke of them in the historic sense. Those were his moments of triumph. When the tale was told he could, like Sieyès, claim for credit: "I survived." And that was important because even she could not hold time at bay for ever. When that day came he would be there. Such was his idea of love.

Today was Gerald's birthday. He was forty. It was hard to take in. He had never been a child; and it was sad to realise that he could be middle-aged without having shared the universal experience. Lionel had sent him a case of champagne, and then worried about it. He always worried about the presents he gave Gerald, whose acknowledgements never failed to carry an undertone of mild reproach. And there was no way of avoiding it. Sometimes he panicked and sent an absurdly costly gift. For these, the reproach was extravagance. The champagne seemed about right. The *Sunday Telegraph* was presenting cases to outstanding cricketers. That, somehow, was a guide line.

Eleanor sent rather mean presents. It was one of her unexpected sides. Even to her lovers she was wont to confine her keepsakes to duplicates of books, lying round the house, often without any reference to the reading taste of the recipient. This trait was put down to the credit of her sense of humour by some. Gerald was not among them.

"I'll ring him up," Lionel decided. "He will be feeling upset. I'd like him to know I was thinking of him."

Gerald sounded testy when he answered the telephone. He always did. He resented the instrument because it enabled people to call him at moments chosen by them. He was notoriously curt on the telephone.

"Hello. Is that you, Gerald? I rang up just to wish you

many happy returns from both of us. I wanted you to know you were in our thoughts, my dear."

"Very considerate of you, father."

"You sound busy. I only wanted to send our good wishes. I hope Caroline is well. I'd like to meet her."

"I'm afraid that is impossible."

"Gerald! You are joking."

"After next Sunday I think you will see it is quite impossible."

"But, my God! You don't mean to say we are not to meet our daughter-in-law before the wedding. Won't she find that odd?"

"I may have to change the wedding plans."

"Don't tell me you've called it off."

"Certainly not. But I am fortunate Caro hasn't. The wedding will probably be private now. Just the family and a few friends."

"I think that is a great idea. I hate big weddings myself. Hello. Hello. I've been cut off." But Lionel hadn't been. Gerald had become suddenly silent.

"I've just posted a letter to you, father. I think you ought to wait until you get it."

"But I shouldn't interfere. What does Caroline say? Does she not want a splash? Some girls love it. They don't feel properly married without the whole regalia—strings of bridesmaids, speeches, pictures in the paper. I thought you were rather keen on the idea of a big wedding yourself."

"Not with Sunday in prospect."

"What is all this about Sunday?"

"You know."

"Oh, *that*! But what difference could *that* make to your wedding plans?"

"I think the family will have been pretty well dragged through the mud."

"I do think you are exaggerating. Our name isn't mentioned, I understand. Anyone who catches on will have known pretty well what to expect. Don't lose your sense of proportion, old chap."

"If I may say so, I seem to be the only member of the family to retain his sense of proportion. But I have been feeling pretty bad since I saw the lawyer. I spoke to the Colonel. He was very good about it. But I shouldn't think he will want the connection advertised."

"I'm very sorry Gerald about it all. You know that. But it is all so long ago. I can't see how you can be affected. You were hardly there when it happened."

"I won't discuss it on the telephone. I've written to you. Wait until you get my letter."

"What is going on? Please tell me. Why should you be writing to me? You sound like a family solicitor."

"If you must know, I've written to say that Mother, on no account, must come to the wedding."

"What utter nonsense!"

"I'm afraid it is no such thing. Caro has had to give up a London wedding on Mother's account. She can hardly expect to be *persona grata* in consequence."

"I really think you must have taken leave of your senses. If your mother's not coming, neither am I."

"That's entirely up to yourself."

"Gerald, you are an insufferable prig. Damn it. She is your mother."

"Will you forgive me, father; but this is the busiest time of the day. I really must—"

"Don't let me hold you up."

"Thank you for calling."

"Not at all."

Lionel sat very still after replacing the receiver, as one might who had picked up something that was razor-sharp to the touch. After encounters of this kind with his son he engaged in an inner debate as to whether a limit should be set to mortification. Because he gave Eleanor latitude as Marie Antoinette, must he tolerate Gerald as Robespierre? It was a strain on his sense of justice because Eleanor was a source of joy to him, and Gerald was as exhilarating as nettle soup. To have Eleanor with him he was prepared to pay a price. He had paid it and suffering Gerald was part of it. But there were times, as now, when Gerald was insufferable. It was very rarely he let him know. He was quite prepared to sympathise with him over Runty's threatened disclosures, but the culprit, after all, was that egregious exhibitionist, and it was unfair to be held responsible for his crimes. Runty, of course, would get off scot free and be paid vast sums for his treachery, while Lionel had to endure his son's self-righteous complaints. And his thoughts turned, as they always did nowadays, when Gerald inspired them, to the contemplation of the idea of his daughter-in-law. Ideally, he could think of nothing which could afford him more pleasure than the marriage of his son. No addition to his life at this juncture could have charmed him more than a daughter-in-law. He had untapped sources of love, and longed to let them pour over; with Eleanor it was impossible; she would simply drown or suffocate; it would be like pouring treacle over a moth; and it would be easier to be demonstrative to a dustbin than to Gerald. What sort of a girl was taking him on and at his age? Could she be mentally retarded? Was he using his mother's scrape as an excuse to hide the humiliating truth? Lionel had chosen to be amused rather than offended by Gerald's insistence on the exclusiveness of his in-laws. Was this a mere cover-up? Were they eccentrics, in hiding in the remotest part of England, unwilling to venture from their cave? That was it! All Gerald's talk of a wedding in London and a reception at St James's Palace had been a smoke-screen. The reality had always been a gargoylish entertainment with the ceremony performed by a half-witted vicar, a relation and hanger-on. Lionel played with this fancy. There was more to support it as a hypothesis than the notion of a lovely girl bride, a modern Maud coming into the garden. One had to face the truth squarely : no pretty girl in her right mind would marry Gerald.

Chapter X

THE MEETING IN Trafalgar Square took place on St Patrick's Day, which commemorates the coming of Christianity to Ireland. At home it is celebrated by a trade procession. Angus finished his own celebration in hospital. But, then, he wasn't Irish. He fought with the staff when they wouldn't let him out; the more he urged the importance of his business, the more convinced they became that the blow had done serious damage. Rita had made no bones about the fact that he was suffering from delusions; and as he had, in her view, brought his troubles on himself, it was decided that there was a risk to the public as well as to the patient in letting him go abroad while still in a paranoiac condition. A psychiatrist in whom Angus—mistaking him for a physician—confided, confirmed that he needed sedation. The Hartleys, to whom the hospital referred at Angus's request, denied all knowledge of him at first; but when a fuller description was given, said that they believed he had written a book, the name of which they couldn't, for the moment, remember. He had called upon them on the morning of St Patrick's Day, and his behaviour had left an impression of eccentricity.

The Sergeant in Bantry on receipt of a call from headquarters in Dublin sent a Guard out to Pamela to tell her that her husband was in hospital in London. He assured her that Angus's condition was not serious, but her presence was required. He had no idea of the nature of the illness, and hazarded a guess that it might be food-poisoning. A cousin of his had gone down with that complaint; and it was probably prevalent in London, the weather being so hot even for the time of year.

Pamela had become really frightened by his silence, and had resolved if she had not heard by Monday to go to London and try to find him. He had given her the impression he was staying at the Savage, but when she rung up, she was told it was not so. It was something to know he was in a safe place; and she speculated what caused him to be there. Most likely drink. In every crisis since she married him Angus had become deliriously drunk. She should have insisted on going to London with him, and reproved herself for letting a tiff prevent her.

When she entered the ward she recognised Angus at once. He was wearing his Glengarry; it gave him a monarchical appearance, and the occupants of the other beds looked suitably cowed.

Not wasting time in greeting he called to her across the ward, "Get me out of this."

He waved a newspaper at her. His bed was covered with newspapers. And when she reached the bed, he thrust under her nose a page which he had underlined in red pencil.

"That will do later on, how are you? I've been so anxious about you. Why didn't you get in touch with me? It was mean of you."

"He's doing fine, ma'am," the occupant of the next bed assured her.

"I'm all right. Runty's gang put me out of the way. I must see the Hartleys at once and get the lawyers going. This may bring down the Government if it is handled properly."

Pamela was relieved to find him in such high spirits and, when she kissed him, not the faintest whiff of whisky on his breath.

"There's nothing wrong with me. The doctor said the crack I got on the head hasn't done me any harm. You had better see the nurse. I don't suppose Runty will try to keep me here. He's done his worst."

Pamela went in search of the Sister in charge of the ward

and found her more than ready to let Angus leave at once. He was creating too much excitement on the ward, she said. But the doctor had given orders that he was not to be let out until he could be handed over to a relation.

"You are Mrs MacDonnell, I take it."

Relieved to discover that she had someone responsible to deal with the nurse discussed the patient's symptoms. He should be kept on sedatives and avoid undue excitement. It would certainly be advisable to get him back to Ireland. But Pamela should see the psychiatrist who had talked to him in hospital. Apparently he had some fixation about Sir Romney Radish; it would be as well to get him out of harm's way. The injury which sent him to hospital arose out of an effort to attack Radish in public. Between their two selves, the Sister confided, Pamela was lucky steps hadn't been taken to charge her husband. If they had he might well have been remanded. He should be taken home as soon as possible. His health had benefited by the few days in hospital.

The Sister hesitated to mention Mrs Mooney, who called solicitously, bringing fruit. Now that she saw what Mrs MacDonnell looked like she realised that she had formed a wholly false impression of her husband. His torn clothes and the absurd Scottish cap that he insisted on wearing in bed, his physical condition which betrayed excessive use of alcohol—there had been nothing about him to impress and she had put him down as a type to be encountered only on the downs on Derby Day. And this was endorsed by the appearance of his only visitor, not his wife and therefore, it was to be assumed, the woman he was living with. She seemed to be a decent creature; but was hardly the wife for a Scottish Chieftain. This American lady was quite the thing. Better not to mention the other. The true explanation of the whole affair was a terrific binge, with all the sordid consequences, undignified for a man of that age. He should have treatment. Preferably elsewhere.

Angus left with his wife in a taxi, getting a splendid send-off from those capable of speech in the ward. He had lent colour to the drabness of their days. And they voted him harmless. When Rita called with a bag of oranges, later in the day, she heard that Angus had gone, leaving no address.

Pamela took her husband straight to her hotel. Unlike him, she believed in travelling in comfort, and he cut an incongruous figure in the lounge. Once in their room, the debate which each had put off until then, broke out at once. His first idea was to ring for a whisky; Pamela thought he ought to go to bed and rest while she booked tickets for their return to Ireland. He insisted that he had a week's work to do in London. Pamela asked for details. When he had finished she declared that he had "gotten himself into a great deal of trouble all through interfering in matters which were no concern of his". He ought to come back to Ireland and settle down to work on his too long delayed *magnum opus*—a history of the Western Isles. He had always said that it would take twenty years. Why was he wasting time on Radish, who meant nothing to him?

"Means nothing to me! Do you consider his raping you means nothing? What do you think I'm made of?"

"That's a load of rubbish. He never raped me."

"I heard you telling the story, regardless of my presence, to that pair of hicks we met in Killarney—all the juicy details."

"I did nothing of the kind. Anyway I was drunk at the time."

"So I am to understand you made the story up for my benefit?"

"Not for yours, honey. I don't know what came over me that evening. I suppose I had a sudden desire to assert myself."

"And the way you did it was to accuse a man of rape."

"Right, he did make a pass at me."

"That's not rape."

"I never said he raped me. I said he had a rather eager manner of approach. You invented the rape theory. Nothing else would do you. So I gave up arguing with you. I thought that perhaps your pride preferred it that way."

"I see; so you let me come over here and get beaten up by gangs and left for dead in the street all because you thought it better to leave me under a false impression about a distinguished public man, a hero in the eyes of many people."

"You keep twisting what I say. You heard me describing the incident to the McElligots. I haven't seen any more of them, by the way. She promised to call me up."

"I'm going to have a whisky. You've got me into such a state of confusion that I really don't know where I stand. There are going to be questions in Parliament; I've set off dynamite in Fleet Street—where is it going to end? Why couldn't you have kept your mouth shut? Who are the McElligots, pray, that you should have chosen them as the repository of your secret?"

"Don't keep harping on that. Tell me what you've been doing. What got you into this state? Why did you come away without any clothes? You look a sight."

Angus gave a version of the events of the last few days. Pamela listened.

"What about this woman you got yourself mixed up with? What have you told her? Nothing about me, I trust. I don't want to find my name in the *News of the World*."

"Rita Mooney, though fallen on evil days, is a woman of integrity. By God! I had forgotten. My article!"

"Your *what*?"

"She was ruined by your friend Runty. No rape in her case, no sensation-seeking for the benefit of callers from Killarney; just a plain account of an experienced lecher taking advantage of a working-class girl. Nothing about that in the *Echo*. I should think not."

"He can't be expected to put everybody in."

"What do you mean by *everybody*?"

"He has lived a long time and I daresay he has passed a good many women through his hands. He married five.

There's me, and now this Mooney woman. I'm sure that doesn't close the score."

"You can sit there and say it as calmly as that."

"Oh, for Heaven's sakes, Angus! Aren't you being a little pharisaical? You've been around quite a bit in your time, or so you've always let on. I can't understand why you've become so censorious all of a sudden. Runty never did you any harm."

"I regard him as the prime example of the rot that has set in all round us. I wish you'd seen him on St Patrick's Day—standing up there, looking like the devil's grand-uncle, preaching sedition. Those Irish cheered him like mad, of course, until he proposed planting Ireland with negroes. That shook them. They were prepared to blow the country up, but not to turn it into Swaziland. He went too far. I don't see why he should be allowed to use this decent woman, and then shake her off as if she was an old coat."

"But if he has to support every woman he slept with, he might as well establish an institution. If every girl you had a romp with in your carefree days turned up now would you admit they all had a claim on you?"

"I wish you wouldn't keep on comparing Runty with me. For one thing I'm not publishing memoirs. I'm not parading my past in the press to satisfy public curiosity. That woman has my article. She put it with the letters. And I never took a note of her address. I think I could find the house. It's near Lords."

"Oh, more lords."

"The cricket ground, you fool."

"Don't be rude. Leave this woman alone, whoever she is. It has nothing to do with you. You've helped her. If she needs money I'm sure she can sell the story and blackmail Runty with the letters. I wouldn't worry about her."

Angus rang the bell. He was going to have a large whisky, a stiff one. Without it he couldn't stand up against this negative attitude. Was he to go home after all he had accomplished, setting London by the ears, and not see the thing through? The Hartleys, for one, would think him an imposter; the secretary woman, who pried into his private affairs, even the chap who obliged with the loan of a typewriter would get to hear that he had been blowing about nothing and looking for notice. He must justify himself. He had his reputation to think of.

"It's frightfully depressing to see how quickly you drop out of things over here. Do you know, even in Fleet Street, they have to be reminded that I'm the Angus MacDonnell who wrote *In the Spring a Young Man's Fancy*. It takes a few minutes before the penny drops. What's the use of fame, Pamela? One struggles to attain it; and how long does it last? I can only be reasonably certain students of English literature in Santiago will never let my name die. I have carved my niche. But, Hell! Who wants to be remembered only by a bunch of spotty students?"

"It's more than most people achieve, honey. Why not learn from this; do more good work. Have you ever thought of moving to Smogg? I've sometimes wondered whether that wouldn't give you a true sense of identity. Perhaps that's what you have really been in search of. No, dear, don't drink any more. You know what the nurse said."

Angus had moved towards the bell. He hesitated and then threw himself on to one of the beds.

"Oh, dear," Pamela said, half to herself, for she knew what this meant. He was in his Dostoievsky mood.

"Even on Smogg there wouldn't be peace. They'd persecute me there."

"I thought there was nothing but sheep on the island."

"If that were so, I'd have moved there long ago. No, even on Smogg, we couldn't escape from people. And the man who claims to own the island would probably challenge my right to the title. I'll prove it in my history. I'm descended from Sorley Boy. Did you know that? I've never told anyone."

"Who was Sorley Boy?"

"Who was Sorley Boy! You married a MacDonnell and

you never heard of Sorley Boy! Ring that bell. I can't go on if I don't get another drop. I've been kept off it for days.

"Sorley Boy, let me tell you, had his family put to the sword by the Earl of Essex on Rathlin Island, and Elizabeth (I wouldn't speak to the present one, not if she were to go down on her knees) was highly diverted by the account. Six hundred of them! A man from Ayr called Crawford afterwards tried to claim that Rathlin was part of Scotland. The MacDonnell of the day disputed this successfully. You know, sometimes I wonder if I made a mistake. Lord Rathlin might be my proper title, not Laird of Smogg. Or, maybe, it isn't too late to claim both. I'll wait until I finish my book. Keep it to yourself in the meantime. Don't entertain the McElligots of Killarney with the possibility. I'll die if I don't get a drink."

For all Pamela's entreaties, he refused to leave London until after what he described as "Bloody Sunday". Until the last he was prepared to live on the telephone, meeting rebuff after rebuff. Where he had called more than once his voice was recognised, and in some instances the receiver was replaced. So far from taking these as personal slights, Angus's spirits mounted. It was evidence, he pointed out to Pamela, of the scope of the conspiracy. The Prime Minister, the Irish Ambassador, the Home Secretary, Canon Collins, the Secretary of the Press Association, even the Governor of the Bank of England (whom in a moment of confusion he had called up) were involved. It would probably be necessary to lodge a protest with the United Nations.

Pamela, intent on getting her husband out of London, heard him mutter something to the effect that the Hartleys had reason to be grateful to him. Seizing on this, she congratulated him. Had he not thrown himself into the controversy the Hartleys might have been unaware of their danger. They owed Angus more than they could ever repay. She saw him softening. She kept it up. He sent a telegram: "Glad I was able to do something. Will keep in touch."

Pamela booked seats for a flight to Dublin, and urged Angus to return before his enemies, maddened by his success, planned punitive action. He saw the force of this, and agreed to come after making a last unavailing attempt to get Radish on the telephone.

The flight to Dublin put Angus into a good temper. Travel-bookings provided an opportunity to call himself the Laird of Smogg without giving rise to confusion. As a result, he received pleasing attentions from air hostesses, and he was invited to sit in places reserved for very important people. Everything, for once, was as it should be.

Pamela had moved their belongings from the house in Kerry, and they returned to their flat in Lower Mount Street. Adjoining Merrion Square, the Arts Council, and the Legislature, their residence was also conveniently situated for visits to Murphy's, a public house down an alley way, within a stone's throw of the flat. There Angus liked to call of an evening to meet young men with revolutionary ideas. Since an evening when powdered glass had been put in the petrol tank, he went on foot and left his car at home.

Pamela was anxious to preserve the mood in which he returned. Very gently, she persuaded him not to go to Murphy's on the first evening. Let her cook him an omelette, and they might open the last bottle of Montrachet. She wanted, she said, to have a quiet talk before he got caught up in the whirl of Dublin life.

He listened to Pamela's narcotic dronings, soothed, for an hour. Then the unsleeping devil in him—a legacy no doubt, from ancestors forever grappling with Vikings—took possession again. He shut Pamela up rather brusquely and spilled brandy on the new carpet in his rush to the telephone. He had suddenly decided to get into action, not to be lulled by dreams. If he could get the Minister for Justice on the telephone (and he hoped by ringing someone who knew someone who knew him intimately to achieve this) he might get the Government to lodge a complaint about his treatment at the hands of the London police.

"For Christ's sake, sit down," Pamela protested, when he failed to establish any contacts. He then decided to ring up someone prominent in the theatre to discuss a plan he had thought of for a new play. Before beginning on it he would require a guarantee of a performance at the Theatre Festival in the autumn. There was nobody to answer him at any of the numbers he rang. The broken English of baby-sitters set his nerves on edge.

"I'm going out," he said. "I'm stifling here."

Pamela sighed and took a novel to bed. Now the wheel would go into rotation again : euphoria followed by paralysing depression, or hysteria, slept upon, and awakening as a thirst for vengeance.

The audience in Murphy's, when Angus appeared, was composed of young men. They greeted him with a welcoming hail. He ordered drinks all round. A fleshy young man in a corner had rolled back his sleeve to show cigarette burns inflicted by the military authorities in Belfast. Another was offering what looked like a page from an evening paper for sale. It was a broad-sheet to which Angus had contributed a poem, written under the influence of punch, on a previous occasion. It dealt with lust, and didn't rhyme. But print lent the verse a pleasing illusion of sense. Angus felt a gentle fondness for it, as for a sickly child, and bought all the broad-sheets from the vendor, whose gratitude was muted because the financial gain was offset by the restriction on publicity (every copy in the same hands). A friend avoided this by appropriating three-quarters of the bundle in the course of the evening. As Angus didn't notice, it was a satisfactory compromise.

He talked away. Names began to drop like the preliminaries of a thunder shower; but nobody ran for shelter. Angus, coming from abroad, was free of the bar at Murphy's. These young men were glad to hear from him, and his tone of incessant denigration was agreeable. Had he boasted of favourable treatment there would have been resentment; but the idea of a conspiracy appealed to them. When someone put his hand on Angus's head to feel the bump, there was a protest from the young man exhibiting his burns. His own head, he said, resembled corrugated iron from the dints of batons on it. He offered to take his shoes off to show scars on his feet; but there was no demand for this. The night was warm, and his feet, someone said, were better off where they were. Angus bought him a drink; and the cloud over the evening passed.

Everyone knew about Radish, or if they didn't before, they did now. Angus had his listeners agog with his account of the efforts to rescue his friends from the old man's malice. They were prejudiced in Radish's favour to begin with; his championship of every revolutionary cause and his recent support for I.R.A. activity made him something of a hero. On a platform Angus might have been out of step with his audience, but in the comparative intimacy of a bar he was able to sway them.

The one objection this group had to Radish was his success; it was consoling therefore to hear that it was undeserved, that he was only a retailer of second-hand ideas in metaphysics, that his scientific work was purely sensational, his literary reputation spurious, his amorous career abortive, his benevolence bogus, his alleged passion for equality a fraud; no one was ever more arrogant in the exercise of aristocratic principles than he.

Then Angus told them how, when he had a chance to expose the old charlatan, a band of roughs was hired to beat him up. The idea was to keep him incommunicado until the publication of Radish's slander on the following Sunday. Of course the press lords were hand and glove with him in it. So was Heath, if the truth were known.

The arrival of the police at this stage interrupted the narrative. It may have been as well. Angus was about to tell these louts about Pamela, to squeeze the last drop out of the Radish theme. Had he done so he would have been ashamed tomorrow. The police left as mysteriously as they came; but their visit, whatever its purpose, dampened the spirits of the party. The young martyr who had pulled his shirt on when the officers of the law were present was inclined to truculence now that they had departed.

"Why do you call yourself the Laird of Smogg?"

"Because I am. And I defy you to maintain the contrary."

"I give you the toast of the Laird of Smogg, the Laird of Eigg, the Laird of Muck, and the Laird of Rhum," said the truculent young man, raising a tumbler filled at Angus's expense, to the company.

Glasses were raised; there were cheers and laughs; not everyone saw the point. Angus's never-resting antennae felt the edge of a hostile wind. He was inclined to sail into it. The MacDonnells died with their boots on. But a voice at his elbow urged withdrawal. He looked round and recognised the perennially smiling face of the editor of the *Celtic Advertiser*, Mr MacWhirry. He had appeared late on the scene with members of the Georgian Society, who were showing the sights of Dublin to London friends; Angus, holding court in Murphy's bar, had been kept for the last.

In a matter of moments he was outside the pub and driving in an automobile worthy of his pretensions towards one of the more splendid hotels. It was exactly what his spirits required at that moment. He had stooped, muddied himself in the process. He should stay with his peers. They were being very flattering to him, and insisted on hearing all over again what had happened in London. He could forgive himself if in this company he gave a confidence which he pledged them to respect—Radish had raped Pamela—in Antananarivo—he could show them the spot if they felt like going to Madagascar. The information produced a solemn silence. No one volunteered for the journey.

"I didn't think he had it in him," someone said at last.

"I hope she is none the worse," added a fair-haired man with eyes as blue as sapphires, but not so soft-looking.

"Why in Antananarivo?"

The speaker was rather drunk, and nobody thought it was worth answering the question. Mr MacWhirry, who had conciliatory qualities in society to offset his trouble-shooting propensities as an editor, took Angus aside.

"Would you consider writing a review of the Radish book for us? You could spread yourself. A page if you need it. I'll see what there is in the till; but we can't give you what you would get from the *New York Times*."

"I'd rather write for you than for the *New York Times*. I'd rather write for your honest little paper than for any of the bloody Fleet Street sheets. When do you want it?"

"You'll have to read the book first. By the end of the month?"

"I'm on. I'll give you value for your money; and you needn't worry about libel. I've seen the letters. I can stand over everything I say. Take my tip. Print 100,000 of the next issue. There will be a run on it from across Channel. I wouldn't be surprised if it led to a question in the House. See Harold Wilson gets a copy. And that red-haired female . . . We are going to town this time."

Angus arrived home very drunk indeed.

Chapter XI

UNDER VERA'S MANAGEMENT life in the Radish home ran with the smoothness of cream down the back of a spoon. It required unceasing vigilance. Romney woke early, and took up whatever he had been reading the night before and continued until Vera, who slept better, woke up. While she was sleeping he felt like a general without an army; her first stretch and yawn was a heartening reveille. With the regularity of army drill the morning routine proceeded. He liked to get up for breakfast, to have the newspapers on the table, and afterwards, in summer, to cross the lawn to a garden-room where he read and wrote until lunch-time. There his letters were waiting for him, and at half-past nine his secretary came and took dictation. She was a worthy but awkwardly-built girl, and he cut down her services to the minimum, finding no pleasure in having her around. She had been engaged by Vera, against whom he felt a grievance every morning when he greeted Miss Patterson. A lovely and enthusiastic girl would have given him heart for his work. It was unimaginative, to say the least, to have saddled him with anyone so uninspiring.

When the letters were disposed of and Miss Patterson dismissed, he played Mozart on the gramophone until he had purged the atmosphere of the effects of her presence; then he moved from an easy chair to his desk and began the day's work.

The proofs of the next volume of his memoirs lay at hand; but he had shirked the monotony of going through these with his secretary. She was reading them at home and bringing in the pages she had passed; these he handed to Vera, who was meticulous. After that he would get old Monty

Melincourt (who had nothing to do these days) to go through them. Only then would he run an eye over the well-tilled ground. One could never, unfortunately, abdicate entirely from proof-reading. There was always something which only the writer could catch no matter how conscientious his substitute.

Romney was officially unaware of certain background activities that were arranged for his comfort. For instance, Vera went through the post before breakfast and set aside any letter which might be troublesome or offensive. These she gave to Miss Patterson to dispose of. But even so, it was not possible to keep all the trouble the world had in store away from him.

Miss Patterson longed to be allowed to play a part in her employer's creative life; he insisted on confining her duties to the dull routine of his daily correspondence; anything to do with income tax or accounts was left to her. Where his exciting work was concerned her assistance was not called upon until it came to proof-reading, and even then she was never mentioned in the acknowledgement put in the front of the volume. Vera was given a paragraph of praise for her patience, etc. etc.

The work to which Radish was devoting himself now was a series of *Aesop's Fables* for our own time. He wrote one every morning; and at night, after dinner, read it to Vera. When he had written a hundred, there would be enough to make a book.

Radish smiled as his pen lightly ran over the paper. The fable for the day was rolling out. It described how a thirsty American on a camel asked the beast to carry him to a well. The camel trotted off, and paused where there was a depression in the sand.

"Say, that's not watah, you son-of-a-bitch," the American said.

The camel ignored him and kicked the ground three times. A spout of oil shot up into the sky.

"Say, that's not watah, you son-of-a-gun," the American said.

The camel winked, and said nothing.

Radish smiled; it was extraordinary with what facility he could pour out this sort of thing. How pleasant life would have been, if instead of exercising his intellect with matter that stretched it beyond its limits, he had discovered earlier this bottomless well of pure inspiration.

He read over what he had written. "Delightful." That was the word the critics used for his last volume of fairy stories. But the illustrations hadn't matched the text. Jackson really must bestir himself and try to get someone else for these. Why confine himself to Britain? Surely there were imaginative draughtsmen in Eastern Europe. This awful provincialism—was there no publisher with vision?

He stopped writing. He was in a temper. Read in a temper, his fable seemed to pale on the page. He read it again. It bored him. To distract himself, he took up a letter in a familiar hand which had come in that morning's post. It was in his publisher's envelope; he had forwarded it. "Strictly private and personal" was written on the envelope. Letters from the publisher were deemed safe by Vera and got through uncensored; this one, had it come under its own steam, would have been the subject of debate with Miss Patterson. It had an unpropitious appearance; the handwriting and stationery alike were depressed. A begging letter would have been Vera's final judgement; and as such it would have been opened and handed over to Miss Patterson to deal with. Radish suspected but did not investigate his wife's conspiracy for his comfort with his secretary, the overall result was a great saving of trouble and vexation; he pretended not to know what was going on, but to the extent that it curtailed his amusement he resented it.

"That was a bit of luck," he said to himself when he took in the nature of the letter; for it was not one which he would have liked either Vera or Miss Patterson to see.

"Dear Romney," it began. "I called twice at your house in

London and was told on each occasion that you were not at home.

"I suppose you thought that I had come to bother you. It must often happen to people who are famous. To you I am probably an incident in the past that you had forgotten and did not want to be reminded of.

"I want to put your mind at rest. I have no claim on you. On the contrary; when you asked me not to give you up I left your letters unanswered; but you knew at the time that I had decided to marry Peter. I thought I should make a clean break. You were married; and you made it very clear to me that you had no intention of breaking up your home. A year later I read that you had married again. I cannot therefore reproach myself for having tried to make a life on my own account.

"I haven't any money, and I know that I could make some by writing about you and using your letters. In the ordinary course this would seem to me to be a shabby thing to do. But I read in the newspaper that you were publishing what is described as 'frank and candid revelations of his associations with women and his tempestuous career as the husband of five of them'.

"Naturally, I was curious to know if I was to be included. I shall have to wait and see. If I am, I don't think you should object if I write my own account of our affair. If I am not, I cannot flatter myself that I am left out because you felt an especial tenderness for me. It will be because I was one of the incidents which you deem beneath your notice.

"As I am not in a similar position, I think I should be allowed the privilege which you have taken with the ladies who qualified for admission to your memoirs.

"I don't want to discuss this through third parties; I ask for one meeting when we can come to an agreement.

"I have no desire to attract publicity. Though I could do with the money, I can get along without it at the moment. But I may be in straits, and if I ever am, I want to have your permission in my hand to dispose of the letters to the best advantage. If you write to me here and say where I am to call on you, I will come at any time you choose and keep you only so long as you wish to talk to me.

Yours,
Rita (Mooney, formerly O'Connor)."

Radish put the letter down and indulged in reverie. A rather commonplace girl with vague notions about improving herself, but with a ravishing figure. She had refused to let him photograph her. But memory needed no aid. He could see her quite distinctly, standing naked in the embrasure of a window with the morning light flooding her in gold. She had been perfectly kind and matter-of-fact, telling him of some young man with whom she had lived for a week, whom she was expected to marry. His image had come between them. Reaching out towards that elusive loveliness, he was haunted by the thought of this Peter, a motor mechanic, who had rifled it. Gladly, at that moment, would he have bartered all his brains and accomplishments to have borrowed Peter's twenty-two-year old body. Never could he rid himself of the thought that she was comparing performances, and her "My, you are clever", "Is there anything you don't know?" and "Now, how do you think of things like that? I couldn't if I sat down for a year and tried", brought no balm to his soul.

She never thought it necessary to pretend, and her assurance that, at his age, he could not expect miracles, was no consolation.

Commonplaces bored him. Half-education had only spoilt what might have been attractive if she was perfectly ingenuous. Once—always allusive—he had burst out :

"For God's sake hold your tongue, and let me love."

And she had flushed and said, "I'm not stopping you."

It had been a humiliating experience, in some ways the most humiliating of his life. He had descended like Jove, but he had not acquitted himself like a god. After that it was all very well to talk about ideal beauty, but one's authority was impugned. He had warned her; he had said that at fifty-seven she couldn't expect prodigies, but he hoped that he could offer her something she wouldn't get from other men. He had discharged the terms of their compact, but he had an uneasy feeling that what had persuaded her to join it was simply his fame. A working-class girl, it was something to have attracted Sir Romney Radish. The intellectual treasure he poured out for her benefit, she found no substitute for the simple requisite of a lover. If she had been less beautiful, it would have been easier to bear. But to have Venus to oneself, and to have taken such feeble advantage of the opportunity was a vision of Hell.

To his philosophical soul there was no comfort in the reflection that a body so sublime was inhabited by so mundane a spirit. It was a shattering criticism of romance. After Helen (his first) he had married women without pretensions to beauty. If one had to deceive oneself, it was easier, he discovered, to imagine physical charms where they were not than to conjure up mind in its absence. In the first case one —literally as well as figuratively—turned off the light; but when a love battle was over there was no way of persuading his clear brain that what was being offered was worth its consideration. He had, of course, met women who were brilliant as well as beautiful; but they were never available. Eleanor Hartley—she was nearest the ideal. So very pretty and gay and witty; but shallow, very shallow. She had given him up for a painter, of whom she expected a great deal—she always did of her favourites. He came—of course—to nothing.

It was one thing being given up by Eleanor—she had never enjoyed the relationship; and she used his false teeth as an excuse for breaking their liaison off—but rejection by Rita O'Connor, on whom he had descended from a cloud, rankled still.

Helen left him, but he had come to the end himself when she did. Catherine went back to New Zealand and married a faith-healer. Olive embarked on good works, on her own account. Neurotic Grace took refuge in the bottle. He turned to Vera then. She was his secretary. He married her in the mood that a battered ship puts into harbour.

"You are my good angel," he told her on that awful day when he saw Helen outside the Athenaeum. She got up, leaving the stew to get cold, and fondled the huge white head. It lay between her breasts like a child on inflated water-wings learning to swim; the simile was appropriate; she came between him and the devouring waves. Fame was his, and applause, and sycophantic attention, and power—up to a point. But outside in the night the wind was howling, and only on her breast was there comfort within.

"There, there."

"Nobody has ever brought me your comfort, Vera. Not even Nanny Evans, who left when I was five. My mother never petted me. She had a physical aversion to her children. Nanny Evans was my true mother. I was a very frightened, lonely child. She used to hear me cry and come in and soothe me, and I clung to her as I cling to you, Vera. I am afraid of the dark. I was always afraid of the dark."

Vera kissed his domed forehead and began to croon. Across the table her stew was sinking under a film of grease. But she did not mind. She loved her Romski. What did it matter that she couldn't understand his books? She understood him. All the others tried to be clever (which bored him) or worked themselves up about 'glaring social injustices' (which meant the expense of time or money). She only watched his engagements, booked his passages, cared for his linen, minded his medicine chest, and took him to her breast. She knew him best. Like lovers returned to earth they began to talk. Tenderness took everything in. Nothing, in this mood, sounded trivial. The sharing of little things was what all those importunate outsiders would never know. Catch-crys and banner-headings for them, hers was humbler and sweeter than that. "Mrs Brown called for the cat." "I gave old Mr Evans the back copies of the *New Statesman*. He sent you his love. Poor lamb. He is not quite sure where he is or what is going on." "That strange man rang up again. Where did he get our telephone number? He says he is going to horsewhip you—on account of his wife—Pamela MacDonnell. I asked him to repeat his name, and assured him that you had never heard of her or mentioned her anywhere. This is the third time he has called. He sounds like an alcoholic. I think we ought to inform the police. He might be violent. He calls himself the Laird of Smogg, but there's no such person, and he doesn't own Smogg. Miss Patterson looked it up for me."

Radish sighed. "I have a good mind to suppress this book. We don't need the money and I can get just as much attention, if I want it, by denouncing Portugal or threatening to move to South Africa. I enjoyed writing it, and your help made it a happy time. My angel! But now it has gone sour. The Hartleys have behaved disgracefully. It was taking a risk, I suppose, when she's alive. I counted on her craze for the right kind of publicity and Lionel's acquiescence in anything that pleased her. Now we have some lunatic threatening me. Yesterday something worse happened. It frightened me and I'm not easily frightened, not of people, not in daytime."

"Darling, what was it? I know my Romski. I knew there was something upsetting him. I saw it the very moment he came in and didn't look at the letters on the hall table and didn't listen to the news on the B.B.C. and gave himself a whisky on the sly, when Vera wasn't in the room. I know my little Romski's little ways. But I waited. You hate to be quizzed. I knew you would tell me. Tell Vera what upset Romski."

Thus encouraged, he told of the apparition outside the Athenaeum.

"But it couldn't be Helen. You told me Helen died years ago."

"So I thought. I was convinced of it. She married a German scientist five years after our divorce. Heidl was his name. They were living in Berlin. I made enquiries after the war, and I was told that the street they lived in was bombed flat. There was no trace of either of them. Being in the academic world he'd have surfaced if he were alive."

"You must have imagined it was she. Sometimes I think I see people I used to know. Then, when whoever it is comes closer, there is only the faintest resemblance. A way of walking or some other peculiarity created an illusion. I'm sure that was it in this case. Did you speak to her?"

"No. She glared at me as if I were a horrible ghost. The awful thing was, I remembered the expression. She used it in a play, the first time I saw her. 'Looking daggers' never meant anything to me until I saw that look on Helen's face. She turned it on me when we broke up. I can see it still."

"That explains it. You saw some woman who had this expression. It brought Helen back so strongly you imagined a total resemblance. If you were to see her again you'd laugh at yourself. She was probably years younger than Helen is now."

"She was a very old woman, but spry. She carried herself well. Helen had a very proud walk. And although the face had got so emaciated and wrinkled I might not have known it, the eyes hadn't changed. She had the most remarkable eyes. And if you annoyed her they shot a death-ray. It was very frightening. I'd forgotten how alarming it was until I saw her staring at me yesterday."

"If it were she, what does it matter? She hasn't bothered you for over fifty years, why should she start now? What can she do? Were you properly divorced?"

"Yes—when she wanted to marry Heidl. We came to terms. She would never take money from me. She was very proud. She would do me a mischief if she could. I read it in her face. Lionel saw. He asked me if I was all right. I must have gone pale."

"But this is ridiculous. Darling Romski, what could a woman you divorced before most people alive today were born—what could she do to you now?"

"She could talk."

"Why? Why now?"

"Vera, darling. I must tell somebody. I can only tell you. Those references to Helen in the book are not true. We didn't fall out over breast-feeding. We quarrelled over the subject admittedly. Whenever I wanted to talk to her she had the baby inside her blouse. It disgusted me. Babies in our family were always put out to nurse until bottles were invented. I changed my views about this later. But it didn't break up our marriage. We disagreed about a great many things. We were both intent on getting our own way. We were very young."

"Why did you leave her?"

"I didn't. I made that up. She left me."

"Oh, that's a little awkward; but cheer up, Romski, perhaps she won't read the book. At her age it's quite an effort to concentrate."

"She hated me. She hates me still. Do you know what she called me?"

"No, darling, but don't go exciting yourself about it now."

"She said I was a *fraud*."

"Oh! The rude thing!"

"She resented our poverty, especially when she heard I gave it up when I married Catherine."

"Don't think about her—tiresome, old creature!"

"I don't want to. God knows I wish I could forget her."

"There, there," said Vera, starting to stroke his hair again.

In the massive comfort of that enfolding breast he soon nodded off.

His memoirs had given Radish pleasure at first. He enjoyed writing about his childhood, and it was interesting to trace the progress of the earnest little boy, who longed to go out to Africa as a missionary, to the young man dazzled by Greek thought, and to follow him through successive stages —the philosopher, the scientist, the sage and reformer, finally the story-teller, the La Fontaine of the age. His was a cerebral life. But the later stuff became rather a chore. The only time when he escaped the gaol of his intellect was when he lost his temper. That was the greatest freedom he knew. He had tried to love through his senses; but he couldn't. He read about people losing themselves in women, but such had not been his experience. He was fascinated and sometimes repelled by their abandonment, and happiest with cool ones, like Eleanor, or mother-substitutes, like Vera.

Here she was, come in with an egg-flip that she made for him—it was the highlight of the morning. She saw that he was leaning back in his chair and had put on music. Still worrying over that Helen creature, evidently.

"Isn't the writing going well?"

There was anxiety in her voice; she lived in dread of the day when Romski realised the truth about his fables. What else would keep him quiet? He would be stumping the country, stirring up trouble, and catching his death of cold.

"I am fed up with these fables. Doodling. That's all it is. Doodling. I've had an inspiration, Vera. We are going to start this evening. I'll dictate to you. I don't want Miss Patterson. In my memoirs I was only putting out a feeler. After the first volume, they bored me stiff. All that stuff about conferences and messages to the world. My heart wasn't in it. But the beginning was an attempt at the book I've always wanted to write : my own version of the Don Juan legend. It has only been used twice in modern times at the level I will maintain. Byron, and Shaw in *Man and Superman*. And Shaw is getting pretty dated. I want to write a Juan for our time. Juan in search of perfection, pursuing women in vain, ever questing. Juan escaping from romantic illusion. Juan apparently engaged in an endless hunt, but in reality in retreat. Juan the victim. It will be quasi-autobiographical. I'll put in what I left out of the memoirs, and draw on imagination. Above all, I'll depend on humour. There will be a thread of philosophy running through it, a word to the wise. For the general reader it will seem a frolic. I'm longing to begin. What I can't understand is why I didn't start long ago. I can't tell you how bored I am with this piffle."

"Don't call it 'piffle', Romski. You mustn't lose faith in yourself. What did Cyril Connolly say about the first volume of fables? 'The purest distillation of the finest intellect of the century.' I think some of these are even better. And you were so pleased with them yourself. Only yesterday I heard you telling John Jackson that you would let everything you have done go if the fables were left to represent you."

"But I've done with them. That's all behind me. I want to go on. That's the crazy thing, Vera. I am eighty-three, and I feel as if the journey was only just beginning. It is as though I was born to accomplish a certain mission. I had a revelation this morning. A woman wrote to me—someone I hadn't seen for more than a quarter of a century—someone quite insignificant, but she was playing her destined part. Her letter made me review my whole life. Everything falls into place. The women who you have said were a waste of my time, seeing that I am not a hedonist at heart, they were necessary to my work. I could have written everything else without them, but not the Juan book. And that is the one which will put me where I belong in literature. It will be my *Faust*."

"This is wonderful. Who did you say wrote you a letter?"

"I didn't say. I said a woman wrote to me. Someone you never heard of. I had forgotten her."

"I didn't see any letter."

"She wrote to the publishers."

"Well, what do you want to do? This other book is announced, and Jackson is looking for an illustrator. Couldn't you wait and let your new idea simmer while you finish off the fables? At the rate you are going, it should only take a few weeks."

"I want to strike while the iron is hot, Vera. At my age I can't let it cool. But I'll compromise. I'll write a fable in the morning, and in the evening, after dinner, we will play some Mozart to get the mood, and I'll dictate to you. We must cancel every engagement. I'm damned if I'll address the

World Council of Churches next week. Send them a telegram."

"What will I say? If I tell a fib and say you are ill, journalists will plague us. Life will be impossible. Make a very short address, and say to the press afterwards that you are making no more public appearances until your book is finished."

"I suppose that is best; but I do grudge the time. I haven't felt such an upsurge of creativity for years. It would be a sin against the light not to respond to it. I tell you what; send Miss Patterson in. I'll dictate to her. I might as well conserve my energies."

Miss Patterson came in, looking portentous.

"Ah, there you are, my dear. I want to speed up the work a bit, and I should be grateful if you would take dictation every morning before you deal with any business. By the way, there were some fables we rejected for the first book. Would you get them out, and I'll see if they can be patched up. I hate wasting anything. When I'm dead they'll dig them up, you may be sure. Someone will want to make money out of them. Before we go on, there's a letter I want you to take, to a Mrs Rita Mooney, over the Express Dairy, Northwick Crescent, St John's Wood, N.W.8.

Dear Rita,

Your letter was sent on to me by my publishers. I shall be in London next week for a meeting of the World Council of Churches, and I could see you at six o'clock on Tuesday at Eaton Square.

Yours,
Romney

Miss Patterson took down the dictation.

"May I have Mrs Mooney's letter for filing?"

"I need it for reference."

"I could let you have a copy."

"I haven't got it here."

"Is it with the rest of your mail?"

"I don't know where it is. I'm trying to think. Ah, now I've got it. Are you ready? *Once upon a time there was a louse who made himself a home in the armpit of a Chinese sailor.*"

The fable unfolded in half an hour. The moral: *Chinese sailors should guard against Yankee lice* took a few minutes to resolve itself while other alternatives were considered.

"Is that everything?"

Romney detected disapproval. Miss Patterson resented his not entrusting her with the letter. He had expected her to express some opinion about the fable. If Cyril Connolly had decided these were masterpieces, surely Miss Patterson shouldn't take one down as if it were a letter to the Revenue Commissioners. If she appealed even a little to his imagination he could see himself dictating "Juan" to her. It would be delightful to recline under a tree with a pretty amanuensis instead of dictating to dear Vera. But the idea of reclining anywhere with Miss Patterson was preposterous. She had an inhibiting influence on him, unlike Vera, from whom he had no secrets, so confident was he of her absolute devotion to his interests. After he died she would guard his reputation like a bull-dog. It was a source of comfort.

But why should he have to put up with Miss Patterson, when England and Wales teemed with attractive typists? Surely a fractional nubility would not have made her less efficient? She had been imposed on him by Vera. Was Vera jealous? Did she think it necessary to take precautions to safeguard her marriage? Suppose—he played with the fancy —he had a pretty typist; was he at eighty-three capable of falling in love with her? And if he were, what would her response be? If favourable, would it be good for the book? Might it not be the essential element for its completion? The last link in the chain of his extraordinary life. Victor Hugo, Rodin, Picasso—they were splendid examples of the influence of Aegipan, the goat-god. Was not he intended by nature for their company? These fables that Connolly and his sort raved about—they were trifles; but they fitted excellently into the pattern of life Vera and her lieutenant, Patterson, had designed for him. They were putting him into a strait-jacket. He might have stayed in it if that letter hadn't come, sounding the pipes of Pan. It was a miracle. He looked up mischievously. Miss Patterson was wrapping her skirt round her knees as if she was folding a parcel in paper. The gesture conveyed disapproval, if not distaste.

"How did it go?"

"I beg your pardon."

"The little tale. Did you like it?"

"I'm not competent to judge."

"Oh, come on. Don't be so modest. You must have an opinion. Why should it not be as good as anyone else's? You are a very capable young woman."

"I try to give satisfaction."

"That is what Jeeves says."

"I'm afraid I can't follow you, Sir Romney."

"Jeeves, you know. Wodehouse's valet."

"I think I should return to my work. I have to list your dividends for the income tax officer in the bank."

"There must be times when you long to escape from this routine. Are you never tempted to throw your cap over the mill?"

"One is human."

"You sound offended. Have I offended you, Miss Patterson?"

"Not in the least. Have you finished? I have quite a lot to do."

"*Miss Patterson.*"

He had hurt her feelings. He knew it from the appearance of her back and the way she was putting her handkerchief to her nose. He had pierced her armour with an idle arrow. How little one knew about people! He had never thought of Miss Patterson as having emotions. Was she in love with him, too?

When it came to evening Romney found difficulty in

waiting until after dinner to begin his new book. He was like an eager bridegroom; and Vera watched him anxiously. She was suspicious of euphoria. Female representatives of revolutionary groups had played on his enthusiasms at similar moments in the past, with embarrassing consequences and unconvincing disavowals.

He was being duped by unscrupulous flatterers who exploited his vanity. What, she wondered, was behind this sudden excitement? The fables were going well. He had made the most extravagant claims on their behalf; now, all of a sudden, he was repudiating them on the strength of a letter. Who was writing to him? Miss Patterson had been quite rude about it. Her conduct today was inexplicable. There was some poltergeist at work. With an uneasy mind Vera took up her notebook. Romski lay back on cushions, his eyes half closed, smiling. She knew that expression, and dreaded it.

"*Juan*," he began, "*was an uncommonly serious little boy. His elder brothers were away at school; his parents took very little interest in him. His upbringing was left to the care of a Welsh nanny.*"

"But that is the beginning of your memoirs, almost word for word, dear."

"Don't interrupt, Vera. Where was I? *Nanny Evans became a substitute for his mother, a remote personage who only appeared when she wanted to find fault. Other little boys, who have suffered similar neglect, have idolised their selfish mothers. Winston Churchill is a case in point. But Juan saw her as an enemy who threatened the nursery kingdom where Nanny Evans reigned supreme.*"

"But this is what you wrote before, dearest. Let me show you."

"Don't interrupt Vera. You will break the flow. *He never thought of women as a separate sex and accepted the physical differences accentuated by dress as he accepted the universe—unquestioning. He was, as I have said, a very devout little boy.*"

"But Romski, dear—"

"Don't interrupt, Vera."

On Sunday the *Echo* came out with the first instalment of the Radish memoirs. There was a photograph of him as a baby in his skin; as a boy in a straw hat; riding a pony; talking to Lytton Strachey at Garsington; accompanying Melba on the flute during a rough passage to America on a French liner; discussing the future with Shaw, Wells, and Chesterton at the Albert Hall. There were photographs of his five wives. Priscilla Blue was numbered among the women who, he said, had most influenced his life. She had introduced him to the 'marvel of modern art'. Their liaison had lasted for a year. It had not worked successfully on the physical plane. Her insistence on fantasy, cats on the bed, incense burning, dancing in veils, Paderewski playing Chopin on the gramophone during congress—these were among his reasons for erotic failure. She broke their affair off, he admitted, when he insisted on removing his dentures before going to bed. They were ill-fitting, and he was liable to swallow them if he went to sleep without taking the precaution, he said, in defence of the practice.

Stoicism marked the behaviour of the persons most affected by these disclosures. Lionel suggested a walk in the woods. He was at his best in such a setting; his knowledge of nature was minute and accurate. He reminded Eleanor—who had always to compare—of what she thought it would be like if she had lived with Thomas Hardy. It was curious how one went on imagining what life would be like with the greatly-gifted, always believing—against the evidence—that it would have been wonderfully satisfying. Their wives so seldom found it so. Her own experiences with genius had convinced her that as a species they were less amenable than Lionel; not so kind, or thoughtful or patient or good-humoured, often not so knowledgeable, certainly not so easy to live with. On this day, when if ever he had reason to be irritated with her, when her infidelity was being gloated over by millions (not all, alas, strangers), he had planned the day so that she would be as happy as her conscience allowed. What could be more pleasant and peaceful than a walk in the woods on a morning precociously springlike, away from the telephone and curious callers, secure in their companionship, that had survived so miraculously? Thanks to him? Well, yes. Thanks to him. But she had always had the sense to realise how good he was, to see him as the centre to which, however centrifugal her romantic impulses, she could eventually return. He carried a basket with their luncheon in it. They had a hut in the woods for shooting-parties where they could eat—although it was a beautiful day for March, it was not really hot enough to sit out for long under the trees.

"It might have been worse," she said, spreading smoked salmon on brown bread.

"Yes, I wonder if they didn't cut it down a bit at the last moment."

"Anyhow, I think the false teeth gives me game, set and match. Funny he put that in."

"Yes. I couldn't have. Is he humbler than I am then? One wouldn't have thought so."

"No. He's as vain as a peacock. But he doesn't have any sense of the ridiculous where he himself is concerned. I think this comes from his scientific research, cutting up rats and guinea pigs. He doesn't think himself unattractive when he talks like that. He sees people as if they were on the table at an anatomy lecture. I don't know how he allows himself to get married. For him it must be like dissecting a corpse."

"Oh, but come . . ."

"I was young then, and he hadn't taken up science. He thought he was Plato in those days; and he talked about beauty in the abstract. I never knew he objected to my veil-dancing. Augustus John said I was like Isadora Duncan. That went to my head, what a baby I was! Now I wish John had kept his mouth shut. I hope he wasn't laughing at me.

You never laugh at me, Lionel. Bless you. Try the *paté*. I bought it for you especially."

After luncheon they strolled homewards, taking a circular path that led out of the woods across meadowland in which enthusiastic sheep were nursing their lambs.

"What a heavenly sight. I see it as a reproach," Eleanor said. Her husband, who was less inclined to spontaneous expression, merely counted the lambs.

"I wonder," Eleanor said when they had successfully climbed a gate and arrived on the road at last, "if Gerald managed after all to get a bit sawn off Runty's piece. It was strange his not telling you how he got on when he went into battle."

"I took that as proof that he got nowhere. When Gerald succeeds in an enterprise he usually likes to let one know."

They proceeded after that for some time in silence; each knew that the other was thinking about their son; tact on her part, loyalty on his, forbade them to pool their reflections.

"Even if he did," Lionel said, after a while, "he will never forgive us for what did get in."

"I don't see why he should hold it against you."

"Gerald regards me as responsible. I neglected my duties as the natural disciplinarian in the home."

"If he had any sense, he'd keep his mouth shut. Those stuffy in-laws of his will probably not read the *Echo*. I should think by the time they have finished the *Field*, their powers of concentration are exhausted."

"I'd like to think so; but you can take it from me, if there is anything unpleasant about one in the paper somebody always makes it his duty to communicate it to the wrong person."

"The whats-a-names know all about us. This won't make any difference. Besides they have Gerald in cold storage. Whenever they have doubts about the marriage they've only to take a peep at him. Buckingham Palace looks rowdy in comparison with that son of ours."

"I hope so. I don't want Gerald to suffer. He is what he is. We made him between us."

"I often wonder about it. If I were addicted to sleep-walking I'd be anxious to make sure that our bedroom door on the honeymoon was locked. Was it? I can't remember."

"Darling, please."

He expostulated, but as he did so had an uncanny feeling of having lived that moment before.

"I'm sorry about that," she said a little later.

"How do you do it, Eleanor? I try my best but I can't keep life at comedy level."

"I know I'm too frivolous."

"By no means. It requires enormous courage to be gay all the time."

" 'Gay' doesn't mean what it used to, darling."

"I'd forgotten. Damn them. They have poisoned all the wells."

There had been no telephone calls, they heard to their surprise when they came home. After dinner they played chess. At eleven Lionel, yawning, said he was going to lock up.

"Don't wait for me, darling. I've letters to write. And bless you for today. I had been dreading it; and it turned out to be the nicest Sunday we've spent for as long as I can remember."

"That's because we were sensible for once in our lives and didn't fill the place with idle people."

"That's because you are an angel," his wife replied, and kissed his hand. When he had gone Eleanor went to her desk and sat in front of a piece of paper, chewing the end of her pen. Then she wrote:

Darling,

I have been so cross with you that I have been afraid to write in case I might say something that afterwards I'd regret. I've been trying ever so hard to remember what your good points were. Lionel tells me everything. You might as well know that. And I think it was stinking of you to write to him without first consulting me. And not very wise either. He only helps when I approve.

If you promise to behave better than last time, I might be persuaded to let you come down next week-end. The Jervises are coming and the Sturgeons. She has that Chinese painter in tow. He might be worth considering for your sets. In a very short time he will be out of reach. I will ask the Fothergills to come to supper on Sunday. I don't know why I should put myself out like this for you or what you have done to deserve it.

Learn to make us love you. You could if you would only try—a little.

> Yours tentatively,
> Eleanor.

She read the letter over and felt a faint thrill. Then she put it in an envelope, addressed it with care to Frederick Parker Esq. and put it in her bag. Going upstairs she took it out again. Somehow, writing it had soiled the day. To tear it up would clean her bib; but tomorrow she knew she would write another. Every day since Lionel mentioned that he had heard from Freddy she had sat down to compose a scolding letter; but each time pride had held her back. What Lionel said today about her keeping life at comedy level gave her courage. So long as she kept that tone up she could keep her pride intact. He was quite right. It did take courage. But the alternative was shrieking boredom. And, anyhow, Lionel knew her inside out, and liked her as she was. If he was happy why should she let her conscience prick her? What harm was she doing him? This debate took place outside Lionel's door. Feeling certain that she was doing the best for everyone she wandered down the fabled track to her own bedroom.

Chapter XII

"FOR CHRIST'S SAKE!" Angus's irritability had
been growing throughout the long evening and the night.
He had read out passages from the review copy to Pamela,
but he had not entrusted her with the research; now, she
was sitting on the arm of his chair, reading over his shoulder.
For some time he had grappled with an impulse to bring
his elbow into her stomach.

There is something particularly frustrating about a search
for a passage in a book. Angus had leaped through the early
chapters; it was unlikely that there would be any reference
to Pamela there; but the possibility was always present that
she might be included in any place at random in some
generalisation. "Among the women I have known" or "I
recall a night in Antananarivo". However, the place to look
was in the later chapters where Radish, a world figure, was
travelling abroad; closeted with Gandhi; dining with Nehru;
in the shade of a tree with Albert Schweitzer; embracing
Einstein; exchanging toasts with Khruschev—and in lighter
moments: the first trip to Hollywood, surrounded by what
now looked like girls dressed up for a village concert; in a
sleigh with Ingrid Bergman; making up a four of tennis with
Royalty at Monaco.

1953 was a busy year. Following the death of Stalin, the
democracies asked themselves was there now, at last, hope
of a fissure in the Russian monolith? The Friends of
Liberty organised a conference at Antananarivo to which
the free governments of the world (including all the countries behind the Iron Curtain) were bidden. I was invited
to address the conference. It was a wonderful opportunity,

and I was anxious to rise to it. My speech to the delegates took slightly over an hour. I had decided to cut it short as fifty-three speeches were listed for two days, and I did not wish to take more than my share of time available. I spoke of the necessity of world brotherhood, the need for complete disarmament by the Great Powers, irrespective of whether the Soviet felt she could safely adopt such a policy in the prevailing climate of opinion. I avoided all reference to Stalin, and concentrated my attack on the military policies of the United States and Britain since the War. I pointed out the dangers of a revived Japan and applauded the indication of revolutionary activity in our former colonies.

The reception was all I could have wished for. The Ghanian delegation embraced me. A dear friend from Zanzibar was in tears. The Soviet representatives maintained the impassive expression which is protocol in their service; but the chief of the delegation spoke to me in a warm fashion, and stood on the rostrum to lead the applause.

Afterwards, at the dinner, he proposed my health in one of the forty toasts, and made flattering references to my work for world peace. I had very little opportunity of seeing Antananarivo, but I returned to England with pleasant recollections of the conference and the part I had been permitted to play in it.

"Not a bloody word about you," Angus need hardly have said. But he did, and in his mood of general irritability, tired after a day of unusual incident, his energies flagging beyond the point when whisky and water could sustain them, he picked on his wife for a quarrel. Had anyone else been there he would have chosen them.

Pamela should have been able to put him in good humour by pointing out that her apprehension was groundless. So far as she was concerned there was nothing to worry about or complain of in this book. Her reputation emerged unscathed.

They had worried for nothing. But in the course of the evening Angus's sense of grievance mounted, and by now transcended any proximate cause. It was as if he had already gone to war with Radish; and the time was past when the hatred engendered by the conflict had anything to do with the issue in dispute.

As he tore at the pages as if to drag out any frightened facts that might be trying to find cover there, one might have thought that the cause of his annoyance was the absence of his wife's name. He had forgotten that his investigation had been considered unnecessary by Radish, who had assured him that Pamela would not appear. If Radish had been present he would have been the object of Angus's wrath. In his absence Pamela had to meet the attack.

"Have you been making a fool of me before this crowd? To listen to you anyone might think you kept up a daily correspondence with your friend Runty. But there wasn't a word about you here. I've read the damn book through."

"I told you I met him only once, at the conference. Apart from the hour we spent on our walk, I didn't get another opportunity to talk to him. I told you the exact truth."

"How have you been feeling lately?"

"All right. Why do you ask?"

"Are you sure you shouldn't see a doctor and have a check-up?"

"Whatever for? Do I not look well?"

"You look fine, but you know—to put it crudely have you noticed any unusual symptoms lately? I thought you looked rather flushed when I came in."

"Naturally. You banged on the door as if you were going to break it down. I was out in the garden. I ran to see what was the matter."

"I still think you ought to see a doctor."

"Who's been talking to you about me, Angus?"

"Nobody. But I may tell you plainly that I believe you imagined all this business with Runty. It happens to women

When they get old they are always telling one about all the proposals they turned down in their time."

"You think I'm going senile. Is that it?"

"No, Pamela. I'm only asking you to remember what your age is."

"I'm fully aware of my age."

"If you were you'd realise that you have made a fool of me with your fantasies. Tell me this : why did nobody hear of this Sabine woman act until the night those McElligots came? Why had it to be trotted out for their benefit?"

"Right! I was drunk."

"You've been drunk before."

"Right! I was goaded into it. You go on and on about yourself. Nobody else is allowed to exist. Just for once something cracked inside me. I decided to get it across to you that I knew something about life before I had the inestimable privilege of having gotten myself married to you. When you refer to Horace, one would think, to hear you, he was some gaffe I made, some youthful indiscretion. Let me tell you, if Kennedy had lived Horace Cannon would be our Ambassador in Paris. I know that for a fact."

"Don't goad me, Pamela. Don't try me too high. God damn it, woman. Haven't I been chasing round London after Radish and his publishers all on your account? What does it matter to me if your Runty ravishes you on every page of his rotten memoirs? I'm sick and tired of the whole thing."

"Right, drop it then. I didn't want publicity. But I think it is too mean that I should be called a liar just because I'm left out. I remember his speech very well. I was sickened by his self-satisfaction and the crowd of sycophants who were licking his boots. He was lapping it up."

"But you didn't refuse to go walking in the moonlight with him."

"Right. I am not denying that he isn't a very interesting man when he's not showing off. One doesn't get to that

184

position on nothing. I liked Runty. I'm not pretending I didn't."

"Perhaps you ought to have gone to see him instead of me. That might have jogged his memory."

"That's a pretty rotten thing to say! I haven't looked sideways at a man since we married. And now you are throwing it in my face. There's no pleasing you, it appears. We had better break this thing up. I've a few years left. I want to enjoy them. I'm tired of acting as a crier for a one-man-band."

Pamela walked out. She had a dignified carriage, due to a straight spine and a strong jaw-line. He couldn't get on without her. Only she knew his weakness and bolstered it. He poured himself out a huge tumbler of whisky. It burned his throat and filled his eyes with tears. He had been fighting for them both. He couldn't afford to discard whatever contribution Pamela had to make to his self-respect. His self-doubting could not be kept down by drink alone or bombast or abuse. *In the Spring a Young Man's Fancy* had made his name. He had that to wave in the face of the world. It had not been forgotten. But when he perused even the longer lists of contemporary writers in the literary magazines he never found himself. The prescience of a professor in Santiago was exhilarating: but it would have helped if there had been distinction of the same kind nearer home.

Even in Ireland, where he threw his weight about and attacked anyone he pleased, maintaining the stance of an alcoholic houyhnhnm at large among yahoos, he had moments of misgiving.

Try as he might to link his name with the great, when he didn't lend a hand, his own tended to be left out. Open letters of advice to Ministers of State did not compensate for the missing sweets of discriminating praise. What was the struggle for? What was he seeking to prove? His eye caught a letter on the desk, a courteous refusal by an editor of an article attacking the moral standards of trade unions. It had spoiled his breakfast. Now he tore it into shreds and thrust it in the grate where it was caught by the last red coal and went up in a sheet of flame.

He watched it flare and flutter and fade; then he returned to his chair, suddenly calm. He saw his way. He saw it clearly. He knew now what the threat of Radish was to their lives. He had treated Pamela as if she were a skittle to be knocked over for his amusement, then discarded and forgotten. No man had the right to treat any woman like that. No man, merely because he was regarded as a Messiah, would treat Angus MacDonnell's wife like that—and get away with it. Now he had an opportunity to show Pamela that, when the need arose, he could be her champion. He could have had his name linked with Romney Radish among Pamela's lovers. Nobody thought the less of George Sand because she had de Musset as well as Chopin on her string. There is an immortality in these sequences—Cleopatra: first with Caesar, then with Antony. The parallel pleased him. He stood up smiling, and carried the proof copy away to bed. Tomorrow he would tackle it again from the beginning, list the persons offended by mention and omission (if he could think of any) and get to work. He would mount a campaign against Radish which, by God's grace, would never be put down. Angus had a purpose, and his eyes were bright with it.

Chapter XIII

COLONEL CHETWYND-SKOPWITH was a man of few words with a perpetual drop on the end of his nose. An east wind, it would seem, blew up whenever he was around. It had not completely blighted his wife. She retained some of the prettiness that had been amply hers when, to the astonishment of the regiment, she accepted Captain (as he was then) Chetwynd-Skopwith's proposal. He had been staring at her very hard for a week and saying nothing. Then he asked her for a dance and proposed immediately afterwards. She accepted, never having the readiness to think of an excuse when confronted with any sudden proposition. He was a man, she told herself, of whom one knew the worst immediately. It was like marrying a bull-dog. She was grateful for his silent kindness and steadiness and decent dullness and was used to nearness in money matters. It had been hell at home; and she was glad to get away.

Caroline had her father's disposition. She would have been admirable on an expedition to the South Pole or in an ascent of Mount Everest. She was suspicious of effeminacy in either men or women, and was as seductive as a tablet of Imperial Leather soap. She saw young men who answered her ideal, but, if they saw her, they came no closer. Then Gerald appeared. It might be over-simplifying his psychology to say that he had spent his life trying to find a woman who was the antithesis of his mother; it was probably truer to say that he avoided any woman who exhibited any of his mother's traits. As Eleanor possessed the characteristics common to all womankind, it was almost impossible to imagine a girl who could answer exactly Gerald's requirements. Then he met Caroline. Striding along beside her, listening to her deep contralto, sharing her frank contempt for every modern amenity, Gerald was stirred.

She could never have found what she wanted in a young man. Nature forbade it, nor could he have discovered in any but a young woman such utter unawareness of life as it has been lived on the planet since the battle of Omdurman.

Caroline's mother regarded her with fascinated awe. When she looked at her daughter she was amazed at the facial likeness to herself at the same age. Caroline was a larger model of the same physical type. The contrast between herself and her daughter in every other respect alarmed the older woman. She could not get over the feeling that nature had used her in some freakish way to play a trick on the adult male population. Caroline was very filial. She called her parents by pet names (which was once the fashion) and being entirely self-sufficient was satisfied with a silent father (Boo) and a mother (Mims), who chatted away like a budgerigar, and to much the same effect. The Chetwynd-Skopwiths were in one respect a safe family to belong to. While critical of ninety-nine per cent of the human race, they regarded any Chetwynd-Skopwith as sacrosanct, and all that was required of him (or her) was attachment to the family. At any Chetwynd-Skopwith entertainment there was always a generous sprinkling of family, of whom nothing was expected but their presence at the table. A visitor was often puzzled by the predominance of guests who looked as if they had been released from a geriatric ward or private asylum for the day. It was sufficient to the host that they bore the magic name. When a Chetwynd-Skopwith broke away from the parent stem he became anathema at once and was deemed dead. There was in every generation a large number of unmarried members of the family. This was approved of; particularly in the case of the women-folk who, when they hadn't the good fortune to mate with cousins, could no longer be Chetwynd-Skopwiths. When money was left to any of these there was invariably a condition attached that Chetwynd-Skopwith be added to whatever was the surname of the beneficiary. Gerald endeared himself enormously to the Colonel by suggesting of his own accord that when he and Caroline came in for Skopwith, they would assume the name.

No expletives or exclamations of joy greeted the announcement, such was not the Colonel's way; he growled and grew red, but Caro, who was present, knew, and she was never more proud of Gerald than at that moment.

His only desire was to build as high a wall between himself and his mother as possible, and it was a lucky coincidence that his plan fitted in so well with the Skopwith scheme of things. His antipathy to intellectual pursuits and suspicion of fellows with ideas, his rigid conservatism and reactionary politics, made him very agreeable to the Colonel. Mims had no ideas of her own; and was only concerned to keep her husband in temper. Nothing had pleased him so much as Gerald's arrival since the news of Bernard Shaw's death. Mims therefore approved of Gerald; and his age didn't upset her as there had never been any youthfulness in her own life. Her husband, when she married him, looked like a tree on the wrong side of a Hebridean hill.

Mims loved parties, even the ghastly ones she gave. And nobody had been more pleased than she by Gerald's programme for the wedding. He shouldn't have interfered; it is not the prerogative of the bridegroom; but Mims had never been allowed to suggest anything at any time in her marriage, and Caro thought Gerald was only one degree less divine than her father: as a result he fell at once into the way of dictating to the two whenever the Colonel was absent.

The Colonel disliked conspicuous expense; but he was not wholly averse to the idea of a blow-out on this occasion. There were a few people who might be the better for a reminder of where the Chetwynd-Skopwiths stood. And to put it with soldierly bluntness, there were people in high places who might go to a London wedding organised by the family, but would shun the journey and hardship involved in a wedding under the auspices at Skopwith, the most inaccessible village in the bleakest reaches of the border country.

It came therefore as a surprise to Mims when Caroline checked her non-stop chatter about the wedding to tell her that Gerald had now decided on a ceremony at the earliest possible date in the Skopwith church.

"By, my dear, it was Gerald who insisted on the Guards' Chapel; and we can't say now that we don't want to use St James's when we put in for it so urgently."

"I'm afraid he's adamant; and you know what Gerald is like when he makes up his mind. Boo is wax in comparison."

"But what is your father going to say? He hates fuss, and after the persuasion I had to get him to agree he won't understand. It is very flighty of Gerald really. And I'm afraid Boo will stick his heels in. He asked to see the list of guests yesterday. There is someone he wants to strike off it. He is quite enjoying all the excitement. I hadn't a proper wedding; and it was such a disappointment. We got married during the war, when doodle-bugs made it impossible to concentrate. The first thing I said when you were born, was 'She's going to have one'. The nurse didn't understand, and I didn't explain; so I wonder what she thought I meant. But I've always been crazy about weddings. It is the best day in a girl's life; she is escaping from one family and doesn't know what is waiting for her in the next.

"I love a wedding, looking at all the people and comparing the bridegroom's friends with the bride's; and then that moment when all heads turn and the organ wheezes, ready to start; and the bride comes in with her father. I feel as if it is the Last Day or the start of the Derby or something when 'Here comes the bride' peals out. And I always cry when I look at the bride."

"Daisy Thorpe will play the organ at Skopwith."

"I know; but it won't be the same thing. Oh, my dear, you've no idea how much I was looking forward to it all. We so seldom have any *fun*. And there's nothing I enjoy so much as a little innocent fun. You don't understand. You like your bird-watching and your hiking trips; your father is lost in his snuff-boxes; but I'm not serious-minded. I need a bit of gaiety occasionally. And I thought we were at last going to have a real break-out. You must talk Gerald round."

"I can't. He's terribly upset, and he dreads publicity. He doesn't want to have anyone at the wedding. Just you and Boo—and the aunts, of course."

"And his parents. They will think it very odd."

"He's not going to invite them."

"Why ever not?"

"Didn't you see the *Sunday Echo*?"

"Are they in trouble? Getting divorced or something? Fancy, at their age."

"Oh, Mims! I mean the Radish article. It was all over the first page of the bit of the paper you pull out."

"Darling, I don't understand. What's Radish? What has that to do with it?"

"Mims! Even you must have heard of Romney Radish. He writes books and makes speeches in favour of Africans and being kinder to queers; and he used to have a nudist colony in his garden until the police arrested someone for climbing up a tree where he could be seen from the road. Someone Boo knew. He was very angry about it. Don't you remember?"

"I think I know who you mean. I sometimes mix him up with the Archbishop of Canterbury. But his hair grows differently. I still don't see what he has got to do with it."

"I don't know if I ought to tell you if you don't know. Gerald is convinced that you and Boo are upset about it."

"You know your father never reads the Sunday papers. He says they cater only for depraved plebeians."

"That's what I told Gerald. But he keeps on about it. You see Mims, I have never told you, but Gerald disapproves terribly of his mother."

"But why? Boo says the Hartleys are nobodys, but she was a Lapworth."

"She is quite notorious. The Lapworths have nothing to do with her; she devotes herself to creepy artists and new writers and every sort of long-haired intellectual. You can imagine what that has meant to Gerald. Besides she got herself talked about. They make no bones of it in the books they write about one another. They make it plain that Gerald's mummy slept with them. It's too awful."

"And what has Gerald's poppa to say about this?"

"That's the extraordinary thing. He doesn't appear to mind. Gerald can't make him out. Now this awful Radish man admits in this article that Gerald's mummy was actually his mistress."

"I don't believe it. People don't say that sort of thing, especially if it's true."

"He gives her another name; but everyone will recognise her, Gerald says. He is terribly upset for my sake, poor darling. He thinks I won't be able to face it : I can't persuade him that I don't really give a damn what his parents do. He thinks it is letting us all down. He is so terribly sensitive to what people say."

"Everyone has these troubles nowadays. I can't think of any family which hasn't. But we must carry on as cheerfully as we can, and hope for the best. It's like the war. It may be you next time."

"Me? Mims!"

"Don't be silly, darling. I mean that nobody can safely say any more 'that couldn't happen in our family'. Let me talk to Gerald."

"It would be no use."

"I do think you are being too pliant. Of course Gerald is entitled to his say, but he can't really expect to be allowed to take over and dictate to everyone. The bride usually gets her own way about the wedding, whatever about later; but we fell in with Gerald's plans. We never intended to have a grand wedding. Boo dislikes any sort of extravagance. And now, when we have it all arranged, Gerald, on a sudden whim, decides to reverse engines. He can't do it. If I am not to tell him, you must."

"I agree with Gerald."

"Since when?"

"I see his point. He has had attention drawn to his family in this contemptible way, and he doesn't want our wedding to degenerate into a peep-show."

"All weddings are peep-shows. Yours won't be any different. Think of the Queen, and what she has had to put up with in her time, poor darling. Gerald will recover. Take it from me."

"But next week there's going to be another instalment, and another the week after that."

"It won't be all about Gerald's mother. Isn't that Radish the man who used to be called Bluebeard, he had so many wives? I think I remember hearing something like that about him. Anyhow I think it is absurd to let him ruin your wedding. It would be different if we intended to invite him. I can see the objection to that."

"I'm sorry. I've made up my mind."

"Then you had better face your father. I won't. Drat Gerald."

"You are not to criticise Gerald to me."

"He is too much concerned with what people will say. People say things whatever you do. What are they going to say when they hear you have suddenly decided you must get married in such a hurry?"

"Mims!"

"Don't look at me as if I were a snow goose. It will seem odd. What excuse shall we give? If I were Gerald, I'd prefer to have my mother libelled by old Radish than to have it said I put my Colonel's daughter in the family way."

"If you only knew how beastly and vulgar you sound."

"I'm sorry, dear. I'm upset. I had so looked forward to the wedding."

Chapter XIV

RITA, BOILING A kettle, heard a letter drop through the letter-box, but she didn't go out at once to see what was there. Nothing tells so much about our lives as our attitude towards the post. It was a long time since Rita rushed for hers.

She was making unusual preparations today for her interview with Romney. She had treated herself to a new pair of shoes, and this morning she had an appointment with the hairdresser. On the way out she saw a large envelope addressed to her. The handwriting was Kate's. Kate was her only Irish correspondent, a spinster cousin of her own age, who lived in Dublin, and for the sake of their fathers—devoted brothers—kept up a rather forced friendship. Each, from time to time, issued an invitation to the other; but neither took it seriously. They could do nothing for one another. Their epistolary manner was low-spirited. Letters usually ended with an admission—to propitiate Providence —that "things could be worse".

Today, Kate was out of place; Rita put her letter in her bag unopened. The hairdresser, as on every occasion, said "your hair could do with a rinse".

Rita had always refused to tamper with nature, which had turned her black hair grey in most places, showing white streaks, like gulls' feathers, when it fell out of place. She had been surveying herself despondently in the looking-glass. That was what Romney would see this afternoon; it was not an inspiring sight. She would read his thoughts in his eyes. He would wonder what he had ever seen in that worn face and dilapidated figure. When she tried to brighten up her appearance as she had this morning by putting a red scarf on, it had the appearance of a rag on a bush. Her teeth needed attention. Poor diet had undermined her complexion. Her hands, which were long, and should have been an asset, had the appearance of out-door work in frosty weather. Altogether she made a depressing spectacle.

"Just a touch, then," she said, and the barber, poised, bottle in hand, let fly.

"That's more like it," he said when the deed was done. But Rita was not convinced; certainly the white and grey were gone; in their place was an over-all look of a carpet on which ink had been spilled—a lacklustre effect. It made her look hard. But she was now launched on an undertaking which would make a nice hole in her savings; from the hairdresser she went behind another screen where a young woman with a moustache took her face in charge. Lights and shadows were put round her eyes. Colours rubbed into her skin.

Under the treatment her scarf took on a certain gaiety. She had her hands manicured, bought a very small bottle of quite expensive scent. In a window, close to the beauty shop, she saw a white blouse with a high fan-collar that would cover the tell-tale craters in her throat. It cost seven pounds. She had never spent so much on a single garment in her life; but she had the money in her bag. She went in and bought it so precipitately—for fear of second thoughts—that the shop-assistant had to remind her to see that it fitted. It did. Almost anything fitted her. She had a quite decent black skirt; with that, the new shoes and blouse, and the red scarf round her head, she was still nervous but not a little exhilarated by the transformation. Men, passing in the street, looked at her; that hadn't happened for years.

Vera prided herself on her good sense. It showed itself in her clothes. Radish, propped up on his pillows, reading Hardy's later love poetry, wished that she wouldn't walk about in her knickers. No matter how hard he tried to concentrate, they seemed to come into view, shattering his mood. He was strangely excited by the prospect of this afternoon's encounter. Visions of Rita rose before him like Botticelli's Venus. But Rita was dark. He liked that better.

Vera went at last, to his infinite relief. Splendid person that she was, matchless in affliction, when the sap was rising in him she loomed over the landscape like an approaching drizzle. Her presence was a reminder of his dependent state, and the flight of years, and the absence of joy.

If only he could have replaced sturdy Vera in her self-service knickers by Rita, as he remembered her, as nature made her. For a moment he imagined himself (it would be used for today's fable) as Faust offering his soul to Mephistopheles for a renewal of that vision. What would he not give if it were vouchsafed to him that for only an hour this afternoon he and she might be young again—really young, not fifty-seven?

Hardy, he suddenly bethought him, wasn't a very happy choice for such a morning. The mistake was very typical. Before meeting women in the past he had sometimes worked away at scientific problems, and that sort of concentration was fatal to the lover's mood. "You are an old stick, really," one girl had said. It had stung.

He should be eating peaches and listening to Chopin or Mozart if he wanted to keep up his spirits, instead of soaking himself in sadness.

> I look and see it there, shrinking, shrinking,
> I look back at it amid the rain
> For the very last time; for my sand is sinking,
> And I shall traverse old love's domain
> Never again.

Vera returned—still in her knickers.

"Won't you catch cold," he enquired testily, hurling Hardy to the end of the bed.

She had come to tell him his breakfast was ready. As he habitually walked about in the nude, looking like the

196

root whose name his family bore, it did not occur to her that she was offending by her homely informality.

Miss Patterson had not accompanied them to London (they were spending three days in the capital), and Vera took down the fable for today.

She noticed something strange in Romski's manner. When he began to describe Faust's vision of a modern Helen, he became unnaturally excited. She wondered whether she had been wise to persuade him to keep his promise to the World Council of Churches tomorrow. He was having a quiet day today. Someone was calling—he hadn't said about what—at six o'clock. In the evening they had seats at Covent Garden. After luncheon he rested. For some reason (undisclosed) he was not going to resume work on his Juan book until he returned to Wales. Vera hoped that by then the fever might have passed. There was no other sign of failure in Romski's mental powers—he was observant, acute, his memory was perfect—but the book was incompatible with sanity. She had taken down enough to make two chapters, and except for the substitution of "Juan" for the first person he was traversing the same ground as in his memoirs. Whenever she tried to point this out, he became angry.

Something was exciting him today. When he became irritable with her or drew attention to her shortcomings, it was usually because he had some other woman in mind.

When she went to see if he needed anything after his nap she was astonished to find him in his dressing-room with an assortment of clothes, shirts, and neckties round him, looking at himself in the mirror.

He was trying out a gear which would have been suitable for a yachting cruise. It enabled him to wear a very boyish shirt with a loose cravat. When Vera came upon him he was contemplating a new hair arrangement, with the locks brushed straight across the head clustering over one ear. She stood fascinated while he shook his head and reverted to his usual parting which, while it revealed thin patches, did not suggest camouflage.

Vera tiptoed out.

When Romski appeared again, looking a little self-conscious in his yachting rig-out, she waited until he made a reference to the unusual heat for March as a justification for his youthful apparel, unsuitable for London at any age; then, as casually as she could manage (her teeth in a slice of toast) she said, "Who are you expecting this evening?"

"Oh, someone who wants to see me. Something to do with copyright."

But she didn't believe him. This visitor was the cause of his eccentric behaviour and preoccupied manner. Who could she be? She tried to piece together the history of the last few days. Miss Patterson had referred to some letter which came via the publisher. That was consistent with a request about copyright; but why was Romski dealing with it himself? This was what he employed an agent for. And why this sudden preoccupation with dress and the attempt to look juvenile. The caller was a woman. Some distinguished and attractive woman, perhaps, someone certainly whom he wished to impress, and didn't want to discuss with her.

When a woman marries a man at seventy who has had four other wives, she cannot be blamed, even when he is eighty-three, if she feels jealous. Romski was behaving so unaccountably about his writing; calling himself "Juan" and repeating what he had already written in his memoirs, it was possible he had involved himself in a senile liaison. But would he have the nerve to conduct it under her nose? She sat with some *petit point* in the front window, where she could see callers. At six o'clock a woman (as she expected) came along the road with the determination in her carriage of one who knows the house she is making for. She looked up and Vera saw a face, no longer young, heavily made-up. A glance at her outfit was enough to decide the rest.

"A tart," she exclaimed, "and a rather shop-soiled one at that."

Romski had contrived to leave the room so that when the bell rang he was in the hall to open the door. Vera ran out on to the landing in time to look down on his bald patch as he followed the woman into his study. The door closed behind him.

The room was lined with books. There was a chair at the writing desk, another facing the window and a seat built into the window. Both made for this. Radish got there first.

"Do sit down. That's the comfortable chair," he said, indicating the one facing the light.

"I prefer a hard chair," Rita said, settling herself uneasily beside the desk. At least she was out of the glare. They looked into each other's eyes, and saw a stranger there.

"You want to talk to me about my letters," Radish said. He hadn't intended to open the conversation in this way. In his imagination he had staged an *après-midi d'un faune*. Now he pulled uneasily at his collar. Why had he put on this absurd sports-shirt? It had caught his attention in a window when he had looked at a group of scantily clad young people go laughing by; and he had gone in and bought it as one might the uniform of a regiment.

The first impression Rita made on him was of a sort of vulgarity he had never learnt how to deal with; but on closer inspection he saw her as essentially pathetic. Her first impression of him was that he had taken leave of his senses; but now as she surveyed the contrast between the juvenile garb and the lined parchment of the skin—the skull looking as if it would at any moment shed its crinkled carapace —she felt a twinge of compassion.

Twenty-six years ago, when he had tried to demonstrate his prowess as a lover, she had had almost the same feeling, but with a significant difference. Then, however inadequate she knew herself to be in innumerable ways, she had been artlessly confident of her own body, and could afford the luxury of pity. Today they were each in the same case. "Aren't we a pair of old fools?" That is what she would have liked to have said. It would have cleared the air. They could have become human; but one didn't say things like that to Romney Radish.

"I'd like to know where I stand."

"Where anyone does who had had letters written to them. They belong to you, but you can't publish them without permission from me."

"I thought—"

"Yes."

But Rita wasn't quite sure what she thought. "Your memoirs—I read the article in the *Echo*—you are telling all about yourself and the people you knew—"

"Well?"

"I sort of wondered where I came in."

"Come in? You don't come in at all."

"You haven't written about us, then?"

"Certainly not."

His tone angered her.

"I didn't know. You didn't seem to mind what you said about other women, I thought you might—"

"Might what?"

"Tell about us."

"There wasn't, as I recollect it, much to tell."

"At that age, you couldn't have expected it, could you? You said so at the time. You told me not to entertain extravagant hopes. I remember that expression 'entertain extravagant hopes'. I don't know why, but it struck me as funny at the time."

"It doesn't strike me as particularly amusing."

"I didn't think people talked like that—not about—well you know. It was as if I was holding an auction."

"I have no recollection of the circumstances."

"I know I treated you badly. You hadn't your heart in it at all really, and I was impressed, being what I was, that you thought me worthy of your attention. There were, after all, hundreds of other girls who had anything I had that you could have picked up, I'm sure, if you went about it the right way. I was flattered. I didn't like to think I'd made no impression, so I wrote to you after each of our little trips to remind you. You were quite cold-blooded about it. And I used to say I wouldn't; and then at the last moment I weakened. It wasn't fair to Peter. But you said your wife perfectly understood that you needed other women. You had such a rich nature; and I was not quite sure about Peter. He drank. I don't think I told you that."

Her auditor gave no sign, so she proceeded.

"After the last time, something happened. You got keen on me. Women do when men please them; but it isn't always the same the other way round. Men take the credit to themselves. You said I gave you back your youth. And then—isn't life perverse?—as soon as you thought you needed me, I felt sure I must marry Peter and put an end to our affair. It wasn't an affair really. I don't flatter myself; but you got hooked just when I decided not to go on."

"You will forgive me; but I am going to the ballet this evening, and I shall have to change."

"What you've on wouldn't do for the ballet certainly."

It was the first indication she had given that she was aware of his dress. Why had he allowed this woman to come and mortify him? She was nobody, nothing, not even a memory—until she resurrected that pain he had suffered very slightly at the time. Had he written to her often? Once, perhaps. He did recall the day when she wrote to tell him she was getting married. He had felt old for the first time. It had induced despair. Then he met Grace.

"If you want money, I'm quite prepared to buy the letters."

"I didn't come here for that. I tried to make that clear. I'm not blackmailing you."

"But you are concerned about the value of those letters. Otherwise you wouldn't have written to me."

"Suppose some time in the future I want to write about

you. It doesn't seem fair that you can spread yourself in the *Sunday Echo* when you don't need the money, and I can't when I do."

"I couldn't have published your letters without your permission."

"But who would want to read them? I'm talking about yours. They are valuable. Besides, there's nothing to stop me telling the whole story without them."

"There's a law of libel."

"It wouldn't be a libel if it was true, and I had the letters to prove it."

"You *are* trying to blackmail me."

"I'm not. I can't understand your attitude. Why do you think it's all right for you to tell about your love affairs, but not for other people to?"

"It is a matter of judgement. The people I mention are interesting in themselves, and they are dead."

"All of them?"

"Yes. Why do you ask?"

"I didn't know."

"If you were contemplating a book, it might be different, but I can't think our brief acquaintance will flesh out a book. I tell you again that I'm prepared to pay you as much as a newspaper will for any letters of mine. If you prefer, the matter can be arranged between solicitors. I don't want you to think I am taking advantage of you."

He would pay her anything to get rid of her. She had depressed him enormously; he couldn't face an evening at the ballet now, dolls jumping about, an audience packed with queers. In fantasy, this morning, he had seen her body: it had been palpable, breathing. But now, looking at that defeated face under its unconvincing war paint, she had no more significance than a road hoarding; and he knew that if she were to undress, her body would not be the one he had seen this morning. An image dispelled by Vera in her serviceable black knickers.

He was losing touch with reality. Now peace was all he

asked for. This woman was merely being a nuisance, a rather sordid nuisance.

"I'll give you anything you ask in reason"—his Adam's apple wobbled—"for the sake of the past."

That was a brain-wave. Until now, he had dispensed with gallantry, and if she had decked herself up like this to call—he was aware of an effort—she was not out of reach of flattery.

"Why do you care? What harm could I do to you? I'd understand if you were a private person; but you have revealed so much about yourself, and you haven't obeyed the ordinary rules even. Trotting off like that with me when you had a perfectly good wife—"

"*Please.*"

"I'm sorry. I didn't come here for money. Honest. I wanted to come to an agreement in case I needed it in the future and got desperate. But I don't pretend I couldn't do with some. And if it makes you happier, I'll sell all the letters for whatever you are prepared to give. I'll leave it to you. I don't want to go to any solicitor. Is that fair?"

"Perfectly. How many letters are there? Have you got them with you?"

"No. They are at home. Let me see—about twelve. Some are quite short, giving train-times, etc. You were very precise. It made me laugh at the time. There were two long letters. One very sad."

"If I say a thousand pounds?"

"That's very generous. But I suppose you can afford it."

"It is more than anyone else will give you for them."

"I don't want to stick you."

"Take it for—"

"For?"

"The sake of old times."

Radish took out his cheque-book and moved towards the desk. Rita got up and let him sit down. He hesitated for a moment, pen in hand, and then resolutely post-dated the cheque a week. She watched his writing. Of all that had happened in this meeting, this was the only episode which brought him back exactly. There was something off-putting —she remembered distinctly—about his precision; it recalled his first amorous approach to her, as systematic as if he were taking her measurements for a coat and skirt.

He read the cheque and then signed it and blotted it carefully.

"There. I want you to leave the letters here tomorrow. Mark the envelope 'personal'."

He made no reference to the post-dating, a token of less than absolute trust, which Rita was too humble to resent. What, after all, did he know about her? And he must think —whatever she said—that she intended to take money in the end. The cheque in her hand sent a glow like brandy through her veins. She could hardly believe it was true. Her face was flushed as she thrust it into her plastic bag under his surveillance. Now that he had concluded the business he looked as if he had cleaned up after a delinquent dog; he was patently on edge and irritated by every second the interview was protracted. She stopped at the door. She would have liked to say something grateful— and gracious—if she could think of it; but there was no encouragement in his face. She read distaste in it for her person, her poverty, and her involvement in his past. How was she to know that he always looked like that when he parted with money?

"Well, it was nice to see you again. And thank you for the cheque. It will come in useful."

He bowed, and closed the door, almost on her heels.

While negotiations were proceeding downstairs, Vera, in her bedroom, put through a telephone call to Miss Patterson in Wales.

"Louise—I hope I am not disturbing you, dear, but I'm very anxious. He is downstairs with some woman, and he has his cheque-book. Did you make an appointment for him with anyone? He hasn't been at all himself since we got here. I can't go into details on the telephone. You did think there was something wrong when we were coming away? Didn't you? All that excitement about this new book. I suspect this woman has something to do with it. What is she up to? If he starts to give away money—where is it all going to end? I wish you were here. What a rock of sense you are, Louise! Where would I be without you?"

Miss Patterson told her about the letter. She was unable to throw any light on the identity of the Mooney woman, but very ready to anticipate trouble from that quarter. Vera, in London, should call on the bank manager and drop a hint. Distraction was needed and absence from unscrupulous influences. What about a trip to China? That was a place where he would get the sort of reception he liked. Failing China, there was always Cuba, but that bait might smell rather mouldy now.

Why not put it to Lord Stoat: let the *Sunday Echo* arrange a visit to China by the one man who had the sort of antiquity the Chinese respected. And that would get over the question of the fare. He might boggle at the fare if it were a private journey. But the idea of a trip to China with all found, at Lord Stoat's expense—what was better calculated to get his mind off whatever was responsible for his recent vagaries?

"I'll talk to the agent," Miss Patterson said, "and you can call at the bank. That's really all we can do."

Vera felt easier in her mind. She could do a great deal for Romski, but he needed mothering; and it was impossible to combine that with the sort of operation she was planning with Miss Patterson. Single-handed, that is. She needed that dedicated woman at her side. Together, they managed Romski better than the directors of any other concern of the same importance in the country.

She couldn't ask Miss Patterson what she most wanted to: should she tackle him about this Mrs Mooney as soon as he returned? That was her own problem. But his appearance when he returned reassured her. Gone was the hectic air of the afternoon. He had dwindled. Even his suit looked sad. He was pettish. Whatever had happened, it had taken a lot of wind out of his sails. Wisely, she made no comment, and prepared an egg-flip instead.

The ballet was a new one with, she thought, a disgusting theme, and music of a dreariness that called for sleep and prevented it. An entertainment of this kind was a challenge to which Romski never failed to respond:

Every morning I rise to greet the dawn, praying it will bring something new. Be it a salute or a challenge I am quivering to respond. I shall never be old so long as I am born again every day.

These were the last words of his memoirs; and he liked to live up to them.

When they got home he ate a smoked salmon sandwich that Vera had in readiness, drank a glass of Ovaltine, and played *Trial by Jury* on the gramophone. The pain of parting was beginning to wear off. Besides he would get a good deal of it back when the sale of his papers went through. The agent was working on it now. He had forgotten that. Vera, missing nothing, saw a smile and threw one back. He pinched her cheek.

Chapter XV

Rita walked the whole way home. She was in a dream. She smiled when she thought of the fantasy she tried to weave round today's visit. A particle of the vanity that persuaded her to let Radish use her in the first place had survived. She had wished to remind him of the body that had distracted him sufficiently to keep him two days and nights on end away from his books. But not completely. Once, on their first week-end, she had followed him downstairs and found him pulling out a tome. Something had occurred to him, and he had wanted to check the reference.

His coldness this afternoon had brought her to her senses. There was no romance or nostalgia, but she was quite unashamedly delighted to have for the first time in her life a lot of money. To her a thousand pounds was exactly what "a lot of money" was. More would have been meaningless, because it would have been out of reach of spending.

It had turned out to be a matter of money; but he had dressed up for the occasion. He looked a guy. What had he expected? If she had thrown herself into his arms, would his vanity have been flattered? Had they both set out like fools and realised their folly together? If so, it had cost him a thousand pounds to bury it. His book was said to tell all about his past, but there was probably a good deal more that he hadn't let out. She remembered in the early days of marriage how she would begin to own up about household bills and not have the courage to tell all—her heart sinking as the total mounted. That was probably how it was with him; he must have picked up girls in the way he picked her up, all over the place. It wasn't pleasant, she found, to have to admit this to herself. She had tried to give an air of romance to his cold-blooded proposal; but she had always known that if she had refused him it would have only cost his vanity a twinkle. There was always someone else to turn to; it must be costing him a pretty penny buying all the letters in.

Or was she the only unconfessed? And was that because she had hurt him? Or was he simply ashamed of her? If he had been, he would never have put on that juvenile rig for today's meeting. He would have not asked to see her. A solicitor could have managed the business. Even if he had once treated her as—what she read was called—"a sex object", he had changed. She became necessary to him. The letters were there to prove it.

She read them over again as soon as she got home, and tried to distinguish between their three meetings. The first was very clear, the others confused, and what was distinct was grotesque: his running into the room that first day in his skin; coming up behind him suddenly and finding him picking his nose; his appearance in drawers. She found it impossible to conjure up one attractive picture; but she felt a sort of tenderness even for the absurdities, because they belonged to her youth, and that seemed very precious now.

When she had read the letters, she made out a receipt for £1,000 and put it with them in an envelope, which she directed as he said. Then she remembered her cousin's unopened letter. She took it out of her bag. It was as arid as ever; enclosing, as her habit was, newspaper cuttings, the relevance of which it was usually impossible to discover, unless they were meant to convey the hopelessness of her task. From such poverty-stricken material, how could she extract anything to entertain a correspondent, the scraps of newspaper seemed to say. There was an account of a threat to the amenities of the residents in Sandymount because of industrial projects in Dublin bay, a report of a pligrimage to Lough Derg, a great list after a public auction in the Mansion House (in which Rita sought her cousin's name in vain), and the prospects of the greyhounds entered for the following evening's races at the stadium. Rita was throwing the depressing little bundle away when her eyes caught a familiar name.

A cutting from the *Celtic Advertiser* announced that in the following issue its readers could expect to find a detailed account of internment conditions in Belfast; an exposé of capitalism in Britain by the Chief of Staff of the I.R.A., Mr Cathal Goulding; a survey of art in Ireland by Sir Basil Goulding; and a review of Sir Romney Radish's first volume of memoirs by Angus MacDonnell, the Laird of Smogg and well-known author of *In the Spring a Young Man's Fancy*.

Rita stared at this, transfixed. It was as though her cousin had been employed to send her a secret message. She felt a dull pain, and recognised the familiar smell of disaster. The date on the page was a few weeks old. There was a shop she knew which stocked a few copies of Irish newspapers for expatriates. If she went there they might have a copy of the *Celtic Advertiser* with the review in it.

As she pulled herself up on her tired legs to go walking again, she was conscious of some power greater than her instinct, which told her to leave well enough alone. She had dismissed the unpredictable Angus from her mind; and when she decided to write to Radish on her own account she had forgotten him. She had suppressed the whole incident so thoroughly that not until she saw his name in the newspaper did it occur to her that Radish had no idea there was an article in existence which told the whole story. What was to prevent Angus from publishing it so long as he didn't pretend that it was written by him? How much had he told in the review? He was quite dotty on the subject of Radish, capable of saying anything. He might even drag in her name. And what would Radish think of her when he read it? He had paid £1,000 for peace of mind. She halted, feeling faint. Without realising it, she had been running. She was sweating and breathless.

"Go home," instinct said. "Forget the *Celtic Advertiser*. Forget them all. You have said good-bye to men. Take a holiday. Go somewhere you have dreamed of—Venice, the

Italian lakes, Amsterdam. Don't bother your head about Radish. Remember the way he looked at you, pinching in his nostrils. He bought the letters. Let him have them. That was the bargain."

But when she got her breath again she went on. There was a copy of the last issue of the *Celtic Advertiser* available. Unsold, it was disinterred from a case of grapefruit in the homely shop.

"It looks like rain," the shopman said, "and then again I think we may have it dry, for the next few days anyhow."

She hadn't, on previous visits, noticed that he had an Irish accent. It struck her today as ominous. She gave a fifty penny piece for the newspaper and forgot to wait for change. He followed her into the street.

"Well for you," he said. She thanked him and went on. There was a forty-year-old photograph of Radish on a centre page, and round it Angus's article sprawled. He had certainly spread himself. She tried to read it, but the print jumped in front of her neglected eyes. She would have to wait until she got home, begin at the beginning, and read it carefully.

Angus sprung to life in the opening paragraph. With a blare of trumpets in his own honour; and a column was taken up by matters in which he was central, Radish peripheral; then, their relative positions having been established to the writer's satisfaction, he charged.

The inconsistencies of that long career were chronicled in detail with mounting disapproval. It would have done as an indictment at the Last Judgement. Still, the substance of the book had not been dealt with. That waited until the last. The reviewer scourged the author in paragraphs of mounting ferocity. His revelations about "a gracious lady whose youthful follies in recollection might have been punishment enough, was stripped for the edification of the public. She must regret the day when she admitted this satyr to her incautious embrace. If—applying the standards of a chaste age—the reader may consider that any woman who encouraged our hero's exploits deserved 'all she gets', what is one to say about the revelations of this Radish's marriages? His nearest rivals in history, ancient and modern, are Kings Solomon and Henry VIII. He would probably prefer comparison with the first, who also had in his time a reputation for wisdom, but the second monarch provides a juster comparison. Henry deprived the wives he suspected of their heads. Radish is satisfied to remove their reputations ("The coward does it with a kiss"). Did these unfortunate women, when they entered into their rash compacts in the registry offices (in which his secular conscience insists his marriage vows be sworn), anticipate that readers of the *Sunday Echo* would be invited to join them under the sheets? But we won't go on. This is a sordid business; and little credit is to be gained by those who have contributed to it. Miserable it is to be mentioned in these pages, happy those who have escaped. Are we paying Radish too great a compliment when we attribute to a belated twinge of conscience his decision to leave unrecorded a cry in the night in Antananarivo and the tears of a working-class home where a welcome intended for a sage was extended, in simple innocence, to a satyr?"

The blow she had expected struck at last. Rita sat very still, her face in her hands. Then she opened a parcel of letters. Taking out the receipt, she replaced it with the cheque and a note.

Dear Romney,

When you gave me this money I did not tell you that I had shown the letters to a journalist. It was, I now realise, very wrong of me. He prepared a newspaper article and tried to sell it on my behalf to a newspaper. I lost touch with him, and only this afternoon read his review of your book in the *Celtic Advertiser*.

I shall write to him and threaten to take proceedings if he doesn't return the story. Meanwhile, I have, I see, given him material to use against you in his ill-natured review.

In the circumstances I can't accept your money. I am enclosing the letters. I don't want to hear any more about them.

Yours sincerely,
Rita Mooney.

She then wrote to Angus and addressed it care of the offending newspaper.

Dear Mr MacDonnell,
　　You had no right whatsoever to make use of what I told you, in your disgraceful notice of Sir Romney's book in that low-class paper. Please return me the article you wrote. If you ever dare to make use of it or to refer to me again, I shall take proceedings against you.

Yours faithfully,
Rita Mooney.

When Sir Romney asked Miss Patterson if she had seen the review of his book which appeared in the *Celtic Advertiser*, she prevaricated. It was one of those which she suppressed. But he was apparently in good humour, and she produced it. He seemed highly amused when he had finished reading. The last paragraph pleased him particularly; he read it aloud and went off, chuckling to himself.

On the following day, by the afternoon post, Rita received a huffy letter from Angus. He had given her the article. He wrote it for her benefit and had gone to considerable trouble. He hadn't a copy of it, and was at a loss to understand her vindictive tone. If ever she thought of coming to Dublin he would be glad to repay her hospitality. She had spoken of the extension to the National Gallery; he would be glad to give her an introduction to the Director, a personal friend, who would show her round the collection. For himself he expected to have very little available time for several years as he had been recently elected local trustee of PEN. This would make taxing demands on his time, what with administrative duties, foreign travel, and incidental entertaining.

After she read this, Rita went to a drawer in which she kept receipts and her more precious papers. There, under an illustrated supplement to a Sunday newspaper, which she had put away because it contained interesting information about attempts to cure arthritis, she discovered the sheets on which Angus, on a borrowed typewriter, had set down her story.

Chapter XVI

THERE HADN'T BEEN a marriage in the Lapworth family for a decade. But one of Eleanor's nieces became engaged to a Guards' officer, and an invitation to the wedding came to Bloomdale. The groom was a Roman Catholic, and the wedding was to take place at Farm Street with a reception afterwards at St James's Palace.

Eleanor didn't keep up with her brother, who came to London as seldom as possible, looked after the family estates, hunted, and led a life as different from his sister's as could be imagined. But they had never fallen out. He much preferred her to his other sister, who was married to a former Colonial Governor, and disapproved of Eleanor, always the prettier sister.

It was galling, Lionel agreed, to find themselves at a family wedding, conducted in the traditional genial spirit, at the moment when Gerald had decided to behave like a lunatic. For he had had his way, and his own wedding was to take place at Skopwith with more hugger-mugger than attended the burial of Polonius.

The Chetwynd-Skopwiths were not family friends of the Lapworths, but the impending connection between the two families caused an invitation to be sent to them. Mims wept when it arrived, on the morning that Gerald delivered his ukase; it would be hard to sit out the ceremony so like what he had planned for Caroline. Gerald had played on his father-in-law's closeness in money matters; prompted by Caroline he had concocted a list of incidental expenses which made the old man pale. He was prepared to undertake them for Caroline's sake, but when he heard that she preferred an economical arrangement, the relief was instantaneous and overwhelming. He took the hopeful view that the Lapworth wedding should console Mims, who would be able to enjoy an identical ceremony, free of charge. The Lapworth invitation was a great event. Gerald was persuaded that his mother's family had made this gesture to show their approval of his decision to save all their faces. He had written to his uncle, tactfully hinting why he had decided on an obscure ceremony. And he would have been surprised to see with what scant attention his letter was read; the last line was not reached before it went into the waste-paper basket (and he had expected his uncle to read between them!). That cheerful extrovert's contempt for his nephew was only increased by the manoeuvre; but Gerald remained convinced that the reason why he was never invited to Lapworth was on account of his mother's notoriety.

The Chetwynd-Skopwiths had never seen a great deal of Gerald; having satisfied themselves about his antecedents they had left him to their daughter; his addition to their table, usually on Sunday evenings, made very little difference. The Colonel hardly ever spoke; Gerald was also silent; such remarks as he made were usually intended to crush rather than to inspire conversation, consisting as they did of plain statements of his own preferences. The two women talked to each other as they had always done, in the tone customary in sick-rooms.

But now Gerald had changed. Everyone noticed it; he was obsessed by the Lapworth wedding and frankly bored his bride's family by returning to the theme on every possible occasion. His uncle he extolled in a way that was quite foreign to him—praise did not come readily to Gerald's lips —he was too vigilant in his search for faults—at the play, for instance, he would be so put out by a solecism in an actor's dress that he couldn't be persuaded to see any merit in the evening. Even the Colonel, a man to support his own side in all weathers, was inclined to complain.

"If Gerald is so keen on big weddings, why did he prevent Caroline from having one?" and, more brusquely, "I'm sick to death of his damned uncle." Caroline, with a woman's intuition, detected some underlying cause connected with their own marriage and Gerald's desire to keep it so private. She decided that he had been more hurt by his mother's recent exposure than he was prepared to admit, and that he was compensating for this by cooking up an excessive enthusiasm for his uncle. She had never heard Gerald mention this relation, except incidentally; and she had gathered that they never saw each other. It was therefore all the more extraordinary.

"I'm afraid Gerald is a weenshy bit of a snob," Mims said. But loyal Caroline flared up at this. She was sorry that when they decided against a large wedding she hadn't got married at once. There seemed to be no point in waiting for six weeks. It was Gerald's latest plan. He was afraid a hasty wedding would be misinterpreted; and after the trouble with his mother, he was running no risks.

Even Caroline—Flora MacDonald and Grace Darling rolled into one—complained to her mother that Gerald seemed more interested in his cousin's wedding than in his own. He was solicitous that they should be dressed to do themselves the greatest credit. He had a new morning coat built for himself and spent hours at Locke's deciding on a suitable hat. There was quite a nasty scene when the day came and Gerald arrived—they were driving to the wedding together—and surveyed the Colonel. He had last invested in glad rags for the Jubilee of King George V, and there was that suggestion of green in the cloth of his suit, that patina only time will bring. His hat besides was defective at the ribbon, and he was wearing black, not grey; a fair and free option certainly; but in the circumstances, Gerald thought, the best foot should have been put forward. He began to fuss, to pick pieces of imaginary fluff off the Colonel's clothes. "Just a moment." "There." "That's better." It was all meant for the best, for something snapped in the older man. "Take your hands off me, damn it." At the best of times he was irate at breakfast. But this was going very far. The day was damaged beyond repair before it had begun. And as always happens, there were mishaps in the women's department—little things certainly, but it all added to the prevailing unease. Mims fought against tears; Caro looked out of the window; dark circles, which nothing could have prevented, round her eyes made her look dreary enough, without a family row. The Colonel and Gerald sat up very stiff, staring ahead. The journey seemed to take hours, and when the driver lost his way in London, the men sought relief in abusing him. It was another of Gerald's mistakes. The Colonel was employing the driver, and there is an old tag to the effect that you insult a man when you insult his servant. The Colonel came loudly to his driver's rescue, and congratulated him on his prescience in avoiding the heaviest traffic.

However, there was relief at Farm Street. Entering a Jesuit Church imposed a temporary sense of camaraderie on the party—a joint raid into enemy territory. Gerald's spirits revived. Here he took command. Debarred from his cousin's entertainments in the past, he was making his first appearance at a family festival, not counting the funeral of a great-uncle when the country had been snowbound and nobody else turned up. He hardly recognised anyone, but assumed that everyone recognised him, and was taking stock of the company. It would have been totally reassuring if the other occupants of the pew into which they had been shown had been even vaguely familiar; but they stood up to let the foursome in with that simulation of petrification which people adopt when someone unknown is passing close.

Seated he stared ahead and only gradually allowed his head to pivot so as to take in his surroundings. Efforts to catch a Lapworth cousin's eye failed. Whoever he could identify he did, in a whisper, to Caroline, and got cross when she showed no disposition to pass the information on.

On the whole he was satisfied with his showing. The Colonel, if antique, looked genuine. Mims had the sort of prettiness which went in the old days with short trips to hill stations in India. Caro was not at her best. It was unfortunate that it was the wrong day of the month for her; and he struggled against a tendency to be peeved on that account. But there was no question about her antecedents. Into any family group at a county show she would have fitted perfectly. Her prettiness—not at its peak, alas!—was laid on a reassuringly substantial frame.

That Gerald had swung the Hartleys into true again was incontestable. Who cared? Gerald, very much; and he assumed that his satisfaction was universally shared. The extension of the wedding invitation to include his in-laws was—as he interpreted it—but the first step to a new cordiality. He would not be surprised if he and Caro were invited to spend next Christmas at Lapworth. This pleasant fancy—in spite of his repeated failure to win a glance of recognition from his cousin—brought balm to Gerald's bruised spirit. He forgot the little differences with the Colonel, no longer saw the dark circles round Caro's eyes, concentrated on the prospect of a dignified future, when the organ gave a preliminary peal and all eyes turned to the door. It was a false alarm; a trial balloon; the bride had not arrived at the church; but Lionel and Eleanor appeared in the door at that instant, and the alerted eyes were on them as they came up the aisle, Lionel looking as always the serene and perfect foil for his ebullient companion. She appeared today like Persephone returning with spring. At her approach every other woman re-arranged some part of dress; old men smiled; and the younger ones put their hands to their neckties. You could feel the change in the atmosphere, as when the prima ballerina comes on. Had the organist played her in, it would have passed without comment. For this was an occasion.

"Who is that?" Caroline asked Gerald. "Ask Gerald who that is," Mims said at the same moment. Not until then had either of them, unprompted, sought any information from him.

For a moment, he hesitated. His mother's presence just

218

then was the worst blow he had ever received. It affected him physically like a collision on horseback with the pommel of his saddle. When he had time to think, it would make him question the justice of Providence. Every calculation had gone astray. He had appeared in the church, he believed, as the saviour of the family honour, in his retinue as in his own person. They could sleep happily in future. And now. . . . How could it be explained? Had everyone gone mad? While he sat dumb he saw his elusive cousin waving at Eleanor, and she was already talking away to the people round her, and smothering laughter. It was too much.

"I haven't the faintest idea," he said.

At that moment, "There's Gerald" fluted back to them as Eleanor stood up and waved at her son.

Chapter XVII

MISS FAIRFAX PUT aside the letter she was writing to her nephew for his birthday. She was sending him the price of a new cricket bat to celebrate it, and to forward his hopes of a place on the junior eleven.

Duty, as ever, called her. She had to ring up that unfriendly editor and tell him about last night's episode. That she had bought a first-class story gave her the necessary encouragement to face the inevitable *froideur* of the editorial manner.

"Where did you say this lady lived?"

"In a home—St Jarlath's—in Putney."

"Not the place that was burnt down last night?"

"Burnt down!"

"It's on the front page of the *Evening Standard*."

Miss Fairfax glanced at the copy on her desk. She had been too busy writing letters to read evening papers in the morning.

"How dreadful. Oh, I can't bear it. Poor Mrs Heidl! Everything burnt!"

"Everything?"

"I mean her—"

"Her what?"

"The piece she had written."

"I thought you said you bought it."

"I did but—"

"I'm afraid I can't follow you. Could I have that piece? It will make a good story."

"First, I must talk to Lord Stoat."

"I thought I understood Lord Stoat was away."

"I'll get him on the telephone."

"Well, be sure to let me have the story in good time for the sub-editors. How much did you say you paid for it?"

"£1,000 down, and another if Lord Stoat approves."

"I hope it's worth it."

"Well—I'd better try to contact him at once."

"Do that. I must look into the fire story. It's a small world."

"Too small," Miss Fairfax thought. She sat very still. The letter to her nephew lay half-written before her. The writing started to blur. What a pity the fees at that school were so heavy.

"Someone on the 'phone for you, Romski. Lord Stoat's secretary, she says. She seems to be very anxious to talk to you."

"I wonder what she wants."

Romney, looking disagreeable, picked the telephone up. Drawing a short dry breath, he announced his presence.

Sensing flurry at the other end, he swung his head round, crane-fashion, as if following the circular flight of a fly on the ceiling, while Miss Fairfax apologised for having called him to the telephone.

"I felt that I must ring you when I read the dreadful news about Mrs Heidl in the *Evening Standard*, have you seen it?"

"What news, Miss—aha—?"

"The fire. The report says that Mrs Heidl was never found. It started in her room, you see."

"Please go slowly. What fire? Who is Mrs Heidl?"

"Mrs Heidl—she said she knew you."

"I thought I heard you say that Mrs Heidl was lost in a fire."

"I'm afraid so. I rang up the police. They think she was the only casualty. I hope I'm doing the right thing; but I felt that I should tell you before I spoke to anyone. I gathered from Mrs Heidl that she had no relations in this country except yourself. I thought you should know. I hope it hasn't been a great shock."

"This is very sad news. Very sad news, indeed. A fire did you say? It was very thoughtful of you to get in touch with me so promptly, Miss . . . Please tell me your name."

"Fairfax."

"Miss Fairfax. May I ask you how you came to know that I had any connection with Mrs Heidl?"

"She told me. She called at the office. She gave me her reminiscences to read. She wanted us to publish them."

"And where are they?"

"That's the thing. I'm afraid they went up in the fire. She was going to bring the manuscript in today, poor woman."

"This is very sad. Very. You haven't a copy of the manuscript?"

"No."

"You are quite certain?"

"Only too sure, Sir Romney, I am very sorry to say."

"Ah, well. Tell me, Miss—er—Fairfax. Did you mention my former connection with Mrs Heidl to anyone?"

"No. I don't think. . . . No, I'm sure I didn't."

"You are *quite* sure?"

"Quite."

"I think it would be just as well if you didn't. Just at the moment, do you understand? There has been so much publicity. I never thought my innocent disclosures would cause such a controversy. May I rely on your discretion?"

"Certainly, Sir Romney. . . . I'm in such trouble at is is."

"What is that? Oh, yes, you did quite right, Miss—er— Fairfax. And now you can rid your mind entirely of the matter. I shall do whatever is necessary. You can put your mind quite at ease. I am very much obliged to you. What a dreadful thing!"

"Dreadful! Good-bye, Sir Romney."

"Good-bye."

"Always thinking of themselves." Miss Fairfax had dealt

with two men this morning; picking up the telephone, she braced herself to deal with a third.

"What was that?" Vera enquired.

"Nothing dear, nothing."

But she noticed that he was unusually thoughtful all day; and when they sat together after dinner, he said with unwonted seriousness, with a beautiful expression on his face:

"Sometimes it is very difficult *not* to believe in the existence of Divine Providence, after all. Sometimes I have an intimation that there is—watching over us, every one of us—*dear* Vera."

All Futura Books are available at your bookshop or newsagent, or can be ordered from the following address: Futura Books, Cash Sales Department, P.O. Box 11, Falmouth, Cornwall.

Please send cheque or postal order (no currency), and allow 55p for postage and packing for the first book plus 22p for the second book and 14p for each additional book ordered up to a maximum charge of £1.75 in U.K.

Customers in Eire and B.F.P.O. please allow 55p for the first book, 22p for the second book plus 14p per copy for the next 7 books, thereafter 8p per book.

Overseas customers please allow £1 for postage and packing for the first book and 25p per copy for each additional book.